THE BUS STC _

THE BUS STOP

DI Jellicoe Book Two

Jack Murray

The Bus Stop

Books by Jack Murray

DI Jellicoe Series
A Time to Kill
The Bus Stop

Kit Aston Series
The Affair of the Christmas Card Killer
The Chess Board Murders
The Phantom
The Frisco Falcon
The Medium Murders
The Bluebeard Club
The French Diplomat Affair (novella)
Haymaker's Last Fight (novelette)

Agatha Aston Series
Black-Eyed Nick
The Witchfinder General Murders

Jack Murray

ISBN: 9798783877001
Imprint: Independently published

The Bus Stop

Monica, Lavinia, Anne and our Angel, Baby Edward ...

Jack Murray

The Bus Stop

Dear Reader

This book covers the sensitive subject of racial prejudice. It is set in 1959 Britain. To convey truthfully the language of the time makes it difficult to avoid using terms which, these days, have quite rightly fallen from use. I have tried as much as possible to avoid using words that are excessively racist but some terms, used by the characters, may be deemed to be so by the reader.

For the record, I abhor racism and the use of language which is racist in meaning, suggestion, or intent. The views of some of the characters in this book are not my own. They belong to the characters and the situation depicted in the book alone. I hope that you can bear this in mind when you read this work of fiction.

Researching this book has given me a greater insight into racism. I hope and pray that we will see an end to this blight that still affects us today and move towards a more inclusive future for all.

Yours Sincerely,

Jack Murray

Late February 1957

The phone rang.

She found phones a little eerie sometimes. Not that this was something she would admit. They had only had a phone installed in the house the previous year. Her husband used it rarely, of course, but once she had overcome her reserve it became like a new toy. Ben always complained she was never off it. When he was around, that was.

But still…

The ringing of the phone seemed to become more insistent the longer you left it as if it could have a life of its own. All you had to do was to pick it up. Put it to your ear. It came alive then.

Yet she could hardly do this. After all, it was not for her. How could it be? Look where she was. Dilys turned her head and surveyed the immediate surroundings. She was standing by the side of the road at a bus stop. It was the twilight hour when day and night meet and arm wrestle over who should rule. Night was winning.

One thing was clear; she was alone. Utterly and verifiably alone. Yet the phone wouldn't stop ringing. Who on earth would ring a public phone box? She looked at her watch. It was five o'clock. It was dark. Utterly and verifiably dark now. Where was the bus? It should have been here ten minutes ago. This was a mistake. Being out here on her own at a time like this.

How stupid.

She stepped out onto the road as if by standing in the middle she would have a better view of the bus coming. There were no cars. There was nothing. She followed the road all the way until it bent away behind the trees.

She was surrounded by trees. This was sheer folly. Why had she come? She should have known he wouldn't show. Yet here she was. Waiting like a fool. Suddenly the rage rose within her like a giant wave. It crashed against the seashore, and she screamed in frustration: at the bus, at men, at the world that seemed to have abandoned her.

The phone wouldn't stop ringing.

In a moment of madness, she stalked over to the red phone box and yanked open the door. Almost ripping the phone from its cradle, she snarled, 'Yes?'

'Who is this?' asked a strange voice. A very strange voice, in fact. It had a sing song quality to it. Like a child yet it was unquestionably a man.

Dilys was stumped at first. Who on earth would call a phone box in the middle of nowhere? It certainly wasn't Jim. The thought of Jim caused the wave of anger to return. It coursed through her like fire raging through a dry forest. Of all the no good, lying tricksters. He was probably having a good old laugh in some pub or other with his friends. He'd be telling them how he'd fooled a silly woman into meeting him in a forest. How she hated him. The anger was swiftly followed by a second wave of emotion. This time it was remorse. Not for herself or her decision to come out that afternoon to meet a man she hardly knew. Instead, it was for a husband who was out on the road. A lorry driver.

She'd known what she was doing when she'd accepted Jim's invitation. Let's go for a walk, he'd said. I'll meet you at the forest. Oh yes. She knew what he wanted. Why don't you collect me, she said? I don't have a car he said. That was a lie.

'Who's this?' asked the sing song voice again, interrupting her thoughts.

'Dilys. Who are you?'

She heard a voice in the background. Muffled. Then the line went dead. Dilys looked at the phone in shock then slammed it down angrily. Even an unknown man, strange as he might be, had stood her up. This really wasn't her day. She stood stupidly and looked at the phone. Then she spun around, pushed the door open, and left the phone box.

Another scan of her watch. Almost five past five. It was becoming very dark now. What if the bus had broken down? Or worse if it had been cancelled. They couldn't just do that, could

The Bus Stop

they? The anger was slowly being replaced by a lurking anxiety. It was chillier. This explained why she was shivering. Mostly.

Then the phone began to ring again.

Dilys couldn't believe it. Of all the nerve.

She turned around and decided it was time to give the caller a piece of her mind. She snatched up the phone but before she could speak the odd voice said, 'Dilys?'

'Who is this?' demanded Dilys angrily. Her anxiety was mixed with genuine rage. Taking it out on this unknown caller was a form of catharsis. The man at the other end began to breathe heavily. Dilys had heard of these phone calls, but she couldn't be sure it was one of those. He seemed too nervous. Child-like.

'Are you at the bus stop?' asked the man. The voice chilled her. This wasn't because it sounded someone trying to scare her. It was the opposite. Its higher pitch, its disingenuousness was like something from a dream. A terrifying dream. She slammed the phone down and stepped backwards from the phone as if it were possessed of an evil spirit.

The phone began to ring again. She stared at it in terror. Then it stopped. Her heart was beating fast now. Her throat felt dry, yet all over her body she was perspiring in the chill of what was now, without question, night. She could not take her eyes off the phone. For what seemed like an eternity she stared at it. Her senses were in a heightened state of alarm. She'd have heard her shadow breathing had it not been night. She stumbled outside into the darkness and the cold. Something seemed to hold her legs for she stood, rooted to the spot, staring at the phone box. A slight breeze tickled her face. The phone was ringing again. It would not stop ringing.

Somewhere in the distance, headlights appeared on the road.

Jack Murray

Late February 1959

Nick Jellicoe gazed at the apartment block. This, at least, looked promising. Built in an art deco style, it had a white stucco façade and curved windows that promised a sea view. The entrance reminded him of his local cinema in London. He suspected two things would result from his trip to view the flat. As a detective, inspector-grade, suspecting things was his stock in trade. His instincts were unerring most of the time. This was probably a less taxing challenge. There was no question he would love the flat. He already liked its exterior. The interior, with a view of the sea, would be a clincher.

And it would cost too much.

A policeman's salary in 1959, outside of London, was just over a thousand pounds a year. The cost of this flat would probably be at least half his monthly salary. He shook his head at the folly of what he was doing. Perhaps he should give up the flat in London. Perhaps? There was no 'perhaps' about it. His life there, for the time being at least, was finished. His wife was dead. He had come to this seaside town for a reason.

Resolve speeded his steps. He climbed the two flights of stairs to the second floor. A man of around fifty smiled thinly at his arrival. Jellicoe suspected he was probably the latest in a long line of visitors. The novelty had long since whittled away at the estate agent's desire to seem welcoming. Jellicoe was probably the last to view the flat that day. They shook hands.

'Mr Jellicoe?'

'Yes. Mr Foster?'

'Please, come this way, sir. The door is open.'

'Have many people been to see it?' asked Jellicoe, stepping into the apartment. It was everything he'd imagine it would be.

4

The Bus Stop

Light flooded in like a high tide and reflected off the spotless white walls giving it an airiness and a buoyancy he had not seen anywhere else. It was tastefully furnished in the G-plan style. A leather sofa that was certainly newer than the old one he and Sylvia owned in London. A teak Aphrormosia sideboard. Jellicoe could put a record player there with his long-playing jazz collection underneath.

There was a teak round dining room table that could seat four. On the other side of the room, near the windows, was a brown drinks trolley. Beside it was a quadrille nest of three tables. It wasn't a large living space but it more than sufficed for his needs.

Jellicoe walked over to the large bay window that curved just at the end. The view was, as he had suspected, wonderful. It was possible to see some of the sea and the pier. Foster was silent. He knew the flat would be sold on its view rather than its size.

'There's only the one bedroom,' said Foster after a long pause. He said it in the manner of a man who knew it didn't matter. The view was everything.

Jellicoe nodded.

'Does it come with the furniture?'

Foster smiled, a trace of embarrassment on his lips.

'No. Although I believe for an extra consideration the furniture can stay.'

They always asked this question. Yet the owner of the apartment wanted to hold out for the extra payment.

'How much extra,' asked Jellicoe, fixing the estate agent with a look that had made criminals wilt. It failed to dent the conscience of an innocent man.

'Ten pounds over twelve months.'

Jellicoe nodded but he was unaccountably irritated by this. He shot the estate agent a glance.

"What does that make it in total for a year?"

The estate agent told him. It was less than he'd anticipated but not by much. He could afford it, but London would have to go. And soon. He'd make a call that day. Perhaps he could sell the furniture. Too many memories. Memories he wanted to forget.

Jellicoe sensed the estate agent was gently leading him towards the bedroom. He followed him into a large bedroom with a double bed and two bed tables. There was a teak wardrobe and matching drawers. Whoever had decided what furniture to include had to be a male, concluded the detective. There was a lack of ornamentation or personality. It was neutral. Anonymous.

Perfect.

'What do I have to do to secure the flat?'

'I need two months advance and the first month,' replied Foster who had to stop himself licking his lips. Jellicoe nodded and took a chequebook out of his breast pocket. He waved it at Foster to confirm if this would be acceptable. The estate agent nodded. Jellicoe took the chequebook over to a table and started writing on it.

'Who do I make it out to?'

'Foster's Estate Agents.'

'Not the owner of the flat?'

'No; he asked that I handle everything.'

'Who is the owner?'

'That is confidential sir.'

Jellicoe wondered if there was some tax issue the owner was keen to avoid. Not his problem. He filled in the rest of the cheque and was about to hand it to Foster when a thought occurred to him.

'When can I have it?'

'As you can see, it's free now. I think when the cheque clears, we will be in a position to hand over the keys.'

Foster took the cheque from Jellicoe's outstretched hand and a little part of the detective died and was born again. He found himself struggling to breathe. His savings had just been wiped out at the stroke of a pen. Foster smiled and thanked Jellicoe, hoping the relief was not obvious in his voice. A few people had viewed. All were interested but no one had committed. He just wanted the rest of this Saturday off.

He thought about his client, the owner. A shrewd man indeed. He'd been right. Someone would pay a little over the odds for the view and the convenience. And that someone would be a single man.

'Is there a Mrs Jellicoe,' asked Foster, out of curiosity.

'Yes,' answered Jellicoe out of instinct then stopped and looked at Foster. 'No. At least there was. She died.'

'Oh. I'm so sorry, sir.'

The Bus Stop

Jellicoe waved his hand to signify that it was not a problem, but the subject was closed. Foster took the hint and stood back as Jellicoe gave the kitchen a cursory look over. A gas cooker and a fridge. What else was needed? No matter, he had all that and a lot more besides. He checked inside the cupboards. They were empty. Jellicoe doubted that would change much. He couldn't afford to eat now anyway. There was no crockery to be seen, either. This was not a problem.

Both his and Sylvia's mother had seen their marriage as an opportunity to rid themselves of all the crockery and bedding they'd accumulated over the years with just this project in mind. The two fathers had looked on, bemused, when he'd gone to each house to pick up the horde. It was a woman thing concluded Jellicoe. From the looks on the faces of his father and father-in-law, they agreed. He remembered his dad picking up one peach-shaped glass dessert plate and saying, 'I don't remember using that. It was wedding gift to us.'

Jellicoe skipped down the stairs in a better mood than when he'd arrived. The breathless high of indulgence was always followed by the low when reality came and the next month was due. This wasn't the only dark spot that lay on the immediate and cloudy horizon. He would have to take his life in his hands and tell Mrs Ramsbottom at the Ramsbottom Guest House that he was leaving.

His time at the guest house had been a mixed one. His initial horror at his accommodation and the food served (a varied set of dishes that all required toast) had gradually softened. This was partly a feeling of guilt. The Ramsbottoms were a decent old couple who would see out the rest of their lives without the two boys who'd gone to war and not returned. Jellicoe could not imagine the sadness they must have felt. Yet neither Ramsbottom spoke of their sons with anything other than pride. There was no bitterness; they'd done their bit. It was a typically British stoicism that Jellicoe admired more than he could say.

It felt strange to have a free afternoon. He'd hardly had any time off since his arrival from London. Perhaps he could join the rest of the civilised world in acquiring a television. The walk from his apartment building into town took around ten minutes. Jellicoe knew of one electronics shop on the High Street. There was an

Italian café beside it. Lunch, purchase a television then join the library. He felt positively giddy with the newfound freedom. It wouldn't last, of course.

The high Street was quiet. This was one of the marked differences he'd noticed from London. Oxford Street was permanently crowded with shops that never seemed to close. This was particularly the case with shops running closing down sales to attract the unwary. Here they closed for the afternoon. High Street on Saturday afternoon was like being in a ghost town. The shop he was looking for was Frederick's Electronics. It was still open but due to close at two o'clock. He had ten minutes. How did people make money here? In London it would have stayed open until five.

The manager of the shop greeted Jellicoe's arrival with a fixed smile of someone who could see the end of the week if only this unwelcome visitor would have the good manners not to outstay his welcome. He was dressed in a dark three-piece suit which he even had a watch chain. The moustache had a military cut to it. So many men still chose to have such facial hair. To Jellicoe it seemed as much a part of a bygone era as the coach and horse. A relic of the officer class who had led men so dismally through two wars. The man was certainly old enough to have served, yet Jellicoe sensed this was unlikely. But he knew better than to judge someone by their appearance.

'I'm looking for a television,' said Jellicoe. This gave the manager some cause for hope on two fronts. There was a business-like cut to the customer's jib that suggested his decision-making would be rapid. And he was clearly in the market to buy. The manager straightened up and switched his smile to full unctuousness.

'Well, you've certainly come to the right place, Mister…?' said Martin Fitzgibbon.

Of course, I have, thought Jellicoe. I'm not a complete idiot.

'Jellicoe.'

'I'm Mr Fitzgibbon,' said the manager waving his arm towards the wall in what he hoped was an expansive manner. While there was no questioning the theatricality of the gesture, its impact was blunted somewhat by the relative modesty of the display. In all,

The Bus Stop

Fredericks range of televisions comprised two: one large, one small.

Jellicoe turned to Fitzgibbon in the hope that the grinning imbecile was going to suggest they retire to the showroom to see the full range of what the shop had to offer. Sadly, it looked as if this was the lot. Nothing in Fitzgibbon's smile suggested anything other than the utmost pride in what they had on offer. This was confirmed a moment later.

'The very latest models, sir,' said the manager before adding what he considered to be the clincher, 'all the way from London.'

'You don't say.'

Jellicoe stepped forward to have a closer look. He ignored the smaller one. The new radio telescope at Jodrell Bank would have had trouble seeing a picture on it from five feet away.

'This is the Ferguson, sir,' said Fitzgibbon, moving over to the larger set. 'Very good choice if I may say. The screen is twenty inches, would you believe?'

'It's very large, certainly,' agreed Jellicoe. And it made their decision to place it alongside the tiddler all the more baffling. Or perhaps it was meant to have this impact. Jellicoe had read an article about the science of shopping recently and how marketing research was being used to understand the psyche of unwary customers. Were they duping him by having such a small set beside the large one? Or was he just a suspicious flat foot? Probably both. But there was no denying the appeal of having such a very large television screen in his living room. Twenty inches! But would it dominate the space, though? Was it vulgar? What kind of picture would twenty inches provide?

He realised he didn't care. He wanted it. Watching sport on a twenty-inch black and white screen would feel like he was actually there at the match. The marvels of technology. A twenty-inch screen.

'I'll take it.'

'Excellent choice sir.'

'When will it be delivered?'

'Three weeks, sir.'

'That's quick.'

'Oh, Ferguson are first class, sir. Many of our customers have been surprised by how quickly these sets are available.' The delight in the sales manager's voice could barely be contained. He'd rounded off Saturday with a wonderful sale and it was still only three minutes to two. Elsie would hear all about this with perhaps a few embellishments to highlight his own role in swinging the customer towards a sale.

At one minute past two, Jellicoe left the shop and proceeded in a southerly direction with a marked skip in his step. Perhaps it was because his wallet was considerably lighter than it had been when he woke up that morning. Such considerations were for another time. First thing Monday morning he would give up the lease on his London flat. He would organise for his belongings to be moved down to the coast. He would make a clean break both from London and the past. From her.

There were still a few weeks to wait for the television. How to fill the time each evening? Across the road was the town bookshop. He popped across the road narrowly avoiding a Ford Anglia driven by a young woman. The bookshop was dark but filled with paperback books. Hardback was now beyond his budget. On the table near the entrance, he saw some detective books. There was also the latest Patricia Highsmith book. He slapped his forehead as he remembered he'd never returned *The Talented Mr Ripley* to Stephen Masterson. He'd post it. From the police station. There were probably other things they'd taken from Masterson's room. They could all go together.

His eye caught another Patricia Highsmith book, *Strangers on a Train*. He remembered enjoying the film. Picking it up, he flicked through it, but he'd already decided to take it. He took it to the counter and paid for it. Soon he was back out on High Street and heading down towards the sea front. He resisted the temptation to stop in at a bookie on the corner. Why give Ronnie Musgrave the business? Ronnie Musgrave was a local gangland leader who owned many businesses on and around the sea front.

Next door to the book shop was Farley's Record Shop. Like Oscar Wilde, Jellicoe was a man who could resist anything except temptation. He walked in and was nearly knocked over by a young man who barged past him. Jellicoe rearranged his hat and raised his eyebrows at Desmond Farley.

Farley's reaction to the shoulder charge was a great booming laugh.

The Bus Stop

'What's wrong with him?' asked Jellicoe.

'Sticky fingers, Nick. Sticky fingers. I took him on last week and then found cash missing. I just caught him in the act.'

'Do you want me…?

Farley waved his arm in a motion that said, just leave it. He then motioned Jellicoe in and over to the counter. Jellicoe followed him. There he handed Jellicoe a newsletter from a record company called Prestige. Jellicoe scanned the list of upcoming releases and then his eyes fixed on one: *Miles Davis and the Modern Jazz Giants*. He read the blurb beside the photograph of the album cover.

'With Monk?'

'With Monk,' confirmed Farley with a grin. 'Can I order you one?'

'Absolutely,' laughed Jellicoe.

'I boiled the kettle. Would you like some tea?' asked Farley. He said the word 'tea' in the manner of an English gentleman. It sounded odd as his usual accent was distinctly Jamaican. Jellicoe accepted happily. While the Jamaican went to the back of the shop to make the tea, Jellicoe glanced down at the counter and saw a number of other newsletters from record companies. On the wall was an area set aside for musicians advertising themselves and night spots. One of them showed a man playing a saxophone: The Tulip Club. Just then Farley arrived with the tea. For the next twenty minutes Jellicoe stayed and chatted with the store owner as jazz music played on the speaker. Half a dozen customers entered the shop to peruse the banks of long-playing records while the two men were chatting. Farley, looking at their age and dress, changed the music to Elvis. He smiled and shrugged at Jellicoe who took this as his cue to leave.

Life, just at that moment, felt good. He felt happier than he could remember in a long time, and that included the days with Sylvia. Turning right off High Street he found himself facing the sea. He breathed in the sea air and for a moment guilt assailed him. Should he not feel greater grief? He exhaled. He had no more guilt to give. No more heartache. What's done was done. Yet the moment this thought passed through his mind it felt like his stomach had been punched. He couldn't breathe. If he could have screamed there and then in the middle of the street, he would have.

He strode towards the sea believing his guilty conscience to be freedom and his anger a sense of shame. But like the tide a few hundred yards away, the pain receded. It would come again, and he wouldn't be ready. This was strangely comforting.

A week later:

There was no condemnation in her eyes nor farewell on her lips. Mrs Ramsbottom stood at the door. Her husband was standing behind her lost somewhere in her shadow. Jellicoe was unsure whether to smile goodbye, hold out his hand or whether just to say, 'So long.' The guilt was overpowering.

'Well, I suppose this is it,' said Jellicoe finally. At his feet were two brown suitcases.

'Yes,' came the reply. There was sadness in the voice and, worse, acceptance. This was the killer. People like the Ramsbottom couple were the salt of the earth. They asked for nothing, expected nothing, and were usually rewarded accordingly.

There was toot on a car horn. Jellicoe turned to acknowledge the driver who, in this case was Detective Constable David Wallace. Then he turned back to the couple and raised his eyebrows in a I-really-must-go-now. Mrs Ramsbottom nodded which released Jellicoe to turn away. He picked up the cases and started to walk towards the car. The sound of the door closing behind him made him feel even worse. The cases were thrown onto the back seat and Jellicoe hopped into the passenger side.

'Thanks, David,' said Jellicoe. 'Not too fast. I want to spend the first night in the flat, not in traction.'

DC David Wallace had a reputation that he was inordinately proud of. It was one that he felt duty bound to live up to every time he stepped into the driving seat of a car. Jellicoe was thrown back on the seat as the car leapt forward with the young detective laughing out loud.

'Very funny,' was Jellicoe's only comment as they crossed the town at a more conservative clip. They reached Jellicoe's new accommodation and Wallace whistled when he saw it.

The Bus Stop

'How can you afford this?' exclaimed the young man.

I can't, thought Jellicoe. Wallace took one of the cases and they headed up to the first floor. Jellicoe opened the door and allowed his colleague in first. Wallace let out another whistle as he saw the sea view.

'Very nice, sir,' He always said 'sir' even though Jellicoe had taken to calling him David. Perhaps it was too soon. He wouldn't encourage that level of familiarity yet. Wallace, as much by the impolite nature of youth as force of habit as a policeman, began a search of the flat. At least, that's what it felt like to Jellicoe, who smiled. It wasn't a large flat, so he was back a minute later grinning like a puppy with a stick to play with.

'Very nice, sir. Very nice.'

'Thanks. And yes, it costs a bucket.'

'I'll bet.'

At this point there was only one thing that was needed.

'Tea?' asked Jellicoe.

'I'd love a cuppa,' said Wallace. 'Do you have anything else coming?'

'Yes, the rest of my furniture is due tomorrow. I had to pay extra for Sunday.' The thought of this stung a little. He would be surviving on beans and toast for a while. The flat, the television, the furniture, the move from London had all but cleared his bank account. The last thing he wanted to do was to ask his father for money. It would be forthcoming with no strings attached. His father, an assistant chief constable in London, could certainly afford to help him. But the thought of asking was something he recoiled from.

The kettle began to boil. Jellicoe put a spoonful of tea leaves into each cup and poured the water in.

'I don't have any sugar,' said Jellicoe.

'That's all right,' replied Wallace hoping there was no disappointment in his voice. He usually took two spoonfuls.

'What are you up to tonight?' asked Jellicoe returning with the tea on a tray.

'I'm going to the pictures,' replied Wallace a little sheepishly.

'What's on?'

'It's an old movie but my mum said it was very good. Dead of Night. Do you know it?' asked Wallace.

'Does that qualify as an old movie? Bloody hell. Yes, I know it. It's wonderful. You'll enjoy it.' Jellicoe was smiling at the young constable. Then he added, 'On your own?'

'No,' said Wallace chuckling and Jellicoe took this to be the end of the conversation.

The Bus Stop

Two days later, Jellicoe arrived at the police station a little later than his usual seven in the morning. Chief Inspector Burnett noted the time and then called him into the office. Jellicoe had spotted where his eyes had gone but was unworried about receiving a ticking off.

'Good to have you join us,' said Burnett by way of welcome.

'I thought you'd miss me,' replied Jellicoe.

'Any reason for your sleep in?' asked Burnett, lighting his pipe. It was still not eight in the morning.

A comfortable bed for a change, thought Jellicoe.

'I moved into the new flat at the weekend.'

'Oh aye. Where might that be?'

'Easterbrook Mansions,' said Jellicoe, making a point of not looking at his chief's face.

'Bloody hell,' exploded Burnett. 'How much are we paying you?'

'Not nearly enough,' responded Jellicoe with a grin.

A new day, a new week had begun. Detective Sergeant Yates watched the exchange. He'd liked to have joined in the banter but felt unsure if it was his place. In the end he kept his counsel. He smiled but would have preferred to have added to the chaffing of the new boy. Or not-so-new boy now. He'd been here about eight weeks. In that time, he'd helped clear up a murder, a bank robbery, and a few smaller misdemeanours. All of which indicated that any spurs to be earned had been earned. Yates had played his own part in these arrests but remained frustratingly just out of reach of the top table.

Wallace entered the office just after eight. This prompted Burnett to shout from his office if he could offer him some tea or toast. Unlike Yates, Wallace was a little bit less concerned about jokes directed squarely at him.

15

'No thanks, sir. You don't put enough butter on the toast. Has anyone ever told you that?'

Jellicoe grinned and waited for the riposte.

'One man did.'

The clock ticked loudly in the brief silence that followed this remark. It signalled that an old Burnett joke was being dusted down and made ready for airing. Moments later it arrived.

'I don't know whatever happened to him. I think he was posted to Frimley-Cockstevens.'

'Where's that?' asked Wallace. This was the standard response to Burnett's made-up towns that usually had a hint of *double entendre* about them. Wallace's smile was as wide as the English Channel less than a mile away.

'Exactly, son.'

*

The call came through just after Wallace had made his second tea run of the day. It was not yet eight-thirty in the morning. Sergeant Ramsay came into the office and asked to speak to Burnett. Ramsay was a serious man at the best of times, but his stern features were softened by the evident sadness at what he was about to communicate.

He knocked on Burnett's door which was usually open. Burnett was a man who liked to hear the sound of his team working. Burnett looked up. He had time for Ramsey, and he could see that something bad had happened.

'Go on,' said Burnett.

'A body has been found, sir.'

'Where?'

'In Fenton Woods, about two miles from town.'

'Suicide?'

Ramsay shook his head gravely. By now, Jellicoe and Wallace were standing at the door with Ramsay. Yates was away to call on a domestic disturbance at the Cornfield estate. Detective Inspector Price and Detective Sergeant Fogg were investigating the theft of a dog. The latter crime would, under normal circumstances, would have been a task for uniformed officers had there not had been a spate of these canine thefts. One of the missing dogs was a Yorkshire terrier called Felicity who just happened to belong to a leading councillor in the town, Erskine Landers. Landers was the

The Bus Stop

son and heir of Gregory Landers, owner of the plastics factory. A case that might normally have sat with uniform was elevated to the level of the detective team. Burnett had made it a major priority principally because Chief Constable Leighton had reminded him that Landers was a useful ally on a council that was not always sympathetic to police budgets.

A few minutes later Jellicoe, Burnett and Wallace were outside at the car park in front of the police station. The sun was shining although it was not particularly warm. They walked towards the dark Wolseley.

'Who has the keys?' asked Burnett looking at Jellicoe hopefully.

Jellicoe indicated with his eyes that it was Wallace.

'Drive slowly,' growled Burnett. He glared at Jellicoe for a moment to let him know what had already been communicated all too clearly in his voice: the prospect of young Wallace behind the wheel was not one he either welcomed or encouraged. Jellicoe smiled but pretended not to notice.

'We're in no rush,' reminded Burnett from the back seat. He had motioned for Jellicoe to sit in front to act as a brake on the young man's enthusiasm for testing the Wolseley's acceleration.

Chastened by the attention, Wallace showed that he could drive sensibly when the situation, or in this case, his boss, demanded it. The road was now familiar to Jellicoe as it led out to the forest area where his first case in the town had been solved. They passed the strange crossroads with the bus stop and the telephone box which seemed to be in the middle of nowhere. They continued until they saw the police car and the ambulance. Another car was also present. This was probably Dr Taylor, the pathologist, guessed Jellicoe

A pair of whiskers attached to a grey homburg appeared, confirming Jellicoe's supposition. He was, as ever, puffing on a pipe. This was probably no bad thing. He'd seen crime scenes corrupted before by unwary policemen flicking ash from their cigarettes. Wallace pulled the police car up alongside Taylor's, earning a backhanded compliment from Burnett.

'See. It wasn't that difficult.'

'No, sir,' replied Wallace, stifling a grin.

Jack Murray

Burnett was out of the car quicker than you could say Nat Lofthouse. He made straight for the attending constable who had just been joined by Dr Taylor.

'Hello sir,' said Constable Wilkins, addressing Burnett as he approached.

'Hello, son,' said Burnett who called almost every constable 'son' except Constable Clarke. It saved him trying to remember their names or getting them wrong. He'd read somewhere that Italian men and women called their latest squeeze 'amore'. He guessed a similar principal was at play. He shook hands with the doctor, 'Hilary.'

'Reg,' said Dr Taylor. 'Bad business.'

Although the two were close friends and had shared more than one consoling Scotch over the years as they found shelter from the blessed harmony of wedlock, their professional relationship invariably required that they meet over a dead body.

'What do we have here?' asked Burnett.

Taylor nodded to Jellicoe and Wallace as they joined the group.

Everyone turned to Constable Wilkins. The constable in question was in his thirties and, as yet, had showed little or no capability in the realms of detection likely to see his elevation beyond the beat. This was his platform now to shine. A chance, in a few short words, to synthesise what they were likely to see and to offer a few suggestions about what should happen next.

He fluffed it.

'Uh, it's a dead woman, sir.'

Burnett glared at the poor constable. Then he made a point of looking around at all the men before replying, 'And here's me thinking that the cream of the police force was just out for a walk in the woods.'

Wilkins offered no response aside from a 'this way'. The group followed the constable towards the thicket of woods about thirty yards away from the main road and partially obscured by shrubbery. Lying uncovered on the ground was the body of a woman. No matter how many times he'd seen a dead body, it never stopped being a shock to Jellicoe. It was momentary and then his training would take over. Training and experience. The

The Bus Stop

policemen stood back and let Taylor make an initial inspection. He crouched down and inspected her head.

'What about the man that rang the station?' asked Jellicoe while Taylor examined the young woman.

'No sign of him, sir. It was anonymous,' replied Wilkins.

'We should test the phone box. He may have rung from there.'

Taylor, rose unsteadily to his feet and turned to the group behind him.

'Young woman. Early thirties, perhaps younger. No sign of a blow to the head although there does seem to be a bruise on her forehead. It's yellowing which suggests that it was made a day or two before she was killed.'

Then he glanced down towards her chest. Her white blouse was stained red where she had unquestionably been stabbed. The quantity of blood loss made the cause of death obvious.

'This is what killed her.'

'Has anyone found the murder weapon?' asked Burnett, turning to Wilkins.

'Not yet, sir.'

'Is there a bag or anything we can use to identify her?'

'No, sir.'

Burnett responded with something approximating a growl. The pressure gauge was rising. Jellicoe nodded to Wallace. The nod meant, start a search, and take Wilkins out of the line of fire. Wallace tapped Wilkins on the shoulder and led him away to organise a search of the area. Jellicoe moved away from the body to scan the surrounding area for anything that might provide help in adding to the story of the woman's last moments.

Taylor continued to talk while Jellicoe moved around the body. He was not interested in what the doctor had to say. The cause of death was obvious. More important questions needed to be answered and the first few minutes at a crime scene were always crucial for him. This was when he registered as much as he could about the position of the body relative to its environment. He was looking for any secret code that may have been left by the murderer in case there was a ritual element to the murder.

A second objective was to register what might be *wrong* with the scene. Was it likely that the murder had occurred there? If so, was it planned or a sudden frenzied attack. He continued patrolling the area around the body, but his brain paused as he returned to listening to Taylor.

'I'll know more later but judging by the loss of blood and the lack of ripping on her blouse apart from this one, I'd say you're looking at a rather large and sharp weapon.'

'Like?' probed Burnett.

'An axe.'

Jellicoe stopped in his tracks and turned to Burnett. He was curious to see how the chief would react. He didn't disappoint. The air was turned a violent shade of blue as Burnett vented his anger at the world. Few things were guaranteed to excite public interest or stoke fear more than the prospect of a mad axe murderer on the loose. To be fair, Jellicoe had never heard of a sane axe murderer.

To give Burnett his due, he was able to maintain a high level of righteous indignation at the world and the deity who had created it for well over a minute and a half. This was no mean feat if you think about it. Hilary Taylor stopped for the entire duration of Burnett's eulogy over the dead body of the woman. Finally, when the fire had burned itself out, Taylor added drily, 'Sorry, old boy. Thought that might upset you.'

Jellicoe was still looking at Burnett when he saw the chief turn to him. The eyes were angry but there was more than a glint of determination in them.

'All right, boy wonder. You'll need to clear this one up double quick otherwise we'll have panic on the streets.'

Boy wonder? Did that make Burnett Batman? Well, the strong moral code and immutable sense of justice was certainly there. Perhaps not the waistline nor the fondness for ale chased down by Scotch while watching cricket. That was pure Burnett. The thought of Bruce Wayne watching a minor counties match at Bovington came mighty close to putting a smile on the detective's face when he least needed it.

'Yes, sir,' replied Jellicoe in an unintentional impression of Wilkins earlier. Jellicoe continued his search around the area. Minor details might be noted now that did not seem important but later might become so. His eyes slid over the ground slowly, like a vacuum cleaner. There nothing obviously wrong with what he saw but it was too early to start making the connections.

The Bus Stop

One thing was clear to Jellicoe: the body had not been moved or dumped here. This was where she had been killed. There was enough blood around the scene but no obvious signs that she had been dragged. Why would you, he thought? They were in the middle of nowhere. A thicket of woods separated the body from the main road.

The killer had left no trace of his or her presence. Just then, Vaughan from the forensics lab bounced over to them like a puppy let off the leash. He was wearing the tweed jacket and sporting round spectacles that forever made him look like a visiting university professor.

Jellicoe went over to say hello to him when he saw a young woman arrive carrying a camera. She breezed past two police constables, much to Jellicoe's surprise and no little concern. There was no question that she would soon be standing over the dead woman and snapping away no doubt for some local rag.

'Excuse me,' said Jellicoe. 'What do you think you're doing?'

The young woman ignored him. Just like that, she ignored him. Then, to add insult to injury, she trained her camera, a Leica, no less, on the dead body and began to take pictures. Jellicoe stalked over and grabbed her arm.

'Just what do you think you are doing?' growled Jellicoe.

The young woman shook her arm free from Jellicoe's grasp and glared back at him. Then a smile broke out across her face. The smile was way too confident for Jellicoe's liking. Something was wrong with this. It was almost as if she were…

The he heard Burnett guffawing. There was no other word for it. Jellicoe glanced in the direction of the chief, and he was bent double laughing. If Burnett was laughing, Taylor was virtually lying on the ground. A seizure was imminent if his level of hilarity increased at the scene he'd witnessed. Jellicoe returned his gaze to the young woman. Her eyebrows were raised in a manner that young women reserve for particularly foolish young men. Jellicoe had no doubt he was squarely in this category just at that moment.

'Is someone going to enlighten me?' asked Jellicoe half turning to the two senior men before returning his gaze to the young woman. There was just enough humour in his expression to leaven the exasperation. Burnett soon returned to his senses,

21

perhaps realising that the moment of humour was perhaps not in the best of taste given the tragedy of the circumstances.

'You haven't met Winifred, obviously,' said Burnett.

Jellicoe turned to the photographer and said, 'Hello, Miss Obviously, unusual name.' He raised one eyebrow as he said this. A glow of satisfaction flickered within him as he realised that this rescue of a potentially disastrous introduction had irritated the new arrival. He raised his hat in a mock salute to the young woman.

'Very funny. If you don't mind, I have work to do,' said Winifred.

Jellicoe stepped backwards and walked over to Burnett.

'There's no sign of anything belonging to either the young woman or the killer. I think Vaughan and Forensics will have a job to locate anything we can use.'

There was nothing in there for Burnett, so he said nothing. He glanced towards Taylor. The doctor had left to join the two ambulancemen. They would remove the body shortly to take to the mortuary.

'Thoughts?' demanded Burnett.

'She was killed here. I can see a few broken branches near where she's lying.' Jellicoe's eyes went from the road to the bus stop and then to the area where the body lay.

'She made a run for it,' said Burnett watching Jellicoe.

'Yes, looks like it. She ran and then turned to face her pursuer. That's when he killed her.'

The two men stopped for moment to consider the fear she must have felt in those final moments. The terror at being pursued by someone with murder in their heart. Jellicoe stopped himself from thinking more. But the image of the axe, raised and ready to inflict its deadly business was overwhelming.

'Aye, lad. Awful,' said Burnett. He turned away and headed over towards Taylor who was kneeling by the body and making some initial observations in a notebook.

The Bus Stop

The search around the area of the body yielded nothing for Forensics. Yet Jellicoe felt like the fingerprint of the crime was laid before them in the trees, on the grass, in the area around them. It wasn't anything so obvious as a murder weapon, or a footprint, or a scrap of cloth. He traced the route back to the road which he believed had been taken by the dead woman and her assailant. Burnett watched him go. He watched the young detective inspect the road for signs of tyre tracks. Then he watched him walk along the road for a hundred yards inspecting one side. Jellicoe crossed over the road and inspected the other.

He was about to cross over the road when a bus came past. Jellicoe stopped to let it go and then crossed over. He stared at the bus as it went into the distance. About a hundred and fifty yards further up the road, it came to a halt. Jellicoe continued to focus on the bus. A thought flickered in his mind. Finally, the bus departed, and Jellicoe wandered back towards Burnett.

'Do you think she took a bus here?' asked Burnett.

Jellicoe grinned for a moment. He glanced back towards the bus and then to his chief.

'Hard to say but it's a possibility. I'm trying to understand the story, but nothing makes sense. If she was meeting someone, wouldn't it be more likely they came in a car? If not, then how did she come here except by bus? If she was on her own, then was it really just bad luck that she met an axe murderer? Well, it was obviously bad luck for her but was it simply a moment of serendipity for the killer?'

'Was it?' asked Burnett.

'No. She met someone here. Or she was meant to meet someone here. Someone she trusted. That person might have killed her. Or it was a random axe murderer wandering the woods

23

at night. The press will love that. Anyway, there's nothing to suggest that it didn't all take place right here.'

'You saw her wedding ring?'

'Yes. Perhaps she was meeting someone that was not her husband.'

'Why wouldn't it be her husband?'

'Too simple. We'll see,' replied Jellicoe.

A shout came up from a few hundred yards away, deeper into the forest. It was Wallace. The two men turned in the direction it had come from.

'Over here,' shouted Wallace.'

Another body? Jellicoe and Burnett began to walk quickly through the wood towards where Wallace and a couple of uniformed officers were searching. Wallace was standing looking down at something. Vaughan joined Jellicoe and the chief as they made their way towards Wallace.

When they reached them, they saw what had attracted their attention. A handbag was lying in the middle of a thicket of bushes. It was brown and made from leather or something meant to look like leather. Vaughan approached the bag first, taking care not to disturb the scene too much. His eyes were glued to the area around the bag rather than the bag itself. He got down on his hands and knees as if in worship. He scanned every leaf on the ground, every twig. There was nothing. Carefully he removed leaves from the top of the bag. He lifted the bag up and placed it in a police bag. There was nothing underneath where the bag had once lay.

Vaughan brought the bag over to the detectives. Burnett nodded towards Wallace in a 'you-found-it' way. Wallace put on some gloves and took the outer bag from Vaughan. He placed it on the ground and crouched down. Carefully opening the woman's bag, he extracted house keys and a purse. He replaced the housekeys as the keyring was leather but contained no name or address. The purse was empty. Wallace looked up at the two senior policemen.

'She wasn't robbed. By the look of things, it's been there a while.'

'Are you saying it does not belong to this woman?'

The Bus Stop

Vaughan shrugged. It was too early to confirm this. Burnett knew this too but, for once, had hoped Forensics might provide an immediate answer.

Jellicoe nodded but did not have to say what was on all their minds. The bag looked like it had been there for a lot longer than the woman was likely to have been dead. He doubted it was her bag. But if it wasn't hers then whose might it be?

The group was approached by the young woman Burnett had called Winifred. She had clearly finished photographing the murder scene.

'They wish to remove the body now, sir. Is this all right?' asked the young woman, ignoring everyone except Burnett.

Burnett nodded and she turned leaving without saying anything else. Jellicoe noted that Wallace gave her a swift appraising glance. It had only occurred to him second time around that, despite her abruptness, she was rather attractive. He was amused by Wallace's reaction. He seemed always to be on the scent.

'If you two stags could stop pawing the ground for a second, we have a murder to investigate,' said Burnett.

'Who is that?' asked Jellicoe as they walked towards the ambulancemen.

'That,' proclaimed Burnett with more than a hint of irritation, 'Is Winifred Leighton. Winnie.' Jellicoe turned to Burnett, but the question died on his lips. 'Yes, our esteemed Chief Constable's daughter is a police photographer. In answer to the question which should be circulating in both yours and young Wallace's mind is "no" and I mean no.'

'I wasn't thinking anything, sir,' lied Wallace. This was met with a hard stare from the chief. Jellicoe wisely chose to ignore the comment altogether. Why add fuel to any flame?

They watched in silence as the woman was put on a stretcher and taken to the waiting ambulance. Dr Taylor had already left. Burnett put a hand on Wallace's arm. He moved his arm like an umpire signalling a four.

'All this, keep searching. Maybe there is another somewhere around here, just in case the one you found is not hers.'

'Yes, sir.'

Jack Murray

'What are you going to do now?' asked Burnett, glancing towards Jellicoe.

'The bus. I want to check on who was driving the buses along this road yesterday. She had to come here somehow.'

'Fine,' agreed Burnett. 'Drop me off at the station. I'll have to let the upstairs know.'

Upstairs, on the third floor of the police station were the offices of the chief constable and superintendent. They were occupied only two days each week. The senior police officers and administration were located in a different town. In fact, if it were the case that it was Leighton's daughter who was the police photographer then it was entirely possible the chief constable would already be making his way over to the town along with his deeply unimpressive, superintendent: Ian Frankie.

Jellicoe drove the Wolseley back to the station but rather than drop off Burnett as he'd requested, he came in with him instead.

'I need DS Yates. He can drop whatever he's on.'

'Aye, do that,' was Burnett's only comment.

Another dark Wolseley was in the car park.

'Looks like our visitors have arrived,' said Burnett drily.

They headed upstairs. Burnett went straight to the office used by Leighton on the third floor while Jellicoe returned to the office used by the detectives to see if Yates had returned. There was no sign of him. He rang down to the front desk and asked someone to call Yates back to the police station. While he waited, he rang the bus station.

'Hello, can you put me through to the manager of the bus station? This is DI Nick Jellicoe. It's a police matter.'

There was a short pause and then a voice came on the line.

'Hello, this Mr Gerard, the manager.'

Mr Gerard? He sounded more like a hairdresser his wife would have spent his money on.

'Hello, this is DI Jellicoe. We are investing a serious crime that took place on the Frimhampton Road yesterday evening. Which buses and drivers would have been on this road then?'

'The sixty-eight runs between here and Frimhampton. Oh wait, yesterday was Sunday so it would be the one-six-eight. It runs once per hour. The same bus would go back and forwards, The route is around twenty to twenty-five minutes. Can you give me a moment to find out more about who was driving yesterday afternoon.?'

'Of course,' replied Jellicoe who was writing down the bus numbers.

Mr Gerard came back a minute later.

'Hello, Mr Jellicoe, it's Mr Gerard again. The driver on the route yesterday afternoon and early evening would have been Chester Johnson.'

'Thanks Mr Gerard, I will need to speak to him. Is he around today?'

'No, he was driving yesterday and Saturday. That means he will be off today and tomorrow.'

Jellicoe had to wait a little longer for the address to come. He thanked the bus station manager and rang off. A uniformed policeman appeared at the door and informed Jellicoe that Yates was on his way back.

Ten minutes later Detective Sergeant Tony Yates appeared in the office. Jellicoe looked up at him as he entered. Yates was younger than Jellicoe by around three years. He was a fascinating mixture of ambition and self-doubt. It was clear he was desperate to advance into more senior roles, but a lack of self-confidence held him back. Jellicoe, who had studied psychology at Cambridge, recognised this as a form of Imposter Syndrome.

Unlike Yates, whose father had been a farm worker before being killed in North Africa, Jellicoe came from police royalty. Two generations of Jellicoe had occupied senior positions in the Metropolitan Police in London. He had been born to do what he was doing. Unlike his father, though, his ambition to senior office was more akin to his grandfather's. He had none. It was the chase that interested him. Meeting criminals, understanding them then using this knowledge to find others. Yates had not had the immersion and the education enjoyed by Jellicoe. It showed. He lacked a quality that Jellicoe, Burnett and even Wallace had, a self-assurance, in the latter's case, over-confidence. This was a pity because Yates, noted Jellicoe, had good instincts.

'A murder?' asked Yates.

'You heard?'

Yates nodded then sat down as Jellicoe filled him in about what they knew. As they were talking, the phone rang. Yates picked it up. He put his hand over the mouthpiece and mouthed the word 'Wallace' to Jellicoe. He listened for a minute and wrote something down. Then he hung up.

'Wallace found a driving license belonging to the woman. Apparently, the killer didn't search inside her coat, not wanting to disturb anything, probably. We have a name and an address.'

'Go on.'

'Mrs Sarah Sutton of 12 Anglesey Drive.'

Jellicoe was already on his feet heading to the door. He grabbed his hat and coat from the coast stand, swiftly followed by Yates. Then he stopped and went over to the handbag they'd found near the scene of the crime. He extracted the keys and put them in his pocket. At least they'd know one way or another if the bag belonged to the woman.

On their way to the car, they passed a lone journalist trooping towards the police station. The word was out. Either a call had been made to them to come and attend an impromptu press conference or the police presence outside of town had been noticed and passed on to the press. Either way, the news would be public soon.

*

Anglesey Drive was on the other side of town in the direction of the town's chief employer, Landers Plastics. It was not a particularly nice part of the town, but neither was it a hot bed of crime. The houses and flats had been thrown up with all the post-war enthusiasm of a government that had no money and architects who were slaves to a philosophy for building living spaces that had little soul and certainly no love for humankind. The beige banks of prefabricated houses fought a battle against the blocks of flats to see who was ugliest.

A ten-minute drive took them to a prefabricated house on an estate that Jellicoe had only visited on a couple of occasions. On one of those he'd been looking for a murderer. The house was the colour of weak urine.

They approached the house like two lionesses hunting their prey. Yates headed around to the back while Jellicoe took route one: the door. He pressed the doorbell. No response. He tried again, a little more insistently this time. Still no response. Yates appeared and shook his head. No one seemed to be in.

28

The Bus Stop

Next Jellicoe tried knocking.

'Mr Sutton. It's the police. Are you in? Please open the door.'

Jellicoe shrugged and took the key they'd found in the bag in the forest out of his pocket. One look at it told him it wasn't the right key. He banged on the door again.

A neighbour appeared. She was in her sixties and wore a pair of horn-rimmed spectacles that did little to hide her age or the abiding impression that they were in the presence of a busybody.

'Are you looking for the Suttons?'

It was an innocent if somewhat redundant question. Jellicoe had, after all, been calling out the name of the husband. Yates looked at the woman, sized her up in a split second and said, 'Madam, this is police business.'

The woman shrugged and nodded. Yates turned his body round to assume the position of someone who was about to ram the door.

'You're not interested in the key then?' Her voice was dripping with dryness.

Yates stopped moments before he was about to bust the door down. The two policemen swung around to the old lady. She certainly had their attention now and Mrs Ethel Peabody was too seasoned a campaigner not to take full advantage.

'Don't worry, I'll be on my way, I know when I'm not wanted,' said Mrs Peabody.

'Madam, excuse me, but did you just say you had a key to the house?'

Mrs Peabody was already entering her house. Jellicoe now had a better view of the old war horse. She was wearing a pair of tattered slippers and stockings that were wrinkling around her ankles. A cigarette hung from her mouth like a parody of James Dean.

Jellicoe leapt over the divide between the two house which in this case was nothing and caught up with the lady. Mrs Peabody feigned surprise at seeing Jellicoe appear on her doorstep.

'Mrs?'

'Peabody.'

'Mrs Peabody, how would you like to help in a criminal investigation?'

Jack Murray

If Mrs Peabody was an old hand at running rings around men in general and uniformed men in particular, then Jellicoe had some front-line experience of dealing with ladies of a certain age, odd hair colour (Mrs Peabody's was a light blue) and a native shrewdness. The lady's eyes widened, and he knew he'd played his cards well. The fact that he was a shade over six feet, had a certain Anthony Steel look about him was an additional weapon in his armoury. He used it shamelessly in this type of situation.

'It's my civic duty, officer,' replied Mrs Peabody holding up a finger. This finger was interpreted by Jellicoe as a request to stay right there while she found the key. She disappeared into the kitchen. Jellicoe heard a drawer scraping open and rustling going on. Then silence. Moments later a match was struck, and Mrs Peabody returned smoking a fresh cigarette and, more importantly, holding a front door key.

'Mrs Peabody, consider yourself part of CID.'

She narrowed her eyes, the mouth remained set but there was a humour in her look. She dropped the keys into Jellicoe's outstretched hand.

'Don't you boys need a search warrant or something?'

'Not when we have cause to believe that a crime has been committed,' lied Jellicoe. It was weak. He knew it. Problem was, so did Mrs Peabody.

'If a crime hadn't been committed why else would you be here?'

As there was no answer to this that wouldn't have heaped further shame on the floundering DI, Jellicoe wisely decided to go on the offensive.

'Do you know the Suttons?'

The old lady took a long drag on her cigarette that seemed to start from the region of her slippered feet. Finally, after what seemed an age, she removed what was left of the cigarette and fixed Jellicoe with a stare.

'Do I know the people living next door to me?'

At any other time, such a question would not have been an unreasonable one. The way Mrs Peabody swilled the words around her mouth then spat them out like a second-rate plonk added further to Jellicoe's sense that he was thoroughly outgunned. He was enjoying the encounter immensely.

The Bus Stop

'Yes, you could put it like that.'

'Yes, I knew them. I wouldn't say they came round for canapes very often, mind.'

Jellicoe wondered for a moment if canapes came in tins these days. It was a passing moment, and he returned his attention to the old lady.

'What can you tell me about them?'

'I don't see much of him, Derek. He's a sailor. Merchant Navy. Always away. Sarah, I see more of. She gave me a set of the keys because she's always losing hers. What's happened?'

'I'd rather not say until I see Mr Sutton.'

Mrs Peabody nodded a thank you to Jellicoe. A shadow passed over her face. There was a genuine sadness behind the horn-rimmed glasses.

'Would you say they were a happy couple?'

'Is any couple really happy?' asked Mrs Peabody rhetorically.

Jellicoe winced at this. He and Sylvia certainly hadn't been. He saw her eyes narrow, and he wondered if she'd read his look. In fact, he guessed she had. It was time to inspect the house. He glanced down at the keys and nodded a thank you. Moments later he was over the invisible fence and standing beside the waiting Yates.

'He's a sailor. May explain why no one answered. Also, might explain why they live here.'

Prefabricated houses had often been handed out to former servicemen from the war. They were a typical government-inspired short-term solution that had become a long-term fixture.

Jellicoe opened the door which led to a thin entrance hallway while Yates made a show of announcing their arrival.

'Mr Sutton, this is the police. Are you there?'

No answer.

Jellicoe waved for Yates to move down the corridor and check the other rooms. He opened the first door on his right which led to the living room. He stopped and stared at what greeted him.

'Tony.

'Yes?'

'Come and see this,' said Jellicoe.

Jack Murray

5

Chief Constable Laurence Leighton breezed out of an office insofar as a man of his enormous stature could, gave a quick nod to his secretary Elodie, and motioned to Superintendent Ian Frankie who was sitting with Chief Inspector Burnett to follow him. On their way out of the outer office, they ran into Leighton's daughter.

'Winnie,' said Leighton, a smile creasing his craggy features as it often did when he saw his daughter before it retreated again when he realised what she wanted to do for a living. Winnie Leighton recognised the look as much as she treasured it.

'You go on. I'll catch up,' said Leighton to the two other men.

Frankie and Burnett marched onwards and downward, down the steps leading to the ground floor where the press conference would be held.

'What was it like?' asked Leighton.

'Bloody. You must catch this man. He used an axe or something like that,' said Winnie with an involuntary shiver. Her father felt as if the chill had been passed on to him. Alas, the prospect of persuading her to live in a convent was now long gone.

'We will. Are you home tonight?'

Winnie nodded before a guilty smile appeared and she added, 'Probably late.'

Leighton suppressed the natural desire of any father of a daughter to tell her not to be too late, that he would be waiting for her and that she should consider the feelings of the armed platoon of Commandos who were following her every move. He shook his head and left her in the corridor. Winnie Leighton watched him go and then proceeded towards her father's office.

Elodie Lumsden greeted Winnie with a smile that had been known to melt hearts at a range of one hundred and fifty-seven yards. And counting.

The Bus Stop

'*Ma cherie*,' said Elodie rising from her seat and giving her friend a hug.

'Are you coming to the Tulip Club tonight? There's dancing.'

'Will your father keep me here late?' asked the young French woman.

'I'll fix him,' replied Winnie. 'Meet me at seven. Maybe we can have something to eat then go on to the club.'

The smile on Elodie's face was the answer that Winnie had been looking for.

*

The members of the press trooped up to the front of the building and were allowed through a side door at the desk currently occupied by Sergeant Alex Crombie. As policemen went, he was unusual. If he stood on tiptoe, he would probably have made the regulation height. His weight was a matter of some unsympathetic humour at the station. No one laughed louder than Crombie.

In his thirteen years on the police force, he had not patrolled the beat once. This was because he was missing a leg. Yet no one questioned his credentials as a policeman. After all, Constable Clarke vouched for him. They'd fought together in Normandy. Crombie was his sergeant then as he was now. It was Clarke's suggestion that he join the police. It was Clarke who'd persuaded Chief Constable Leighton to take him. The benefits became apparent quickly. Crombie was the best desk sergeant anyone could remember because he combined limitless supplies of patience with more than a modicum of common sense and a humanity that was manifest in his beaming Pickwickian countenance. Even the petty criminals who regularly ended up before him called him 'Crumbs'.

'Crumbs' Crombie's patience was being tested to the fullest just as the pressmen filtered into the building. Old Mrs Bickerstaff was reporting a crime. She did this on an almost weekly basis. No arrest had yet resulted from the intelligence provided by Mrs Bickerstaff. And she'd been doing this for nigh on twenty years. But she lived in hope. She was a small of height but powerful of stature. Her head was wrapped in a battle-red paisley scarf, and she was in a combative mood that called to mind Churchill at his most bulldog-ish.

Jack Murray

'There's a pack of them out there,' she proclaimed. Crombie eyed the pressmen passing behind Mrs Bickerstaff and couldn't have agreed more. 'Howling they are. Someone should go in with a gun. If my Bill were still alive, he'd have done something about it.'

Bill Bickerstaff, according to his loyal widow, would have solved half if not three quarters of the crime in the town with the aid of his trusty shotgun. Crombie shuddered at the thought and did what he usually did when Mrs Bickerstaff appeared. He smiled benignly and took down the details of the latest crime or disturbance that had passed under her merciless gaze. At the end of her report, Crombie promised to do all in his power to deal with the problem. He smiled and nodded to Jellicoe who entered as he said this. Jellicoe grinned back at Crombie. Mrs Bickerstaff was a police station legend. Then again, so was Sergeant Crombie

*

Chief Inspector Reg Burnett's usual welcome to the members of the press was somewhere between a scowl and outright antagonism. As a result, the newsmen being aware of this considered him fair game. They competed with one another to be the first to get him to explode in annoyance. Of course, this would be more of a challenge with the chief constable and the superintendent present. Still, it was worth a shot.

Leighton opened proceedings by reading a statement to the assembled press. The press in question were not the elite of London's Fleet Street but local editors and staffers from towns in the county. The chief constable was well-liked and respected. A big bear of a man, he'd played rugby for the county. He had no enemies in the press. The same could not be said for his right-hand man, Superintendent Ian Frankie.

Frankie's face had a permanently wounded expression of a pantomime dame who is being made fun of. Whereas Leighton had a constant air of amused discerning, with Frankie it was a watchful tense balancing act that one was permanently engaged in. He glared at the press with a disciplined intensity.

'Gentleman,' began Leighton, holding a piece of paper before him. There were no ladies present. 'A body was found three hours ago in Fenton Woods on the Frimhampton road. We have reason to believe that her death is because of foul play. The woman has

The Bus Stop

been identified and we are currently trying to locate the next of kin. For a number of reasons, I cannot go into detail beyond telling you that the woman is in her early thirties. She lives locally. Chief Inspector Burnett will lead the investigation although both myself and Superintendent Frankie will be on hand to provide support. Are there any questions?'

There were eight pressmen in the room. All eight hands went up at once. This was part of a well-choreographed routine. Leighton would always choose the most senior newsman in the room to ask the first question. This was Cecil Lords. He owned the local Tribune, was President emeritus of the rugby club and had been a Freemason since the age of twelve, or so it seemed. He and Burnett had cordially detested one another for twenty years and counting. Burnett rolled his eyes when Leighton said, 'Cecil?'

Lords considered standing up but then thought better of it. He was wearing a yellow pullover and polo shirt with grey slacks. Had he not received the call from a fellow Freemason, personally, he might have gone out for his fourball at the golf club. But murder was murder. It sold newspapers. Best to show a face, he thought. The face, in question, was of a sixty-three-year-old man, ruddy of cheek, grey of hair and rheumy of eye.

'Two questions, chief constable. Firstly, when will you release the name of the victim? And do you know if the murderer has struck before?'

It was all Burnett could do to stop himself snorting.

'As Chief Inspector Burnett will be conducting the investigation, I think it best that he answers you, Cecil.'

The face of the chief inspector fell at this neat dodge by his boss. It was picked up by a few of the pressmen in the room. Burnett saw smiles erupt around the room and he scowled by way of response.

'Well, Cecil,' replied Burnett, drawing out the two syllables of the editor's name a beat or two longer than was necessary, 'I think that we will look to release the name of the victim tomorrow at the earliest. In answer to your second question, we are not ruling anything out at this stage.'

Burnett finished this information-packed bulletin with a liquid smile and a pair of raised eyebrows. All this was designed to irritate Lords. A warm glow erupted within Burnett when he saw that it had. More hands went up at this stage and Burnett took the next question which he answered at inordinate and unnecessary length.

*

'I do wish you would make more of an effort with Cecil,' said Leighton to Burnett afterwards back in his office.

'Yes, sir,' said Burnett with a look of glee on his face which told Leighton that his instruction would be happily ignored. Frankie, who had been unusually silent throughout the press conference, spoke at last.

'Are you sure Jellicoe is the right man to lead the investigations? Seems a bit odd to me.'

Leighton was surprised by this.

'Really? I thought he was quite bright.'

'He did well in the Solomon case,' pointed out Burnett.

'He would,' replied Frankie.

Leighton looked at Frankie, a trace of irritation on his face. 'I'm not sure I know what you mean by that, Ian.'

'I mean,' replied Frankie with an exaggerated patience that was certainly trying Burnett's if not Leighton's, 'that the Solomon case was fine for Jellicoe. A criminal straight from the pages of detective fiction. This is just a simple case of murder. Probably domestic. It will require thorough, old-fashioned police work not dramatic flights of fancy from Mr Jellicoe.'

In some respects, this assessment chimed with what Burnett thought. The probability that the murderer was the husband was high yet something about this case already worried him. The location of the body for one. The fact that the husband, subject to confirmation, may have been at sea.

'Mark my words,' continued the Superintendent. 'This is a straightforward domestic. Someone like Price may not be spectacular but he gets results. He's dogged. This case needs a dog who'll get hold of the bone and not let go.'

Leighton winced at the mention of the word 'dog'. He'd had quite enough of that subject already, in private, from Cecil Lords. It was obvious the newspaper owner had his sights set on the gypsy camp outside town. This was going to be a headache.

Burnett regarded Frankie's instincts in much the same way as he treated ballroom dancing with his wife. Ideally, it should be

The Bus Stop

avoided at all costs, but when the music started, keep as much distance as possible and avoid being trampled on.

'A simple domestic case, then, Ian,' said Leighton.

'As I said, mark my words,' replied Frankie, primly.

6

'Interesting,' said Yates as he looked at the wall.

'Is it relevant?' asked Jellicoe. Yates did not answer as it sounded as if the detective inspector was talking to himself. Jellicoe stepped forward to look more closely at the photographs on the mantlepiece. They were arranged underneath a large Union Jack flag which occupied a place that one might normally have placed a mirror or a banal landscape.

The first thing that Jellicoe had noticed was the signed picture of Oswald Moseley. He crouched down and read what was written.

Dear Robert, Thank you for all your help. Oswald

Yates bent down to read the inscription. He looked across at the other framed photographs. He pointed to a picture of a young woman. She was smiling the smile of youth. The smile that had something to look forward to. Instead, her future would see her face down, alone in a forest with an enormous wound on her chest.

'Yes,' replied Jellicoe. 'That looks like her, all right. Look over here.'

Jellicoe pointed to a picture of Sarah Sutton on her wedding day with a man he assumed to be Derek Sutton. She was very attractive. Yates asked the same question that was on Jellicoe's mind.

'I wonder who Robert is. A family member?'

'Yes, I was thinking that. Look at this group photograph. That's Moseley in the middle. He was surrounded by a group of young men. Behind them was the British Union of Fascists flag. Jellicoe remembered that it was red with a white and blue circle in the middle with bolt of lightning or some such thing. Jellicoe scanned the faces. His guess was that Derek and Sarah Sutton would have been too young to be members of the party which

The Bus Stop

enjoyed its heyday just before the outbreak of the war twenty years previously.

One young man attracted his attention. He pointed to him. Yates leaned closer in.

'Could be his father,' agreed Yates. He stood back from the mantlepiece. None of the other photos were political in nature. Jellicoe walked over to a magazine rack. There were a few 'Do It Yourself' magazines but nothing else of interest. In the corner of the room was a banner which looked like it had been folded over. Yates strode over and extracted it from the space between the wall and the sideboard. He unfurled it slowly. The banner was around eight feet wide.

The two detectives stood back to view it in full. The cotton sheet was a navy-blue colour on which there was writing in large white letters.

BRITAIN FOR THE BRITISH

'Well, he's not wrong in my view,' said Yates before adding, 'but I wouldn't have any truck with Moseley and those fascist thugs.'

Jellicoe looked at Yates but decided not to delve further into his sergeant's thoughts on immigration. After rolling the banner up again and replacing it, they searched the room for anything that would help them contact Derek Sutton or provide a clue as to why his wife had been so brutally murdered. Yates opened the drawers in the sideboard. He found some papers related to the Merchant Navy. He wrote some details in his notebook before carefully replacing them and continued to work through the remaining contents of the drawer.

In another part of the room, Jellicoe located some photograph albums. The first was a wedding album. The couple had married in August 1956 at a Registry Office. The man in the photograph on the mantlepiece looked like Sarah Sutton's father. Jellicoe put the album down and picked up the second album.

It was quite thick and seemed to cover the years between 1948 and the present day. Jellicoe leafed through the book. Family photographs of Sarah Sutton mixed with other pictures of groups of men including her father. They were taken at meetings protesting the arrival of Black Caribbean families to live and work in Britain.

Then he struck gold.

'Take a look at this,' he said to Yates who was scribbling in his notebook.

The detective sergeant strolled over to look at the photograph Jellicoe was pointing to. It showed the couple standing in a group that included both fathers.

'Do you think they met at one of these protests?' asked Yates.

'Looks that way. Even if they didn't, I'm not sure its material. The fact is they both shared similar political views. This means if Sutton killed his wife, it wasn't because of politics.'

They searched the house thoroughly for the next hour without uncovering anything that seemed of interest. They replaced everything but made notes where/when necessary. One thing was clear from their search. There were no other dead bodies. Their need to confirm this would be used by Jellicoe as the rationale for searching the house without a warrant.

They left the house and Jellicoe hopped over the invisible boundary to Mrs Peabody's house. He knocked on the door. She answered it quickly. An old cigarette still hung sorrowfully from her mouth. Jellicoe resisted the temptation to hold his hand out and catch the ash which was threatening to fall any second. He held up the keys and thanked her.

'Find anything?'

Jellicoe shook his head then added, 'Interesting couple.'

Mrs Peabody's mouth formed into a sneer, 'Best to avoid politics with them.'

'You didn't agree with them?'

'My husband fought against the fascists in Spain and then again in North Africa. He was good man, my husband.'

Jellicoe nodded and thought to say something but realised there was nothing he could say. So many lives lost. Yet he was living in a free country thanks to people like her husband. A country which allowed freedom of speech, freedom to protest things you opposed. Sometimes this protest appeared to be illiberal, to go against the very generosity of spirit that had seen the nation go to war to protect people living in a foreign land. It was a paradox. Yet Jellicoe wouldn't have it any other way.

The Bus Stop

*

'They did what?' exploded Superintendent Frankie. He had stayed behind to keep a close eye on the first day of the investigation while Leighton had left soon after meeting Burnett when the press conference had finished.

Burnett deliberately put the pipe in his mouth at this point. It was a manoeuvre he developed to irritate impatient people like Frankie. Then he replied just a beat before Frankie's pressure gauge reached the red zone.

'Good police work in my book. They had genuine cause to believe that a crime may have taken place and that Derek Sutton's life was in danger. They had to go in.'

'I hope they didn't conduct a search.'

'Of course, they did,' answered Burnett in manner that bordered on contempt. Frankie was seething by both the answer and the tone but equally he knew he would have done the same.

'Then please tell me they didn't make it look obvious.'

'They didn't. The next-door neighbour gave them a key. Jellicoe and Yates know their way around. Nothing was disturbed but they picked up a lot of useful information that may help us.'

'Such as?'

'The dead woman and her husband were connected to right wing politics. Protests about Black Caribbean immigration and the like into the country. Her father knew Oswald Moseley.'

Frankie shifted uncomfortably in his seat. 'Is this relevant?'

'Who knows. It might be a motive. It might not. At least we know who the husband is now, what he does and where we can reach him. That's saved us a lot of time on its own.'

'What does he do?'

'A merchant seaman, apparently. We're trying to contact his ship at the moment.'

'Well, if he's on board the ship that lets him off the hook.'

'Aye,' replied Burnett, hoping that the boat had docked, and they had a gift-wrapped suspect.'

*

Jellicoe and Yates met up with Wallace back at the police station. They found that Detective Inspector Price and Detective Sergeant Fogg had returned from investigating the dog-napping cases.

'Have you had a sniff yet?' asked Jellicoe trying to restrain a smile.

Price seemed to miss the joke, but Fogg raised a smile.

'Not a scent.'

'No leads then?' pressed Jellicoe.

Wallace turned away and headed out of the office. Even Yates was smiling.

'We went to the gypsy camp on the edge of town. Bloody hell there are a lot of them. Mean looking lot, too,' said Price.

Rather you than me, agreed Jellicoe. He hated dealing with the travelling community. In his experience there was usually something going on that wasn't legal. Sometimes this was because they were made to feel such pariahs. Invariably, they were very tight knit. They brooked no outside interference, and this made investigating anything next to impossible. The best they could do was alert the heads of the community if crimes were being committed by their group and then hope some sort of justice would be served to those responsible. Jellicoe took Price aside and mentioned this.

Price, in his short acquaintance, had struck Jellicoe as a decent if uninspired police officer. Solid in character, a detailed if rather slow thinker. He had no doubt that the Welshman would get to the bottom of the disappearances. He doubted there would be a happy ending for the owners.

They discussed the murder for a few minutes. Price suggested that they investigate political connections while they waited to hear from the inquiry to the Merchant Navy. Jellicoe agreed although Yates was already on this.

Burnett appeared in the office following his meeting with the superintendent. Experience warned Jellicoe that the chief's level of grumpiness usually increased in direct proportion to the amount of time that Superintendent Frankie spent at their police station.

'Have we solved the murder yet?' barked Burnett.

Jellicoe resisted the temptation to suggest they were waiting for him to show them how. Sometimes comedy is all about the timing of the joke as much as it is the timing in its telling. Silence was its own answer. He looked around him. Yates was on a phone and pretending to ignore the conversation. Price and Fogg were

The Bus Stop

staring dumbly at him and Jellicoe, as ever, had that half-smile that could bug him so much.

'I'll take that as a "no", then. What are you doing?'

Jellicoe told him what the others were doing.

'What about you?'

'I'm going to visit Chester Johnson, the bus driver. Fancy a trip out of the office?'

Burnett wasn't sure whether to say yes, which was the truth, or to be angry that the young pup had guessed that the time spent with Frankie would have acted as a spur to be somewhere else, far away. He growled something by way of response which Jellicoe took to be yes.

'I'll find someone to drive us,' said Jellicoe heading towards the door. Wallace looked up hopefully from his desk.

'Not you,' snarled Burnett on his way past. He pretended not to hear the laughter as he exited through the office door. They headed for an unofficial mess room to find a driver. Sitting in the middle of the room when they opened the door was Constable Leonard 'Clarkey' Clarke. His rough-hewn features made him look like an oil painting. By Picasso. His face went one direction, his nose another. Cauliflowered ears suggested either a congenital illness or years spent in the front row of a rugby scrum.

'Clarkey, just the man I was looking for,' exclaimed Burnett.

'Reg, sorry Chief, what can I do you for?'

'Fancy hunting down a murderer?'

Clarke drained the tea from his blue-grey cup and stood to his feet. He was not especially tall, but he was wide. Very wide.

'I fancy that a lot. Where are we off to?'

Burnett threw him the keys to the Wolseley with the promise that he would tell him on the way, mainly because he didn't know. Jellicoe provided the address when they reached the car. Clarke climbed into the driver's seat while the two detectives sat in the back. Burnett had visibly begun to relax, having ensured that he would soon be putting distance between himself and the beloved superintendent. It also helped that the distance would be covered at a more sedate pace than would have been likely with Wallace at the wheel.

Johnson lived in a flat which was at the eastern end of town, the opposite part from where Jellicoe had visited Sutton's house with Yates. It was certainly no more picturesque. This part of town had been redeveloped using tower blocks. Although none were higher than five storeys there was a hard-hearted modernity that radiated a disregard for either how they looked or what they might be like to live in. Where an architect or a town planner saw an efficient and modern way of living, Jellicoe saw the future of crime.

'Lovely,' said Burnett sourly as they emerged from the car. Some boys were playing football on the street nearby. They stopped and looked at the three men who, even if the uniformed Clarke had not been with them would have been clearly identifiable as police. 'Perhaps you should stay here, Clarkey. Wouldn't want any damage to the car from that football.'

Clarke smiled and fixed his eyes on the boys, none of whom were likely yet to be teenagers. He nodded as the two detectives left him on his own to defend the vehicle against the eight boys who were now more interested in them than their game.

Burnett led the way up the steps that led to the second floor of the flats. A sign read, 'Flats 8 – 15'.

'Flat thirteen you say?' asked Burnett.

'Yes,' replied Jellicoe.

They trooped along an outdoor concrete corridor. There were puddles where the rain had come in from the previous morning. There was no obvious sign of how it would drain beyond the hope that it would eventually evaporate. Jellicoe shook his head. The flat was the last but one on the corridor. They knocked on the yellow door.

'Mr Johnson, this is the police. Can you open up please?'

A voice from inside shouted back, 'I'm coming, man.' It was an American accent. This made Burnett raise his eyebrows a notch. Jellicoe shrugged. He was more used to Americans in London. This would be the first he'd met since his arrival at his new posting.

Burnett's rose even further moments later when the door opened. Chester Johnson was close to six feet four and built on similarly epic proportions. But this isn't what surprised Burnett.

Chester Johnson was black.

The Bus Stop

7

'May we come in Mr Johnson,' said Jellicoe when he realised that Burnett had momentarily been disconcerted by the sight of Chester Johnson. He wasn't alone in this. Johnson was equally taken aback by the two policemen.

'Yeah, man, come in,' replied the big American standing back to let the two policemen pass.

They entered the flat which was small but tidy. The furniture was older than both the flat and probably its owner. Johnson gestured for them to sit down on a small two-seater sofa. There was music playing on a record player, Louis Armstrong. Johnson sauntered over to the record player and delicately lifted the needle from the disc. He switched off the player and turned to his visitors. He saw the look on Jellicoe's face and grinned.

'Want me to keep it on?'

Jellicoe would have said yes had Burnett not been there. Instead, he smiled ruefully and shook his head. Johnson took the long player out and placed it carefully inside its sleeve. Then he put the record below to join what looked like around fifty other discs. There was nothing hurried about his movements. He had all the time in the world.

'Can I get you gentleman a cup of tea?' asked Johnson. It was what you did in England, he supposed, when policemen came calling. He almost smiled at the contrast with his home.

Both policemen declined the offer, so Johnson sat down on an armchair. 'What can I do for you gentlemen?' asked Johnson.

His voice was, to Jellicoe's ears, from a southern state in America. Johnson leaned forward, resting two large arms on his knee. Both arms were clearly visible as he was wearing a vest. Jellicoe judged him to be in his forties. There was a hint of grey at the sides of his head, but his face looked quite young. Of more interest was the mark on his left bicep. Unless Jellicoe was

5

mistaken, it was a bullet hole. Johnson saw the direction of Jellicoe's gaze and grinned.

'Something I picked up fifteen years ago.'

'France?' asked Jellicoe.

'No, I made it into Germany before I caught one. Two, in fact. I was back fighting two weeks later.'

The voice was slow but attractive. This was a man who seemed relaxed with himself and utterly unworried by the presence of two policemen in his flat. In situations like this, Jellicoe fell back on his training. Not the police training which was to question everything and make no assumptions. His earlier training from Cambridge, studying people. Johnson had faced worse things than two British policemen in his life. He appeared to have not a shred of guilt on his conscience. Or he was a good actor. But then again, wasn't everyone? Burnett spoke next. It was time to get down to business.

'Were you driving the sixty-eight-bus yesterday afternoon between midday and eight pm?'

'Yesterday it would have been the one-six-eight but yes, I was driving then.'

Johnson paused and waited for the next question. This told Jellicoe something important. He'd been arrested before. Often. Or he'd spent a lot of time with policemen. He knew not to ask questions. He knew he had to allow them to ask theirs and wait until *they* were good and ready before explaining why they were there.

'Can you tell us if you picked up a young woman coming from the town who would have stopped at the bus stop near Fenton Woods?'

Johnson nodded. Jellicoe and Burnett both leaned forward in what seemed like a choreographed move yet was purely instinctive. Jellicoe almost laughed.

'Yeah, there was woman. She got on at the town centre, near the bank that was robbed.'

'What did she look like?'

'Brown hair, I think. She wore a scarf. Early thirties. Slender, attractive. She stayed until that stop. I asked her was she sure? It wasn't dark but the light was going.'

'What did she say?'

The Bus Stop

Johnson was silent for a moment. Then he said, 'Nothing. She just got off.'

'Did she not hear you?'

'She heard all right. It happens sometimes. I ignore it.'

'You don't feel offended?' asked Burnett.

'I do but I'm also used to it, sir.'

Burnett nodded and sat back.

'What time was this?' asked Jellicoe, making notes.

'We left on time at four forty-five. So, I would have dropped her off around four fifty-five.'

'That was the last you saw of her?' asked Burnett.

'Yes, sir,' replied Johnson but Jellicoe, who was studying him intensely, saw the eyes shift slightly before returning to Burnett.

'Where you surprised that she got off at such a late hour?' asked Jellicoe.

'Yes, sir, I was surprised. She'd paid to return to town, you see.'

'Can you think of why she would have wanted to get off?' pressed Jellicoe.

'We passed a broken-down car further back. There was a guy beside it. Bonnet was up like he was wanting to see what was wrong.'

'Do you think she was going to him?'

'I don't know, sir. But we were still in the middle of Fenton Woods so I can't think of any other reason.'

'Can you describe the car?'

Johnson shrugged and looked away as if trying to excavate his memory for what the car may have looked like.

'No, sir. It was white. A saloon car but I don't know what make. I didn't see the number plate.'

'What about him?'

Johnson shrugged again.

'White guy. Dark hair. Moustache. Tall but I can't remember much more. We passed him so quickly and it was dark.'

'Was there anyone else on the bus when you picked up this lady, either direction?'

'On the way out, yes. The bus was quite full, but no one got out where the lady did. On the way back the bus was empty. One old lady got out the stop before where I picked this woman up but that was it.'

A silence fell on the three men. Then, Jellicoe probed a little further on the man with the broken-down car, but the driver's memory was too vague.

'How long have you been with the bus company?'

'Eight years this September.'

'Married?'

Was that shadow that seemed to pass over his eyes. There was certainly a pause.

'I was, sir. I was. It didn't work out.'

'Where is she now?' asked Burnett.

'In Exeter. She remarried. Her name is Linda Patterson. Patterson is her new married name. We don't have much contact now.'

'Children?' asked Jellicoe.

'She didn't want any. I did. I guess you should know these things before you marry.'

You can never know who you are marrying, thought Jellicoe. Or maybe you do. The heart blinds you to what the eyes see clearly. This can be a defence for some, a delusion willingly accepted by others and for people like Jellicoe, it was an open wound that bled freely during the marriage until she was murdered.

Johnson smiled ruefully and shook his head after he'd spoken. He still hadn't asked about why the policemen were there. The only thing missing was beer because it felt like a few old friends swapping war stories. Thought of the war prompted the next thought from Jellicoe.

'You were stationed here during the war?'

'Yes, sir. Gordian. Arrived early 1944. Stationed in Gordian. That's where I met Linda. Then June 6th I was on a ship heading over the channel. I wasn't back until early forty-five then I was back out again until the end of the year. In Berlin mostly. They asked me do I want to go home, and I said, "No, sir". I'll stay right here thank you very much.'

'Where was home?' asked Jellicoe.

'Alabama.'

Jellicoe was gratified he'd placed the accent correctly.

The Bus Stop

'I suppose there wouldn't have been much of a welcome home for a soldier like you.'

Johnson burst out laughing and shook his head like he'd heard the best joke in a while.

'No sir. It's different here, that's for sure.'

'Is it? You said the lady didn't seem to have much time for you.'

Johnson shrugged but the smile remained. He stretched his big arms out and shrugged.

'You get that everywhere, sir. Hell, even some of the guys I was fighting with were like that. They changed their tune when I was saving their hide. But it's better here, that's for sure. Look at you gentlemen, for example. Back home they'd call me "Boy" and they sure wouldn't have bothered asking me questions when they could kick my butt instead.'

'If you don't mind me saying, Mr Johnson, you don't seem very curious about why we're here.'

'I am, sir. But I figured you'd tell me in your own good time. Did something happen to the young lady?'

'She's dead,' said Burnett, fixing his eyes on the bus driver. 'Murdered.'

Johnson's mouth dropped open.

'No, sir. No that can't be. Who would do that?'

'That's what we want to find out. By the sounds of it, Mr Johnson, you were the last person to see her alive,' said Burnett.

'That's not quite right, sir,' pointed out Johnson. 'The murderer was.'

*

Constable Clarke faced a big problem now. Two of the boys were racing towards him at full speed. There was a hard glint in their eyes. Clarke was unsure how he would be able to handle two of them, despite their small size. Seconds later they were on him. He fell to the ground with a thud that seemed to shake the foundations of the building. He watched as the ball flew past him. A groan went up from one of Clarke's teammates.

'No point in complaining, lad,' said Clarke, climbing slowly to his feet. 'You're the one that should've been defending.'

'You're the one that should've been keepin' goal,' replied the boy sulkily.

49

Jack Murray

This was a fair point. Clarke had been charged with keeping goal but had decided to make a foray up the pitch when his team had been on the attack. Once they'd lost the ball, he'd been caught out of position.

Three boys looked up at him accusingly. He held up his hands in acknowledgment that he *might* have done a little better.

Then, to make matters worse, he heard a cruel laugh coming from a few yards away.

'He's right, Clarkey. You sold the ranch there, good and proper,' said Burnett.

Clarke turned around and saw the two detectives standing on steps. Both wore wide grins.

'Right lads, time to go. There's no more I can teach you. Just remember me when you're playing for United or Spurs.'

This comment was met with an entirely predictable hail of abuse from the adults watching and the young footballers. Clarke picked up his helmet and walked to the car with the Burnett and Jellicoe.

'So taught them everything you know then, Clarkey.'

'No chief. I taught them everything they know but not everything I know.'

'Lucky them,' said Burnett drily.

'How was the interview, chief?'

Burnett and Jellicoe glanced at one another. Jellicoe wondered if Burnett had the same feeling he'd developed during the meeting. Johnson was unquestionably a suspect. Which was a pity because Jellicoe had quite liked him. But that wasn't the problem they faced.

'I think we could have a bit of trouble with this one,' said Burnett grimly.

'With Johnson?' asked Clarke.

'No, this case, Clarkey. This is going to explode in all our faces and no mistake.'

'Why do you say that chief?'

Burnett told him.

The Bus Stop

8

Back at the police station, Burnett called a meeting of the investigating team. For the moment this excluded Price and Fogg who were left to follow up on the disappearance of dogs in the town. Wallace and Yates joined Jellicoe and Burnet in the office.

'Shut the door,' ordered Burnett. He related the outcome of the interview with Johnson. Then he turned to the other two detectives.

'What have you learned?'

As the more senior man, Yates spoke first.

'I followed up on Sutton. He is a midshipman on a vessel called Pericles. It is not due to arrive at Southampton until tomorrow. Around eleven in the morning they said. It's been at sea since last Tuesday. So that effectively rules out Sutton as the killer.'

Burnett nodded at this. He turned to Jellicoe, 'You and Yates go there tomorrow. You'll have to tell him.'

Jellicoe had long since accepted that it would probably fall on him to break the bad news about his wife. It was something he'd done many times. It was never easy. Invariably the people he had to break the bad news to were usually understanding of this and made it easy for him.

Then Burnett added, 'Someone will have to tell the father. Do we have his details?'

Wallace piped up at this point, 'Yes, sir. I have them here.' He held up a notebook. 'He lives in London. He's a pharmacist.'

'Give me the details,' said Burnett taking the notebook from the young detective constable. 'I'll have someone from the Met visit him. The father will have to come down and identify the body.'

Burnett read through the notes and shook his head.

'Sounds like a charmer. He was a member of the fascists until they were banned. Joined Moseley's party afterwards.' Burnett read through the next pages of notes. A frown creased his face. 'What's this? Some bird's telephone number?'

Wallace grinned before replying, 'I wish. I saw something in the wood that I wanted to check on.'

'Well concentrate on Johnson for the moment. You too, Yates. I want to know everything about him. What he eats for breakfast, his favourite drink. What did he do in the war? I want it all. Right now, he is our chief suspect. And given the views of the father and the husband, this could get messy. No slip ups. Don't talk to the press. Don't even hint to the press what we are looking at here. If that cretin, Cecil Lords, gets hold of this, he'll play merry hell. Does anyone know if the post-mortem has been completed?'

The change of tack with this final question from Burnett was greeted with blank faces. This brought a snarl from the chief and a wave of the hand to indicate they were all dismissed.

Except Jellicoe.

When the two junior detectives had left the office, Burnett fixed his gaze on Jellicoe.

'Did Johnson do this?'

Jellicoe was too experienced to admit his gut instinct was 'no'. First impressions were important and provided more clues than you knew. It often wasn't until the very end of the investigative process when you understood better the narrative of the crime that you saw how many things, you'd sensed at the start, were true. Johnson was a black man implicated in the murder of a woman who had close connections to political groups who had views antagonistic to his presence in the country. It was too easy a fit, yet it couldn't be ignored either. Burnett was right. This could become messy very quickly.

'His surprise seemed genuine but that means nothing. Her views and his colour might be significant. Let's see what Yates and Wallace come up with. Has he been in trouble before? He's been with the police before, that's for sure. Is he violent, though? Didn't seem so to me. But as an ex-serviceman he will have either killed or been around death. He'll have experienced racial abuse before, much worse than this. Has he reacted to it before? At the moment, he has two things might save him.'

The Bus Stop

'Yes,' agreed Burnett. 'Did anyone see Sarah Sutton get off the bus? I'm thinking about the anonymous caller.'

'And did anyone see the car that was broken down?'

'Find out. In the meantime, Let's see what Hilary has come up with.'

The two men headed down to the bowels of the building where there was a small mortuary. The lighting in this part of the police station always struck Jellicoe as in need of updating. It felt as if he was going back to the Victorian era. Green tiled walls, low wattage light and a lack of heat were in marked contrast to the modernity of the police station on the two floors above.

'Hello, Reg,' greeted Taylor from behind his desk. He held up a brown envelope. 'Just had this typed up. What do you want to know?'

'Only the bits I'm likely to understand,' came the response from Burnett.

The two men laughed as they usually did even though the joke was decades old. Jellicoe smiled more at the idea they would still enjoy this moment than the joke itself.

'She was in her early thirties. No sign of any sexual assault. Cause of death was by two blows from a large sharp object that could be an axe. I've found traces of rusted metal which I passed on to the Forensics Lab. I don't know if it's relevant but there is some indication that she was once pregnant. I don't know if she miscarried or if she took the back street route.'

Jellicoe and Burnett looked at one another. This was interesting but not yet material. It would be filed away for future use. Or ignored. You couldn't always tell.

'You mentioned she had some bruising that may not have been caused during this murder,' said Jellicoe.

'Yes. It looks like she's been beaten at some point in the last two days. Can't say it was the murderer of course. The one observation that it may not be is that there are no signs of restraint either on her wrists or her ankles. These sorts of bruises are suggestive of domestic violence rather than murder.'

'Can't be the husband; he's out at sea,' said Burnett.

'Hello sailor,' replied Taylor, with a knowing smile.

There was little Taylor was going to add to their understanding beyond what he'd said so the meeting was a brief

53

one. Jellicoe headed up the stairs while Burnett and Taylor stayed behind possibly to enjoy a glass of malt whisky. It was after five in the afternoon and the day was ending for them all.

Back at the office, he met Vaughan who was standing with Yates and Wallace. He had the Forensics report.

'Anything of interest?' asked Jellicoe.

'Nothing around the dead body I'm afraid. I haven't had a chance to look at something Dr Taylor gave me, but I did find a lot of fingerprints in the telephone box further down the road, including those belonging to the dead woman. She was obviously making a call. There are a lot of prints on the phone but I have the more recent ones so we may have those of our anonymous caller.'

Jellicoe, turned to Wallace to ask something but the detective constable held his hand up.

'I have called the Post Office to find out every call made from that call box in the last twenty-four hours.'

Jellicoe nodded and then a thought struck him.

'Is there any chance you can widen that search. Make it for the last week. Also, does that include calls going into the phone box.'

Wallace looked at him strangely. Then again, Jellicoe was unquestionably a bit different from the rest. The questions he asked were sometimes odd. Yet there was no doubt he was smart.

'It would, I suppose,' replied Wallace who was clearly uncertain, 'but I'll check.'

'Thanks. Do you know when we might have this?'

Wallace looked a little downcast at this. This was a question he had asked. The response from the Post Office was unsurprising.

'He said it might take a day or two.'

'And the handbag?' asked Jellicoe, turning to Vaughan.

'Mrs Sutton's fingerprints weren't on the bag, I'm afraid,' said Vaughan.

'It's not her bag,' conceded Jellicoe. 'The housekeys weren't for the Sutton house either. I'll break the good news to the chief.'

This was disappointing but better than nothing. At least they could remove the bag from their thinking. There was little more that could be accomplished at that moment and Burnett had

The Bus Stop

already headed out the door, followed soon after by Yates. Jellicoe nodded to Wallace to leave.

A few minutes later, Jellicoe decided to it was time to go home. For the first time since arriving at his new posting, he had a place that felt like home. He headed down the stairs and saw Yates saying goodbye to Elodie Lumsden. Jellicoe wondered if Yates had asked her out yet. He never inquired about Yates's love life, but he would have been a poor psychologist, not to mention detective, if he did not recognise the signs of yearning in his sergeant. Yates saw Jellicoe and held the door open for him.

'Age before beauty?' asked Jellicoe wryly.

'You read my mind, sir.'

Jellicoe laughed. He glanced at Yates and asked, 'How is Miss Lumsden?'

Even in the dark, Jellicoe could see Yates was slightly uncomfortable. For a moment Jellicoe regretted putting him on the spot. It was, after all, none of his business.

'She's very well. I think she and Miss Leighton are planning to go to the Tulip Club, tonight.'

'Where?' asked Jellicoe. He hadn't really been interested in exploring the night life of the town. The names of the hot night spots, except those that were run by the two main gangs in the town, were unfamiliar to him, but the Tulip Club rang a bell. Then he remembered seeing a card in Farley's record shop advertising the club.

'It's just off the high street. An underground club. Plays jungle music,' continued Yates.

Jellicoe stopped and looked at his sergeant with a frown.

'Jungle music?'

'You know. Jazz and the like.'

'I see. What music do you like then?'

'Rock 'n' roll. Elvis, Jerry Lee Lewis. People like that.'

Jellicoe wasn't sure whether to laugh or to be dismayed both by the ignorance of his sergeant as well as the overtones of prejudice.

'You do know that Elvis and Jerry Lee Lewis are really just doing what Chuck Berry and Little Richard were doing years before?'

'No comparison, sir, in my book.'

Jack Murray

They parted on this dissonant note. Ten minutes later after a grind through the late evening traffic, Jellicoe was climbing the steps to his new flat. On his way up the steps, a black cat ran in front of him almost causing him to trip. He'd seen the cat around the apartment block but was unsure of who it belonged to. He arrived at his door just as his next-door neighbour was leaving. June Peters was a young woman about his age. She and her husband had seemed friendly enough, but they also kept their distance. Jellicoe had seen the look of wariness creep into their eyes whenever he'd mentioned his profession. It had been the same in London. One of the reasons Sylvia had been desperate for him to show more interest in promotion than actual detective work was her desire to avoid such encounters. Jellicoe said hello but did not detain her to chat. There was relief on both sides.

The flat was now almost fully furnished. His things had arrived from London including his prized long playing record collection and the Dansette record player. He walked straight over to it. There was already a record sitting on the turntable. *Ascenseur pour l'échafaud* by Miles Davis. He'd picked the album up in Paris when he'd travelled there for a romantic weekend with Sylvia. They spent the weekend arguing.

He switched on the Dansette and placed the needle on the first track of the record. A lone trumpet played a melancholy opening. The flat was still dark as he'd not switched on the light. It felt right. He almost wanted to sit down on the sofa and let the music wash over him. To add light would have ruined the mood of the piece. And nothing should do this. He stood for a moment and listened to the trumpet speak to him. When the first track finished, he was woken by the sound of a jauntier more playful piece. He took off his coat and threw it on the sofa. He sat down and shut his eyes. His mind left the room. For twelve minutes he listened without moving. Then the needle slipped off the final track. He replaced it carefully on its stand and stood up.

It was time to think of what he would eat. There wasn't much to think about. He went into the kitchen and opened the cupboard. Despite being quite full, the cupboard was lacking somewhat in variety which was ironic given how much of it was made by Heinz. The bulk of the tins on display were Heinz Beans. There was one lone tin of Spaghetti. It would never be consumed.

The Bus Stop

He'd bought two. The first one had proven to be something of a disappointment. Perhaps his only problem had been the fact that he had a point of comparison with the spaghetti Bolognese he'd enjoyed when travelling through Italy on his honeymoon. He smiled at the shamelessness of the American manufacturer and picked a tin of beans and set it down on the counter. It would be beans on toast.

Again.

As he was eating, he thought about the conversation he'd had with Yates. The Tulip Club sounded interesting. It was a surprise that there was a club playing jazz in the town. It was a bigger surprise he hadn't heard about it. A thought passed through his mind; it would be good to hear live jazz music once more. This had nothing whatsoever to do with the fact that Winnie Leighton would potentially be there.

Nothing whatsoever.

9

Jellicoe elected to walk to the Tulip Club. The walk into town took him down a hill which gave him a view of the lights reflecting onto the flat-iron sea. To reach the High Street took around twelve minutes but Jellicoe was in no rush. At the High Street he'd have to ask directions. He was still wearing the same suit he'd worn at work, the same mackintosh, and the same trilby hat. He couldn't have looked more like a policeman than if he'd started twirling a truncheon and whistling "An Ordinary Copper", the theme tune to the popular BBC television series featuring a policeman, 'Dixon of Dock Green'.

It was close to eight when he reached the High Street. Making a beeline for a taxi-rank he asked for directions to the club. The taxi driver was as tall as him but around twenty years older. He looked Jellicoe up and down for a moment and a cruel grin spread over his face. Jellicoe couldn't decide if the smile was to do with him disliking 'jungle music' or that he'd been made as a member of the force.

'Take the second left and then first right, mate,' said the driver.

Jellicoe thanked him and followed the directions given. The Tulip Club was situated on a street so dark; it was like a black pall had been thrown over narrow gap either side of the alley. There was no streetlight. In fact, the only light on the street was the bright white lights of the club set against a red sign.

The closer Jellicoe came to the club, the more evident was the sound of the music. It was jazz all right and his heart began to race in anticipation. Standing outside the club were two women, a blonde and brunette. Beside them was a man. He was black. As Jellicoe approached, he was aware that all three pairs of eyes were on him. He nodded to the man who was built to epic dimensions. He was a doorman.

The Bus Stop

Jellicoe descended the steps to the basement club. Each step seemed to make the music grow louder and the smoke thicker. He opened the door and was hit by a wall of noise. The place was jumping. Nothing was still, not the bodies, not the band, not the walls, not the air. Everything moved as if tied by some invisible thread to the music's pulse.

Jellicoe walked in, eyes straight ahead and made for the bar. The music was old-style jazz with more than a hint of Dixie. The tempo was fast, perhaps faster than Jellicoe preferred. Couples were on the dance floor moving their bodies in a visceral response to the rhythm and propulsion of the music. The atmosphere crackled with energy and something else which reminded Jellicoe of something that had been absent from his life for too long. But he was in mourning, wasn't he? You don't go to a jazz club when you grieve. He smiled grimly at his own hypocrisy.

He reached the bar and thought to order a Guinness. Then he changed his mind and asked for a martini instead. The barman was black, he glanced briefly at Jellicoe and then ignored him. Jellicoe did not have turn to face the room to suspect that a large proportion of the clientele would be black, too.

The music came to an end, and this seemed to signal a break for the band. There was a good round of applause for their efforts. The barman finally appeared alongside him. Jellicoe ordered a martini and turned to face the crowd again. The martini arrived and he took a sip. Whether it was the barman's skills, the atmosphere or the music, Jellicoe did not know but it was the best martini he'd ever tasted.

On closer inspection, the crowd was more equally split between black and white people than he'd suspected. He couldn't see either Elodie Lumsden or Winnie Leighton but then again, it was crowded and despite the small size of the venue, there were lots of brick pillars, nooks, and crannies for two girls to disappear into. With men friends perhaps.

The walls were all naked brick decorated by monochrome pictures of jazz greats. Jellicoe sat at the bar looking as unobtrusive as a nun at an orgy. He sensed the wariness around him. He didn't need to think long to know why this should be so. Everything about him was an answer to the question posed.

Jack Murray

Alone he sat, sipping his martini, scanning the room for the two young women. Then he sensed someone sitting down alongside him. He turned to the person who'd sat next to him.

'Hello, sir,' said Chester Johnson.

The look of surprise on Jellicoe's face seemed genuine enough but Johnson couldn't be certain. Jellicoe smiled in recognition. A silence settled between them. It was clear something was on the American's mind, so Jellicoe waited. Johnson chose the direct approach.

'Am I under suspicion, sir?'

The directness of the question numbed Jellicoe's brain momentarily. Rather than answer the question openly he replied, 'You're not under surveillance, Mr Johnson, if that's what you're thinking. I happen to like jazz. I wasn't aware of this place until yesterday.'

Jellicoe used his eyes to indicate the Tulip Club.

'Who do you like?' asked Johnson. There was a trace of suspicion still in his voice.

'Miles Davis for one. I was introduced to Ornette Coleman recently,' said Jellicoe, thinking of Solomon, 'but I'm not sure.' Johnson winced at the mention of Coleman. This made Jellicoe smile and the two men both relaxed at that moment. 'You're not a fan, then?'

'No, sir. I like Miles Davis, too,' said the American. 'Sonny Rollins, Charlie Mingus, Monk. They're all good.'

'Do you play?' asked Jellicoe. The American burst out laughing at this which made Jellicoe regret the question. 'I'm sorry, I didn't mean to imply…'

Johnson was too amused though and waved his hand. Finally, he said, 'You think all black people play jazz?' He started laughing again which made Jellicoe feel like fool. But there was something in the laughter that suggested something else was amusing him. 'I'm sorry, man, I'm just joshing. What time you get here?'

'A few minutes ago,' answered Jellicoe, confused.

'Ahh. That explains it. I'm in the band,' continued Johnson before adding, 'Trumpet.'

'You've studied music.'

'I studied Satchmo, sir. That's all I needed.'

The Bus Stop

Jellicoe smiled at this, but an uncomfortable thought was beginning to take root in his mind. Soon he would have to bring the amiable American in for questioning. Perhaps this conversation was not such a good idea and not just because it could be used by a clever lawyer to argue that he'd spoken to a suspect without cautioning him; he *liked* Johnson.

'Do you like Louis Armstrong?' asked Johnson.

'I prefer his singing. The trumpet seems too strong sometimes. He can play, though.'

'He surely can,' smiled Johnson. 'Speaking of which, I'll have to go now. Duty calls.'

Johnson left his seat and disappeared into the crowd. There was no longer an invisible barrier around Jellicoe. The presence of Johnson had, somehow, validated him in the eyes of the crowd. And people wanted to buy some drinks before the music started again.

Including Elodie Lumsden.

'Detective Inspector,' said Elodie, tapping him on the shoulder.

'Hello, Elodie,' smiled Jellicoe.

'I haven't seen you here before.'

'I hadn't heard of this place until this afternoon. What brings you here?'

'Dancing,' smiled Elodie. 'Are you here to dance?'

'No, absolutely not. I love jazz music. Can I buy you a drink?' asked Jellicoe. He deliberately excluded mentioning Winnie Leighton. No point in giving the game away that he knew they'd be together. Just then the music started again. Elodie said something that Jellicoe could not quite catch. She collected two drinks and motioned for him to come over with her. This was an offer he wasn't likely to refuse. He picked up his martini and followed the young French woman through the crowd to a table at the back. The table was empty. Elodie indicated with her eyes to the small dance floor in the middle of the room.

Winnie Leighton was dancing with a tall, good-looking black man. He was wearing an expensive, well-cut suit. It was obvious they were good friends by the mutual smiles on their faces. Jellicoe felt a stab of jealousy at seeing her so lost in the presence of

61

someone else. Other thoughts crossed his mind unbidden and unwelcome. He turned away and sat down beside Elodie.

'That's Jonathan,' said Elodie, which was one of those infuriating explanations that only women were capable of giving. It wasn't just the detective in Jellicoe that needed more specific information as to the nature of the relationship between the pair. He was certainly holding her closely enough to suggest they were more than pen pals. Jellicoe turned to Elodie. She was eyeing him closely and this made him realise he was giving too much away.

'You like jazz?' asked Jellicoe. For some reason he'd assumed someone so young would prefer rock 'n' roll.

Elodie laughed and replied, 'I like dancing.'

Jellicoe wasn't sure if this was a hint. He became uncomfortably aware that his palms were sweating. Some psychologist you are thought Jellicoe. He decided that it was a hint.

'Would you like to dance? I'm not very good, though.'

Elodie smiled and shrugged. She stood up and held her hand out. Jellicoe held his breath hoping that it might calm him a little. An attractive French girl wanted to dance with him. There were probably a number of worse things that life could throw at you at this point. Jellicoe wasn't in a mood to think of them. His mind was focused on the task of not stepping on her toes.

Jellicoe's hand reached down to her waist. His hand sent a signal to his brain and that signal read – she's very slim. Elodie began to move to the music and Jellicoe began to follow her movement. The band were playing a version of 'Some Day My Prince Will Come' in a way that would have been utterly unrecognisable to Snow White. So were the young French woman's movements. They managed the improbable feat of being flirtatious, innocent, and primeval. Soon, Jellicoe was lost in the music, the movement, and the mayhem of the dance floor. It was a couple of songs before he woke up from this dream, bathed in sweat.

Elodie led him back to their seats. Winnie Leighton was sitting with the man Elodie had called Jonathan. Winnie looked up at him archly and said, 'This is a surprise Detective Inspector.'

'Hello, Miss Obviously.'

'Very funny.'

The Bus Stop

'So, I'm told,' replied Jellicoe. Then he reached out his hand towards Jonathan. 'Hello, I'm Nick Jellicoe.'

'Jonathan Richards,' came the reply. There was half-smile on his face as if he recognised the discomfort of Jellicoe. 'You work with these ladies.'

'Yes. And you?'

'I'm a doctor.'

Jellicoe was surprised then angry at himself for being surprised. 'At the hospital or General Practice?'

'I'm a surgeon at the hospital.'

Jellicoe was aware that Winnie Leighton's smile was growing wider by the second. Another thought was running alongside this: he was fast running out of questions he could ask that did not seem as if he was interrogating him. He changed tack.

'You have my admiration. I've attended enough post-mortems to know I couldn't do what you do.'

Richards laughed at this and the table, all at once, seemed to relax from the unusual tenseness that had developed since the two men had met. On closer inspection, Richards looked to be a similar age to Jellicoe. His accent was public school. Jellicoe didn't want to think about his bedside manner.

'Let me buy some more drinks,' offered Jellicoe but Richards put a hand on his arm.

'It would probably be quicker if I do.' This was said matter-of-factly. It was certainly true. Jellicoe shrugged and grinned ruefully. He watched the doctor rise and leave the table. Then with a sinking heart he turned to face the inquisitorial grins of the two young women.

*

A little over a mile away, two men were chugging along on a Norton Denominator motorcycle and sidecar that had seen better days and those days were ten years earlier. The motorcycle pootled un-merrily along, coughing like an aging chain-smoker. The two men had been driving around the residential area making enough noise to wake up a judge, a managing director and two head teachers all living in the area.

'They're not biting tonight,' said Eddie 'Tripod' Tilly. 'Tripod' had been his nickname at school, and it had stuck with him in the twelve years since he'd left with, it must be said, little regret on either side. It was either a compliment or a millstone depending on Eddie's rather volatile mood. In what may have been a cruel joke on the part of Mother Nature, she had compensated for his rather diminutive stature by over endowing him elsewhere. The impact was rather akin to that most essential item of a photographer's camera equipment.

With Eddie tonight was his best and, possibly, only friend, Lee 'Ginger' Rogers. Ginger was neither red-headed, female nor likely to win any ballroom dancing competitions without the threat of violence towards those judging him. In this latter respect, lay his true calling. Ginger was as big as Eddie was small. What he lacked in Eddie's native guile he more than made up for in terms of his predisposition towards hitting people. Hard. They made a good team and had stuck together if not through thick, then certainly, thin, since their school days.

'Must be one around,' said Ginger hopefully. He was an optimist at heart. A thug, too, but his heart and mind were always open to the possibility of a serendipitous outcome unlike his good friend who was prone to depressive rage. Good fortune was to smile upon them.

A poodle named Daphne had temporarily escaped its owner, Jolyon Roehampton, General Secretary of the Bowls Club. Roehampton had unwisely decided to attempt a late-night stroll with his constipated canine. The intention had been to rid Daphne of the prodigious intake of Whiskas she'd enjoyed earlier that evening due to a miscommunication between husband and wife. Both had fed her. Daphne was unquestionably going to feel the effects of this soon. Outside she and Roehampton had ventured. It was a chilly evening and neither particularly wanted to make the trip. One moment Daphne was on the lead, the next she had put fifty yards between herself and her sixty-year-old owner.

'Look,' exclaimed Ginger, as the black poodle trotted into view.

'Good spot,' replied Eddie. The poodle had come round the corner and slowed down following the initial blissful moment of freedom.

She settled by a tree and adopted a position that might kindly have been described as ready to open fire. So engaged was she in

The Bus Stop

her task that she failed to detect the sound of Ginger creeping up behind her. One moment she was offering up a sacrifice to Hecate, the next she was in a canvas bag yelping indignantly at her treatment.

Jolyon Roehampton came puffing around the corner just in time to see the coughing, spluttering motorcycle chug off. He couldn't make out the licence plate on the rust bucket thirty yards ahead of him. This could mean only one thing. The dastardly dognappers had struck again. Already two members of the club had lost their pets.

His purloined pooch was number three.

Jack Murray

The drive to Southampton took less than an hour. The two men joked that Wallace would probably have made it in half an hour. Jellicoe rolled his eyes in a young-people-of-today manner even though he was only thirty-one himself.

The police car arrived at a barrier and was waved through when Yates displayed his warrant card at the guardhouse. They drove on ahead towards the dock stopping briefly to find out where they should go to meet the arrival of Pericles. The sky overhead hung heavy with intent. Jellicoe looked up from inside the car and began to think of the many things he would rather be doing at seven in the morning.

As soon as the two policemen emerged from the car, the first spit of rain greeted them. Jellicoe had a feeling that his mackintosh and trilby would struggle against the likely downpour unless they found cover quickly. The two men rushed to stand in the doorway of an office building that provided a good view of the port. It was shut.

'I thought these things were open twenty-four hours,' said Yates in a voice that came within a whisker of petulance.

'Apparently not,' said Jellicoe marching back towards the car. The two men sat in the front. Neither said anything. Instead, they looked through the rain-slapped windscreen at the charcoal-green sea. In the distance they could see a grey hulk labouring towards them, smoke belching from a funnel.

For fifteen minutes they watched the boat slowly sail to the dock. The rain did not stop. It fell in icy sheets. The two men glanced at one another dejectedly. At some point they would have to brave the elements. A man approached them to ask their business. Yates's warrant card once more worked its magic.

Ten minutes after the ship docked and twenty-five minutes after the two policemen had arrived, they found themselves

The Bus Stop

walking up the metal gangplank to the boat. At the entrance was a rather confused-looking sailor. This time Yates did not have to produce identification. It was obvious what they were even if the purpose of their visit was not.

'Can you take us to the captain?' asked Jellicoe wishing he could have said something along the lines of take me to your leader. Perhaps one day he would get to utter this line.

The crewman nodded and asked them to follow him. He led them along a narrow corridor with white metal walls. At the end of the corridor, they reached a heavy metal door that led to steps.

A minute later they were standing on the deck. Ahead they could see a couple of uniformed officers. The crewman approached the one of the men. He was a lot younger than Jellicoe had imagined he would be. This was, presumably, the captain. He nodded to the crewman and then approached Jellicoe and Yates.

'Hello, I'm Captain Marchbank,' said the captain holding out his hand. 'How can I help you?' His voice was clipped but he appeared friendly enough.

Jellicoe replied, 'Hello, sir. I am Detective Inspector Jellicoe, and this is Detective Sergeant Yates. We've come to meet Seaman Derek Sutton. We have some news to communicate to him.'

The captain looked at them with a frown.

'I'm sorry, gentlemen, but your trip has been a wasted one. Sutton was signed off this trip by the doctor.'

Jellicoe turned to Yates whose face was ashen. This had been his job and, once more, he'd neglected to check on an important detail.

'I see,' said Jellicoe trying not to appear angry. 'Are you able to share with us the nature of his illness?'

'I don't see why not. As you may imagine, long stretches at sea can play havoc with one's personal life. Marriages can often fail. Sutton told us that he was experiencing such difficulties and requested compassionate leave. We granted it of course.'

'When was this?'

'It was just before we left for Gibraltar. That's a week ago now.'

Jellicoe did not have to look at Yates to know that the sergeant was feeling mortified. This was a major oversight. They hurriedly

67

left the ship. As soon as they were off, Yates apologised for not asking the obvious question. Jellicoe nodded but remained tight-lipped on the journey home. It would fall to him to tell Burnett. He would receive, deservedly, a share of the censure.

They arrived back at the police station an hour later. Parked outside was a car in the spot normally reserved for Leighton and Frankie. This was turning into the morning from hell. Not only would he have to deal with Burnett's response; he would also potentially face the wrath of Widow Twanky.

'Let me tell the chief,' Yates suggested as they entered the police station.

'No, leave it with me. In the meantime, find Sutton. Get over to the house. Get round the neighbours. Find him and find him soon. Take Wallace with you.'

The two detectives arrived in the office just as Frankie was addressing the detectives with Burnett standing alongside him.

'Glad you could join us,' said Burnett sourly. Jellicoe winced as he suspected that his mood was unlikely to improve when they dropped the bombshell about Derek Sutton. Burnett must have had an inkling that something had happened as a frown creased his forehead when he saw Jellicoe's face.

'As I was saying,' said Frankie in a voice pregnant with schoolmasterly censure, 'our number one suspect has to be the bus driver. I don't need to tell you that this is going to play hell with the press when they realise that the victim's father is a friend of Oswald Mosely. Whatever your views may be about the arrival of black people from the empire, these cannot be communicated outside this building. Do I make myself clear?'

If ever a man was incapable of delivering a call to arms in the manner of Henry V on St Swithin's day, it was Superintendent Frankie. There was a muted murmur that sounded enough like a 'yes sir' to pass muster.

'Now,' continued Frankie, just as a couple of the detectives looked like they would make their escape. This amused Jellicoe as they had to sit down again. 'Price and Fogg will pick up Johnson for questioning. The victim's father, Mr Bowles, is due here around eleven. On no account can he meet Johnson. The chief inspector and I will deal with Mr Bowles.'

The Bus Stop

Silence followed this statement. Frankie looked around him at the sea of blank-bored faces. He was used to this. Rallying the troops had never been his strong point. He'd often thought of joining a Toastmasters club or some such thing to improve his rather leaden delivery. Even he accepted that it lacked a certain spark.

Frankie was a detail man. Someone who ensured an investigation ticked along. Someone who held people accountable. Leighton could never do what he did. Quite how the big lug had ever made it to the top was beyond his understanding. Or perhaps he knew. Being a Mason helped. Being a minor rugger hero helped. Frankie was neither. Not through choice either. The invitation to join the Masons had never come. And he hated rugby. Tennis was his game. There weren't many senior policemen who played tennis. It was socially enjoyable but professionally useless. He may as well have been a black belt in knitting.

Frankie turned to Jellicoe. A chill ran though him as he realised that he was seconds away from humiliation.

'Detective Inspector Jellicoe,' said Frankie with what sounded like a combination of relish and distaste. This was no mean feat acknowledged Jellicoe as his heart was sinking. 'I was expecting Mr Sutton to be with you. Where is he now?'

Yates stood up and seemed about to speak when Jellicoe touched his arm.

'Derek Sutton was not on the Pericles. He was signed off on compassionate leave a week ago. This is something that was not communicated to us when we inquired of Sutton. We have let the appropriate people know of our unhappiness at this waste of police time.'

Yates resisted glancing sharply at Jellicoe for this flagrant lie. He suppressed a smile and crossed his fingers.

'What?' exploded Frankie. 'I shall have a bloody word.'

'No need, sir,' said Jellicoe. 'My feelings were made clear, and we may need their help at a future point in the investigation. Clearly this puts Derek Sutton in the frame, sir, as you originally suggested.'

It was all Yates could do to stop himself laughing now. Jellicoe was laying it on thick, a fact that the Burnett was all too aware of.

Jack Murray

As Newton once observed, every action has an equal and opposite reaction. Jellicoe knew that in buttering up the superintendent, he was probably earning the disapproval of Burnett. He risked a glance in the chief inspector's direction. Burnett's face would have had the Medusa running for cover.

'You're right, Jellicoe. This does put a new complexion on matters. Very well, we need to find Sutton.' If Burnett's face was one of controlled fury, the superintendent's face took on the beatific aspect that can only be acquired by a man who has been proven right but is too modest to say so. Frankie then proved there is an exception to every rule.

'I knew this was a domestic.'

Jellicoe put a finger up to speak.

'Sir, there is no way we can avoid speaking to Mr Bowles about Sutton. He might be able to tell us where is.'

Frankie's eyebrows came close to shooting through the roof at this suggestion while Burnett's reddening face suggested that Jellicoe was unlikely to escape with anything less than a kneecapping.

'Very good, Jellicoe. I was wondering who would suggest this,' said Frankie shamelessly.

By now Yates was digging his nails into the palm of his hand to stop himself laughing. He had to hand it to Jellicoe, his face was straight as he came out with the most outrageous obfuscation Yates had heard in a long time. Even more incredibly, he'd come out of it smelling roses. There was so much he needed to learn. His approach would have been honesty. To reach the top, he badly needed to add nuance to his communication skills.

The meeting broke up when news came through that Sarah Sutton's father had arrived at the front desk. On the way out, Burnett glanced at Jellicoe and said, 'A word when I come back.'

Jellicoe suspected that the word would be short and Anglo-Saxon in either tone or origin. He smiled at the chief which he suspected would further enrage him. There was some comfort to be taken from that.

The two senior officers descended the stairs at a clip. Neither wanted to keep the bereaved father waiting. Robert Bowles had been taken to a downstairs office, away from the unceasing traffic of victims and criminals coming into and out of the police station.

The Bus Stop

Burnett entered the room first followed by the superintendent. Bowles was in his sixties guessed Burnett. His dark hair was running to grey and thinning at the temples. He was a severe looking man dressed in a dark suit and a navy overcoat. The first thought that struck Burnett was how at odds his well-cut suit seemed in comparison to the rather modest living accommodation of his daughter. As usual, Burnett detected the faint flicker of hope in the man's eyes: the hope that the person he had come to identify would turn out to be someone else. Frankie spoke first.

'Mr Bowles,' said Frankie holding out his hand, 'I am Superintendent Frankie. This is Chief Inspector Burnett.'

They shook hands and Bowles said immediately, 'Can we?' He left the rest unsaid.

Frankie nodded, saying, 'This way, Mr Bowles.'

Dr Taylor met the three men in the mortuary. He refrained from expressing condolences. It was very rare but not unprecedented that the victim was unknown to the person believed to be next of kin. He led Bowles into a cold room where the body of Sarah Sutton lay covered from head to foot with a blue cotton sheet.'

Taylor stood at the head of the table and fixed his eyes on Bowles. He received a nod and pulled back the sheet. One moment Bowles was standing erect like a military man, then his face and body seemed to dissolve before Taylor's eyes. He'd seen the strongest of men crumple in a similar fashion. You never became inured to it.

'I'm so sorry, Mr Bowles.'

But Bowles could not hear him. He was lost in memory, in desolation, in an unwilling effort to find his breath through the sobs that wracked his body. Finally, through his agony he found his voice. It was hoarse with grief.

'Find who did this. Find the man who killed my daughter.'

11

Her screams grew louder.

She wouldn't stop. His eyes widened. Sweat beaded his forehead. His old foes: heat, and fear. He wasn't sure how he would be able to stand it. He'd survived hell already, or so he thought. In fact, the landings were only the beginning.

The noise outside the house was deafening. It never ended. It never would end. This would be what it was like, even if not every day. It would be a constant threat. The gunfire; the explosions; the killing. What would one more death be?

He looked down at the girl, but his eyes were blinded by sweat and tears. He could no longer hear the terrified screams, the begging. Everything was drowned out by the sound of his heart beating, the blood rushing around his head and his conscience yelling at him. Outside he heard someone banging at the door. They were shouting.

Shouting.

Shouting.

He woke up bathed in sweat. But the shouting did not stop. Nor the banging. If anything, it was growing louder.

There was someone at his door. He rose from the bed and stumbled drunkenly out of the room just as his door came off its hinges and two policemen holding a battering ram fell into his front room. They looked at him and he looked at them. He was dressed in white and blue striped flannel pyjama bottoms. His torso was bare. It glistened black in the morning light. His stomach fell over the top of his pyjamas. He looked down and was conscious of his vulnerability. But he was too confused, too drowsy to understand what he was seeing. Was this part of the dream. He'd never had this happen before.

Then two men stepped through the door and past the two uniformed police officers. The older man said, 'Mr Johnson, I'm

The Bus Stop

arresting you in connection with the death of a woman two days ago. You do not have to say anything. But it may harm your defence if you do not mention when questioned something which you later rely on in court. Anything you do say may be given in evidence.'

And then Chester Johnson knew the nightmare was only beginning.

*

'As you originally bloody suggested?' roared Burnett at Jellicoe. He didn't have to shout of course. But then how else would the rest of the men in the office know that he was in a fury about Jellicoe buttering up the superintendent so barefacedly. 'What the bloody hell was all that? Who forgot to check if Sutton was on the bloody ship?' Jellicoe was about to answer the question when Burnett waved his hand dismissively. 'I know all right. You don't have to tell me. But you should have checked with Yates if he'd asked.'

This was true. Jellicoe nodded. They'd wasted a lot of the morning and given Sutton another few hours of a head start.

'When can I speak to Mr Bowles?' asked Jellicoe.

'You're assuming a lot, lad. After this balls-up maybe I should just hand it over to Price like Widow Twanky wants.'

Jellicoe realised he'd earned that one and said nothing. When Burnett was in one of the moods, it was best to wait until the storm had subsided. He would see sense then. For a minute there was silence in the office.

'Where is Mr Bowles now?' asked Jellicoe when he felt sufficient time had elapsed.

'With the super. He's having a cup of tea. I'm sure he'd take something stronger. Compassionate leave you say?'

'Yes. They didn't say much more but it suggests to me that there were problems in the marriage. I think we should tell Mr Bowles that Sutton wasn't on the ship. See what he says.'

Burnett glared at Jellicoe, not because he was angry. He'd had the same thought. The father had questions to answer however he might be feeling. Yet, Jellicoe knew about loss. What they wanted to do was cynical and manipulative, but this was a murder inquiry. Burnett seemed to understand this too but, unlike Jellicoe, he was a father.

73

'Not yet,' said Burnett at length. 'Anyway, we'll have to question the bus driver first. Price is arresting him now.'

'Arresting him?' exclaimed Jellicoe. 'Why? We don't have any evidence.'

'Ah you weren't here. That's right, you were off on some joyride to Southampton. Your boy Wallace came up with the goods. While we were waiting for the US Army to come back to us on Johnson's war record, your boy did a check on him. It turned up something interesting.'

Jellicoe's eyes narrowed.

'Go on,' said Jellicoe. Burnett smiled the contented smile of a boss who is, for once, in possession of an important piece of information that his subordinate does not have.

'Johnson was accused of rape in 1944 while stationed in Gordian. The case was dropped after a couple of weeks. Anyway, you and Wallace can go down there and find out more about what happened. Let Wallace drive. You'll be back before you've left,' cackled Burnett. In fact, he enjoyed his own joke so much that he took out his pipe and lit it.

'Who is going to question Johnson?' asked Jellicoe.

'Price will. Twanky wants him involved, I told you.'

Jellicoe nodded and there was some relief on hearing this. There was little point in being evasive about the previous night. Burnett was looking at him suspiciously. 'What's wrong with you? If it were me, I'd be raging that Price is questioning the man you put us on to. What's got into you? Are you some bleeding heart for our black friend?'

Jellicoe told him about the previous night. Oddly this did not cause a further explosion. Perhaps it was the soothing effect of the pipe that allowed the chief a few extra seconds of reflection.

'Yes. Probably for the best. What did you talk about? Nothing about the case, I hope.'

The tone of Burnett suggested he knew that Jellicoe would have more sense than to do this, but he needed to check anyway.

'Jazz, sir. We talked about the musicians we liked.'

'Jazz?' said Burnett in an amused tone. 'I had you down as opera and ballet. Fat ladies wailing then popping their clogs and the like.'

'You're obviously a bit of a fan.'

The Bus Stop

*

Jellicoe handed over the car keys to Wallace with a heavy heart. Wallace held out his hand with his usual enthusiasm. He caught the look in Jellicoe's eye, and this made his grin grow wider.

'Don't worry, sir, you can trust me.'

They climbed into the car and set off in the direction of Penzance in Cornwall. As it was Wallace who had uncovered the fact about Johnson's past, Jellicoe felt it deserved some acknowledgment.

'Good work on finding out about that business back in forty-four. What made you think of it?'

'I was reading last year about the war and the role played by the Americans. There were a nearly two million of them over here just before the invasion. The book also said there were around one hundred thousand black Americans with them. Segregated, of course.'

'Why do you say "of course"?'

'That's how they do it over there. They tried to do it over here, too.'

Jellicoe said nothing and allowed Wallace to continue.

'Anyway, the book said there was some crime involving the new arrivals. Usually assaults and fights. Theft, too, I gather. So, I thought I should check with the police station in the town near where he was stationed. This is when I'd a stroke of luck. One of the chaps I spoke to at Penzance Police Station remembered the case. He said the case was dropped but couldn't recall why. Promised he'd dig out the file.'

'That'll take a while if it was 1944. We may have to help him,' responded Jellicoe wryly. Then he settled back as they had a long drive ahead to the Devon town where Johnson had been stationed.

They drove through the rain at speed that was just on the right side of sensible. Despite this, Jellicoe still felt a few moments of anxiety as his exuberant detective constable rounded corners as if he was driving at Le Mans. The journey took a shade under two hours by which the time the weather had changed from miserable to ghastly.

Jack Murray

The port town of Penzance contained no pirates, much to Jellicoe's disappointment. As they drove along the sea front looking at the buildings that had probably been there for a few hundred years, he could just imagine the gangs of thugs press-ganging poor drunks onto the ships. He was glad to be living in a more enlightened age. Just then they passed a wall with a CND painted on it.

Wallace pointed to a red brick building, The Penzance Police Enquiry Office. He parked the car outside just as the heavens unleashed their worst. The two men were drenched in the short walk from the car park to the police station.

'Hello,' said Wallace stepping forward and showing his warrant card. Jellicoe noted the smile on the old desk sergeant who had made them as detectives immediately. 'We've come to see Sergeant Fulton.'

'That would be me, Mr Wallace,' replied Fulton with a broad grin. 'Let me find someone to take over here and we'll get you gentlemen a cup of tea. I might even find a biscuit if I'm lucky.'

This was exactly what was needed for the two men. They stepped behind the desk and waited for Fulton to return. When he did, he led them through to an interview room while he trooped off to arrange tea. He returned a minute later with the good news that the tea was on its way.

Fulton sat down and immediately had a confession to make. He smiled sadly and said, 'Look, I had a look around for the file I mentioned and I'm afraid there's nothing here that pre-dates 1950. It's all been packed away and put in some warehouse. It could take days to find what you're looking for. I'm sorry.'

'That's all right,' said Jellicoe, 'I can understand. Perhaps you can tell us what you remember of the case and if there's anyone else, we can speak to.'

'Truth to tell,' admitted Fulton, 'I don't remember much. When those black boys came over in forty-three, I think we were all a bit concerned. The other soldiers, the white ones, that is, warned us against associating with them. Not just the ranks, either. Senior officers came along, too, saying this. Many of the black boys were stationed in the area around Penzance. They weren't doing the fighting as such. It was mostly manual work, supply, and the like. It was like the Americans didn't trust 'em in a

76

The Bus Stop

fight. Anyway, once they were over, we could see that most of them were well-behaved. Better behaved certainly than many of the white Americans.'

'Did you have much trouble with the American soldiers?' asked Jellicoe.

'No more than you would expect. Usually alcohol was involved: fights and the like. I suppose the reason why I remember the Johnson boy was because it was so unusual. And then the case was dropped. I think the girl changed her mind. She may have been pressured into making the accusation because it was a coloured boy but that was the last that I heard of it. I'm sorry I can't tell you much more.'

Jellicoe nodded then asked Fulton, 'Where did all this take place?'

'In a nearby village, Gordian. Many of the coloured boys, and they were just boys most of them, were stationed in and around there. If I remember correctly, the young girl was the daughter of the pub owner in the village. I can't believe there's more than one pub there so you shouldn't have too much trouble finding it. He might still be landlord for all I know. Wouldn't be a surprise.'

Jellicoe and Wallace thanked the policeman which signalled the end of the meeting. They asked for directions to Gordian to which Fulton drew them a map. He left them with the less-than-comforting assurance, 'Ten minutes outside Penzance unless you're caught behind a tractor in which case it could be half an hour.'

It took twenty minutes in the end but only because Jellicoe misread the map much to the amusement and good-natured chaffing of Wallace. The drive took them through an odd mixture of moor, woods then farmland as if Mother Nature couldn't decide what she wanted so threw everything together.

They entered the village just after three thirty. Jellicoe was feeling the effects of a long day on the road. He also realised that he hadn't eaten. The combination of hunger and fatigue were rarely good companions at the best of times. He hoped the pub served food whether or not the landlord was the same one who'd been there during the war.

The village was bustling with activity as there was a small market lining the streets. The traffic, such as it was, moved at a snail's pace. Thatched cottages with exposed stone walls mixed with whitewashed shops. They passed an old forge and a water mill.

'Picturesque. It feels like another time,' said Wallace

Jellicoe couldn't have agreed more. He wondered how the arrival of thousands of American soldiers in the district would have gone down, especially ones of a different colour. Yet as soon as he thought this, he saw a black couple walking down the street pushing a toddler in a pram. The car continued down the street towards the pub which was situated at the far end. The sign for the pub was made from wood. It read: *The Hare and Hounds*.

The police car pulled up outside. The weather was milder now. The rain had stopped but there was a nip to the air. They men rushed towards the entrance and were greeted by a roaring fire inside.

Jellicoe had seen enough westerns to know how it looked when two strangers strode into a saloon. He was expecting the music to stop and the clientele to halt what they were doing and stare at them.

Nobody so much as glanced in their direction. This was hardly a surprise as the bar only had three people and they were silently absorbed in a game of cards. Matches lay strewn over the table. A big stakes game seemingly.

A young man stood behind the bar. He smiled a greeting at them. To Jellicoe's eyes he was too young to own a bar never mind be the father of the young woman who had claimed to have been attacked by Johnson.

'Hello, new to town?'

Town was something of an exaggeration, but Jellicoe let that one pass.

'Yes,' said Jellicoe, eyeing a board that promised pork pies. 'Do you have any pies left?'

'We do,' replied the young man.

Jellicoe breathed a sigh of relief and ordered a couple for him and Wallace plus two half pints of bitter. There wasn't any Guinness. While the barman went to tell the kitchen to heat up the pork pies, Jellicoe looked around the bar. It was relatively small but, then again, so was Gordian. The brick walls showed wartime photographs. The two detectives noted that among them

The Bus Stop

were photographs of black servicemen. Jellicoe indicated with his head for Wallace to have a look at the pictures while he paid for the drinks and lunch. The barman soon placed the two half pints on the bar and collected the money from Jellicoe.

'I don't suppose the man that owned the bar during the war is still around?' asked Jellicoe.

'Grandad? Yes. He's still the owner last I heard,' grinned the young man.

'Can we meet him? I'm Detective Inspector Jellicoe and this is Detective Constable Wallace. We're investigating a suspicious death,' explained Jellicoe. 'Your grandfather may be able to help us with some information related to a man we are questioning about the death. Where can we find your grandfather?'

The young man pointed to the three men in the corner playing poker.

'That's him in the plaid shirt.'

The man in the plaid shirt sensed someone was looking at him. He glanced up and saw Jellicoe. A frown or at least a look of curiosity crossed his face. He folded his hand and stood up. He was a big man, certainly taller than the six-foot Jellicoe and broad with it. Jellicoe doubted there had been much trouble in the pub over the years with such a man behind the bar. He was around seventy years of age and had a grey beard, clear blue eyes and craggy good looks that gave him the appearance of Ernest Hemingway.

Jellicoe thanked the boy and brought the pints over to a table. Wallace was still examining the photographs. He turned to Jellicoe and said, 'Sir, over here. Look.'

Jellicoe pulled his eyes away from the owner of the pub and rose from the table to join Wallace. He was standing in front of a photograph of a dozen servicemen, all black, taken inside the pub. One of the men was Chester Johnson. All of them were smiling.

As they looked at the photograph, Jellicoe sensed rather than heard the arrival of the old man.

'Hello, gentlemen,' said the man. His voice had an attractive west country burr to it. 'Are you looking for someone?'

Jellicoe turned to the man and introduced himself and Wallace. He shook hands with the man who introduced himself as Thomas Adams.

'Mr Adams, we're policemen as you may have guessed. We're investigating the death of a young woman. One of the men we are questioning is this man here. I believe you know him.'

Jellicoe pointed to Chester Johnson. He was quite unprepared for the reaction.

'Yes, I know him. Chester is my son-in-law.'

The Bus Stop

12

Gordian, Devon: January 1944

We knew about them before we saw them. A man from the Ministry came to visit the village. He spoke at the village hall. Afterwards he came for a drink. He told us about life in America, about segregation and how this would apply in the army too. That's why they had to put those boys in separate places from the white boys. Afterwards I can tell you we had a might more sympathy for the coloured boys than we would otherwise have had. They had things rough. I don't know about you, but I don't much like it when people are treated badly for no reason. I don't much like being told how I should treat people either. And I certainly don't like being told how I should run my business.

The next people to visit were these American officers. Most of them were decent and respectful but there was one major I remember. I didn't like him. Clements, that was his name. You know the sort. Expects everyone to kow-tow to him. He didn't have much time for the coloured boys. He used words I wouldn't repeat. And I'm thinking, they're on our side fighting for freedom when they're not even free in their own country. Remember that name, by the way: Clements. He's part of this.

They started to arrive just after the new year. By the end of January, there were thousands of soldiers stationed around the area. It wasn't just the black soldiers. There were some white ones too. But most of them came a bit later. We didn't see much of them in the first couple of weeks. They were building their camp and then bit by bit they began to be introduced to the local farms to do work there. A lot of them had worked on farms. A few of the farm owners drink here. That's when I began to hear about how good the black soldiers were. I don't know what it was like for them over there but over here they knew how to work. That's not all. We kept hearing about how respectful they were, too. Helpful. Like they would do odd jobs on the farms. Fixing things. Old Hodgson had his barn fixed up good as new. Cost him nothing. That's when I heard that the farmers were having them stay to dinner.

Jack Murray

Towards the end of January a few of them came into the village for the first time. By then we'd heard enough to know they were all right. They had money too. They'd buy things in our shops. A few came into the pub. They all called me 'sir'. I can tell you I've been called a few things in my life but never 'sir' and I was in France in seventeen and eighteen, mind. A sergeant. Even my boys back then didn't call me sir.

Chester was among those boys. They'd come in and have a drink of beer. He was the loudest of them. Always a bit confident was Chester. I think it helped that my Linda was behind the bar. There weren't many young men in the village before and during the war then suddenly there were hundreds of them. All black of course. You stop seeing their colour after they've fixed your drainpipe and spent hundreds of pounds in your bar. I think Linda liked the attention particularly as it was so respectful. Not like the white soldiers later.

One night Chester asked me did I allow music in the bar. I said yes but not after ten o'clock. Folk go to bed early around here. The next night he and two other of the boys come in. He played some of the jazz music on his trumpet. One of the others had a guitar and the third had a double base made from an old box, a plank, and some tennis string. That was some night. Of course, we loved it. A bit of life in the place. By then some of our girls had taken to going out with them soldiers. Nothing untoward. They always treated the girls well. We even had some dancing in the pub.

For a month or two there was no problems. It was when some of those white American soldiers arrived that the problems began. At first, they seemed to take over the town and the coloured soldiers disappeared. They were a rowdier lot. I didn't much like the way they treated the people in the village. They seemed to think we should be grateful for them being there. We were but didn't like having it shoved down our throats.

Then there was my daughter. She was always a little bit quiet and never one to go after the boys. Maybe they were a bit scared of me. Anyway, she was friendly with the soldiers but didn't step out with any of them, either the coloured or the white ones. A few of the white soldiers took exception to this and called her snooty.

What with this and the rowdiness, I was getting a bit angry and said as much to their captain. He was pretty decent about it and told the men to calm down a bit. I asked him why the coloured soldiers were no longer around. He told me they'd been ordered to stay away.

I didn't like that and said so. He wasn't a bad fellah and I think he agreed with me though he never said it. There was nothing he could do to change things. It went on like this for a week or two and then a few of the

The Bus Stop

coloured soldiers came into town. During the day it didn't matter so much, and they weren't around at night. Then I heard that Stan who runs the shop and post office was threatened by one of the officers for serving the coloured soldiers. He said that they'd stop using his shop if he continued.

Stan told him where to go.

Then Chester reappeared one night with his friends. He came into the bar, and you could have heard a pin drop. Like one of those westerns with Randolph Scott. A few of the white soldiers told the black men to leave. I told the white soldiers to leave, instead. They were just boys really. They tried it on with me and I just swatted one. The others took off. After that the black soldiers returned in the evenings. Chester even started playing music again with the other two.

At first there was no problem. I think the word had got round that I wouldn't stand for it. Then this chap Clements appears again all full of himself. He goes to my daughter and demands to see me like he owns the place. I was out somewhere at that moment.

Anyway, I arrives, and he tells me straight that I wasn't to serve the coloured boys anymore. I laughed in his face; I did. I told him that it was my bar, my village, and my country he was in. He had no right to tell me what I could or couldn't do. The nerve of him. I still think of him now. He's in one of the photos on the wall. Always good for a laugh when we look at him, Idiot.

Two things happened after that. Well, three, as you'll hear. The first thing was that the white soldiers stopped coming to the bar. I think it was orders. A lot of them mixed fine with the coloured soldiers so it was a pity for them. The second was that Chester asked me if he could take my daughter out for a walk some afternoons when he'd finished work. I said it was up to her. Back then the boys just went for a walk. I'm sure there was no more to it, but they were well-behaved. They just wanted the company, and the girls wanted the company too. You know how it is.

Anyway, Linda said yes to Chester. So, they went out for a stroll along the river. They came back after two hours, and Chester went on his way. Now, I remember Linda had seemed a little upset. I asked her if everything was all right. She seemed to calm a bit and then I felt better. The next day a military policeman comes in and informs me that Chester had been arrested and was on a charge of rape. I asked who he'd done this to. He said it was my daughter.

Of course, Linda said it was a lot of rot. But by then Chester had been taken to Penzance as it was not a military matter. I asked Linda straight if she were hiding something. Then she burst into tears. She was crying her eyes out. I can tell you I feared the worst at that moment.

Jack Murray

Then she stops crying and tells me that she and Chester had kissed. Some of the white soldiers had seen them kissing and followed the two of them home from the river, giving Chester a hard time. She was crying because she felt embarrassed about telling me. I told her not to worry but that she had to go Penzance and clear the matter up.

Well, despite Linda denying anything had happened, it still took a few days for Chester to be freed. First, a colonel came to the pub to question Linda. Clements was with him. They tried everything they could to get Linda to say that Chester had imposed himself on her. But Linda was having none of it. I spoke to the colonel and told him what I thought of the way he'd questioned my daughter. But then he did a strange thing. He admitted he'd been hard on her because he believed both her and Chester. He knew there was a problem with prejudice, and he knew, although he didn't say, that Clements was the problem. I quite liked the colonel after that. He was a good man.

Chester was finally released and for a while he and Linda saw a good deal of each other. But around April, he was moved away. That was that, although they began writing to one another. I didn't have a problem with it as I knew he'd be off to France soon enough.

For a while they wrote frequently and then it stopped soon after the invasion. We thought he was dead. There was no news and Linda expected the worst. Then around a year later we had a letter from Chester telling us that he was in Berlin. They began to correspond again. Chester said he wanted come back to England.

Well, he did come back in 1946. He found work on one of the farms. He was good with engines. Anyway, he and my daughter began to step out again and they married a year later.

*

Jellicoe had listened intently throughout and did not ask any questions. Adams was a natural storyteller, and it was quite a story. Both policemen had another half pint and Adams insisted that it was on the house. Wallace made notes as Adams related the events of fifteen years ago. It did not prove that Johnson was innocent of killing Sarah Sutton but, at least, it meant that there was no reason to suspect him based on what had happened in the village of Gordian.

'How was he when he returned from Germany?' asked Jellicoe.

'War changes a man, Mr Jellicoe. You see things and do things no man should ever have to do. It affected Chester all right. Still

The Bus Stop

well-mannered mind. But he was not the carefree boy who'd left a year earlier. He'd grown up a bit. He was more serious. Mature even. Still likeable but he wanted to make a life here. Make his way in the world. He certainly had no intention of returning home. England was home as far as he was concerned.'

'Do you mind me asking one more question Mr Adams?'

'Of course.'

'Johnson and your daughter are divorced. What led to this?'

A shadow passed over the pub owner's face. Perhaps even a hint of embarrassment. He shrugged and put his hands up.

'Marriage is,' he stopped to find the right words, 'not easy. I liked Chester. He still writes to me every so often. But Linda was too young maybe. This was her first real boyfriend and Chester was a bit different. He wore a uniform, too. It can turn a girl's head. At first, she liked this about him but afterwards it became too much. I think she was a little embarrassed to be with a coloured man. Maybe the bus uniform wasn't the same. She never said anything to me, but I could guess. Anyway, a few years later, she met someone. Began to carry on with him. I knew nothing about it, nor did Chester. She left him in the end, Chester that is. Chose the other man. I wasn't happy about it. But what can you do? She is my daughter after all. The two of them are married now. Even have a young lad. I don't have anything against Chester. I'd shake his hand now if I saw him. He always treated my Linda well.'

'Does your daughter have any contact with Johnson now?' asked Jellicoe.

Adams shook his head sadly and glanced away. His breathing was heavy now as if fatigued by the conversation and his answer, when it came, was barely a whisper in a wind of regret and things long avoided.

'I never ask, Mr Jellicoe.'

Jack Murray

It was night-time as Jellicoe climbed the steps to his flat. Beans on toast awaited him. Once upon a time he ate well. Sylvia, of course. couldn't boil an egg but they had Mrs Howard who came in and 'did for them'. Sylvia had insisted. Sylvia had paid. At least her father had. Jellicoe thought wistfully of the additional income they'd once enjoyed. His lifestyle eight months on was a far cry from those days. He'd hated it at the time; the feeling that he was in a prison of his own making. Now, walking along the corridor outside the flat that overlooked the carpark, he wondered if his manner back then had been on the wrong side of ungrateful.

There were puddles on the concrete outside his door. All the other flats had some sort of welcome mat for people to wipe their feet. He laughed bitterly at his lack of foresight. Civilised behaviour stops here, he thought. Just then his eyes caught a familiar figure standing on the wall. It was the little black cat he'd seen around the flats. It looked at him warily, crouched slightly, ready to escape.

'Hello, Monk,' said Jellicoe. He'd christened the cat after his favourite pianist Thelonious Monk. A thought struck him at once both absurd and worrying. Had he named the cat deliberately after someone who was black or as a tribute to the man? He recognised that the cat's colour had played a part in his choice of name. Did this make him prejudiced? At that moment he felt a chill that was not just a result of the cold night air.

The flat's interior was no warmer than outside. He had resisted using central heating too much as the rent on the flat was costing a fortune as it was. Fishing a small plate out of the cupboard in the kitchen, he poured a splash of milk on it and brought the plate outside. Monk stared at him curiously. Jellicoe set the plate down and closed the door behind him.

The Bus Stop

Beans first or some music? This was his decision every evening.

Music won out. He found his favourite Thelonious Monk record, *Brilliant Corners*. The album included another musician that Jellicoe followed avidly, Sonny Rollins. He sat down and listened to the start of *Pannonica* and realised he'd put side two on first. He stayed slumped on the sofa, unable to move to change it. Unaccountably it irritated him that he was listening to the 'wrong' side. It affected his enjoyment of the music. He was used to the order the music came in. Like starting a movie halfway through, it felt as if he'd missed the first act, the context, the slow build-up of ideas and themes that melded together over the course of the two sides to become a whole, coherent, and objective work of art.

And he was bored of eating beans.

The next morning, he stepped out the front door and saw that the cat had drunk the milk. He turned back inside and took the plate with him. A quick swish under the kitchen sink taps and then some more milk was added. He brought the plate out and set it down outside his door. There was no sign of Monk. He made a point to ask the neighbours if anyone had claimed him. He arrived at the office just as Burnett was bringing his usual morning sunshine.

'What time do you call this?' snapped Burnett as they climbed the steps of the police station together. Jellicoe smiled and decided not to point out he was no later than his chief. He was glad to see that Burnett was irritated because he'd failed to get a rise out of him. 'I don't want to hear anything of your trip to no man's land until I've had another cup of tea.'

It was an article of faith in the station that Burnett was not at his best first thing in the morning. Like a neanderthal with a hangover was how Clarkey described him. Affectionately. The first cup of tea at the station saw his distinctly grizzly manner recover slowly to being somewhat bearish. It was an improvement of sorts but rarely lasted the morning before signs of regression were evident.

The tea was waiting for Burnett as he arrived inside his office. This was the result of a logistical arrangement within the station that saw the desk sergeant call up to the mess room to put the kettle on. The kettle had been filled in anticipation of the chief's

87

arrival. A few years previously, a hapless constable had not understood the morning arrangement and no tea had been left at Burnett's desk. He was now in Bitchfield, Yorkshire, according to Burnett's oft-repeated joke.

Burnett drained the tea at a single gulp. Jellicoe liked his tea hot. But Burnett's ability to neck it straight down while still, technically, just under boiling was excessive by any standards. He set the cup down and looked at Jellicoe looking at him.

'Yes?'

'Nothing,' said Jellicoe. 'Actually, I don't suppose you want to hear about the trip to Penzance?'

The expression on Burnett's face suggested both yes and be quick about it. Burnett listened without commenting on Jellicoe's verbal report. At the end he said two words.

'Proves nothing.'

'True. Has Derek Sutton made an appearance yet?' asked Jellicoe. He assumed that Burnett would have more up to date news on this.

'No. He went to visit his sister in London but left her two days ago to come back here. So, we still need to find him. For all we know he could be dead in a ditch in Dorking.'

Jellicoe decided against complimenting the chief on his alliteration. There were other ways to fillet a fish.

'Or absconding to Amsterdam.'

Burnett shot Jellicoe a look that was trying to work out if his inspector was making fun of him. He growled at Jellicoe, correctly believing he was deliberately provoking him.

'Go and interview Johnson. Widow Twanky and Price are getting nowhere.'

'Are you joining me?'

'No. On second thoughts, yes. What's Wallace doing?'

Wallace had mentioned something about wanting to return to the scene of the crime. He mentioned seeing a houseboat moored at the canal that bordered the wood. Burnett nodded but had nothing to say on this.

'The lawyer is arriving at nine. We had to appoint him one.'

'He was questioned without a lawyer yesterday?' asked Jellicoe, surprised.

The Bus Stop

'This isn't Ronnie Musgrave or Johnny Warwick we're talking about here. He should consider himself lucky. If he'd been back home, he'd be hanging from a tree by now.'

Jellicoe glanced sharply at Burnett. The chief's humour could run to quite dark, but this would have been in poor taste. For once, Burnett was unusually serious-minded rather than angry. It was there again, a sense that Burnett had more sympathy for the American than he was likely to admit.

They walked along the corridor to the interview room to await the arrival of Johnson. It was a further five minutes before they heard him shuffle along the corridor. His manner had changed considerably from when Jellicoe had seen him at the Tulip Club. He was a big man, but he appeared to have shrunk. His shoulders sloped, his head hung down and he held his two handcuffed hands out as if in prayer to a deity that had never listened to him or to people like him.

'Hello, Mr Johnson,' said Jellicoe. He motioned with his head for the handcuffs to be removed.

'Hello, sir,' mumbled the American.

'We have appointed a lawyer for you, Mr Johnson.'

'Thank you,' replied Johnson without much feeling

The lawyer appeared a few minutes later. Jellicoe had seen him before. Albert Castle often took cases such as this where the person being questioned was unable to afford a defence. Castle introduced himself to Johnson and confirmed he had made himself familiar with the key elements of the case.

The police often used Castle and not just because he was cheap. Unlike Uriah Elliot of Elliot, Elliot, and Hardy, who was the lawyer of gang leader Ronnie Musgrave, Castle was no shark. He let the police get on with their job, ensuring only that the treatment of his client was fair and that the police did not overstep the mark. This helped the police as it protected them later at trial. One or two of the police, DS Fogg in particular, were known to enjoy a more robust approach to questioning. Jellicoe had little time for Fogg nor, he suspected, did Burnett. This opinion was not shared by Frankie and Leighton: both seemed to appreciate the gifts he brought to the force, so his position was safe. He was never likely to be in the frame for Detective Inspector, nor did he want to be. He knew his level.

After the formal preliminaries were over, Jellicoe began the interview.

'Mr Johnson, as we have stated, you have not been charged yet. We recommend that you answer these questions as fully as possible for the reasons stated. Do you like living in England, Mr Johnson?'

If Johnson was surprised by this question, it would be fair to say Burnett's jaw dropped. It was all he could do to stop himself snapping at Jellicoe about what this had to do with anything.

'Yes, sir. I do.'

'Why?'

Johnson smiled. It was a sad smile; bitter experience and pain were etched deeply into the upward curve of his mouth.

'You're fair here. You give people a chance,' replied Johnson in his slow, soft southern accent.

'Is this what happened in Gordian? You were given a chance?'

Johnson looked surprised at first but then suspicion clouded his eyes.

'It wasn't anyone's fault except that Major.'

'Clements?'

'Yes. That was a bad man. People like that are why I wanted to live here after the war.'

'You were treated fairly.'

'I was. Right from the start. Mr Adams, Linda, the whole village was like something you see in the movies. It was a dream for us coloured boys. We wanted to do work and the people treated us right,' said Johnson, shaking his head wistfully.

'Yet there were some who did not,' responded Jellicoe.

'On my own side usually.'

'English too?'

'Some but I learned to ignore the comments a long time ago, sir. You never goin' to convince some people so why try?'

'Does it make you angry when you encounter prejudice?'

'It don't make me happy, that's for sure,' countered Johnson. There was more feeling in his voice now. A hint of anger or, perhaps, irritation at the questioning. Throughout the interview, Castle's eyes shifted around the room as if he was looking for something interesting to look at. Once or twice Jellicoe felt that he should intervene. He didn't. Jellicoe pressed on.

The Bus Stop

'That night when you picked up Mrs Sutton. How did she treat you?'

Johnson shrugged and looked away. There was a moment's pause before he said, 'I didn't notice anything. She paid for her ticket and sat down.'

'Just thinking about when she got off,' said Jellicoe. 'You asked her if she was sure if she wanted to get off in such a remote place. You said that she ignored you. And that you were used to it.'

'Yes, sir,' replied Johnson warily. He could see where this was going.

'You must have been angry,' said Jellicoe, sympathetically.

'I told you, sir, I'm used to it.'

'No one should be used to this, Chester. You must have been angry.'

'No, sir,' said Johnson quietly.

'Come on admit it, Johnson,' interjected Burnett, picking up on the theme developed by Jellicoe. 'You were angry. You said something. Anyone would have. You had some words.'

'No, sir. That's not true.'

'Of course, it is, Johnson,' said Burnett. Louder this time. 'You were seething with her. Who was she to ignore you? You were trying to help. And she treats you like dirt. I'd have said something.'

'No, sir. She just left and I said nothing.'

'What were your exact words, Chester?'

'I asked her if, she was sure. I said it was dark.'

'Nothing else?' asked Jellicoe immediately.

'No. She just got off and that was it. I drove away.'

'No one else was on the bus though.'

Johnson laughed but it was a worried laugh. The he frowned, 'What are you sayin'? Look I didn't do nothing. She got off the bus. That was it. That was the last I saw of her. I'm telling you the truth. You can't pin this on me. You can't pin this on me just because I'm coloured.'

At this point, Castle spoke for the first time since the beginning of the interview.

'Chief Inspector Burnett, unless you have something to charge my client with, you must release him.'

14

Silence followed the interjection by the lawyer. Almost on principle Burnett liked to tweak their nose a bit by creating a trivial point of procedure that would act to rain on the parade of a lawyer who was acting presumptuously. Just at that moment, Superintendent Frankie's face appeared at the window with all the welcome bonhomie of a mourner at a children's party. He pointed at the two policemen and made a stiff 'come hither' motion.

Burnett made a half-hearted attempt at excusing himself but gave up midway through. Jellicoe followed him out of the room. The corridor was empty. The two detectives went towards their main office on the assumption that the superintendent wanted to put on a show. He rarely turned down an opportunity to do so. Sure enough, Frankie was waiting in the detectives' office. This was his stage. In his hand was a prop: the local, weekly newspaper.

'Have you seen the morning newspaper?' asked Frankie.

'No, it hadn't arrived. Or maybe you nicked it, sir,' replied Burnett acidly. There were a couple of smiles from the other detectives at Burnett's response.

Frankie held the newspaper up for everyone to see. The Tribune had a stark headline in large black letters decorating its front page.

BLACK BUS DRIVER HELD FOR MURDER

'Someone in here has leaked that we are holding Chester Johnson. When I find out who, I promise you,' snarled Frankie, 'I will have their guts for garters.'

For once Jellicoe and Burnett were in sympathy with the superintendent. Leaks such as this rarely aided an investigation, they certainly ramped up the pressure among those who were on a case, and they undermined morale as well as trust.

The Bus Stop

'Later today we intended having another press conference to announce the name of the victim. Now we will have a lot of unwelcome attention from far afield and all because someone has taken thirty pieces of silver. Now, is there any chance you've made progress with Johnson. Can we charge him?'

'No, sir, we'll have to let him go.'

It was almost possible to see the steam being emitted from Frankie's ears.

'There must be something we can hold him on. He had means, he had opportunity and surely to God if we can't show a motive here then we're sorely lacking in imagination. The bus was late arriving despite having no one on it. He could have stopped and killed Sutton before resuming his journey.'

'It left late sir. Engine problems,' replied Burnett. 'There are a lot of witnesses to this. But never mind that, we don't have a murder weapon, and no one saw him with an axe at the bus depot. It would have been a difficult thing to hide, sir.'

The last words were said in such a matter-of-fact voice that Frankie instantly guessed, correctly, he was being mocked.

'Fine, Chief Inspector,' said Frankie pointing to the window and the outside world. 'But what do you think is going to happen now when we release him?'

This had been on Jellicoe's mind, and he didn't doubt, Burnett's, too. It would be like being thrown to the wolves. He would have to be suspended by the bus company. Jellicoe wondered if this would be on full pay. But Frankie had not stopped talking.

'He will no doubt need police protection. I can just see some of the more extreme elements in society donning their white sheets and looking to dispense summary justice.'

This was unlikely but the police force could not take the risk. A uniformed officer would have to be stationed at the flat for the time being. Partly for protection, partly to prevent him absconding.

Burnett had no retort to this as, in his heart, he found it hard to disagree. Silence followed this rather bleak assessment of the situation.

'We'll release him now, sir, before the pack arrives.'

Frankie shook his head in disgust which probably meant 'yes'. Burnett motioned with his head towards Yates to go and see to this. Yates, happy to be out of the venomous atmosphere in the office, leapt off his seat to comply. At this point the ever-theatrical superintendent usually flounced off leaving his men to reflect on how they could have done their jobs better. He didn't disappoint. With another shake of the head, he stalked out of the office, eyes fixed ahead like a man of destiny.

Jellicoe watched him leave the office then turned to Burnett. They shared a look and a truth unuttered. Frankie was right. To admit this in the open confines of the office with Burnett within earshot was to risk disgrace.

The two men moved to Jellicoe's office to discuss what to do next. Price was called in too. The door was closed, and they sat down. Burnett spent a minute fiddling with his pipe. Both Price and Jellicoe waited for this little ceremony to reach its conclusion. Finally, Burnett was puffing away like Maigret just after he'd stubbed his toe.

'So, we can't pin it on Johnson and there's no sign of Sutton. No one has come forward about the white car that was parked or broken down. In short, we have nothing. Absolutely nothing and the press are banging the drum.'

This was as good a summary as any. At this moment, the next step was to assure Burnett there was a next step.

'Can I speak to Bowles?' asked Jellicoe. 'We need to find out more about Sutton.'

'I agree. We don't know how things were with his missus, for a start,' agreed Price.

'He might know some friends or distant family he could be staying with.'

Burnett nodded. It wasn't much but at least it might throw up some leads. At that moment they had nothing.

'Fine. Go. Take Yates when he comes back,' ordered Burnett. He turned to Price and said, 'Can you get some uniform and go door to door about the white car. Someone may have seen something. There's always curtain twitchers.'

'But it broke down on the edge of town,' pointed out Price.

'It had to get there to break down. Someone may have seen it between 4pm and 6pm or so. And make sure someone from

The Bus Stop

uniform is stationed outside Johnson's flat. I can sense trouble coming. I can feel it in my water.'

So could Jellicoe but there was little point on adding to the sense of gloom that had fallen over the room. He felt his stomach tighten. Vultures were circling overhead. The hyenas would be along soon.

*

The Clifftops was the best hotel in the town. It was situated, as the name suggested so imaginatively, at the top of a cliff. Jellicoe had visited the beautiful white hotel overlooking the town once before on a previous case. He and Yates strolled through the lobby of the hotel and made their way through to the restaurant where they had arranged to meet Bowles.

They saw him sitting alone by a window smoking. Sensing their arrival his eyes shifted towards them. Shafts of sunlight streamed through the window. His brylcreemed hair shone brilliantly in the light. The clipped moustache was stiff like a wing commander's; the eyes were cold, blue chips of rationality, hatred, and sadness. To Jellicoe he seemed like a ghost from another age.

Bowles stood up and shook hands with Jellicoe and Yates and gestured towards the two empty seats. His fingers were stained mahogany from nicotine. He looked at Jellicoe for a moment and seemed on the point of saying something but then thought better of it. He settled on a more general welcome.

'May I offer you tea?'

Yates took him up on his offer while Jellicoe declined. As they waited for the tea to arrive, Bowles remained silent. Both detectives followed his lead. Despite the severity of his appearance, he was a man in mourning. The rage was in his eyes, though. To whom it would be directed was something Jellicoe needed to understand.

The interview began a few minutes later after the polite inquiries about accommodation had been dispensed with. Jellicoe found himself fascinated by Bowles. His movements had the precision of a dancer then he would sit perfectly still like a big cat staking its prey. There was a quiet power within him.

'Have you made any progress in your search for Derek?' asked Bowles. The hint of suppressed anger was there at the mention of his son-in-law.

'I'm afraid not, sir,' replied Jellicoe. He went to see his sister in London but left two days ago, three now. Can you tell us where else he may have gone?'

'I can't.'

Jellicoe was surprised by how much of this was unsurprising.

'You didn't like him, did you?'

The tone of Jellicoe's voice angered Bowles. For a moment his face erupted in rage, and he stiffened even more. Then as quickly as he had tensed up his body relaxed. A thin smile convulsed on his lips, bitter and angry.

'No, Inspector. I didn't like him.'

'Have you been to their house?'

The breathing of Bowles became more sonorous as he tried to control the surge of lava that was threatening to explode.

'No,' snapped Bowles. 'Nor will I.'

Well, that was clear enough, thought Jellicoe. Yet, the question remained about how far he should push this with a man who was grieving.

'Can you tell me more about why you would say this?'

Bowles glared at Jellicoe. It was as if there was a transference of the hatred and pain he was feeling, and it was being directed at the detective. Bowles was silent for a minute. The only noise was the bustle of people entering and leaving the restaurant.

'Derek Sutton,' the words were spat out, 'was, is, a man of dubious moral character. A charmer I will concede but not someone I would ever have chosen for my daughter to marry.'

Bowles shook his head and then it drooped. Regret dripped from every word. The pain of only a father can feel when they lose their daughter not once but twice.

'She wouldn't listen to me,' he continued a few moments later. Then he stopped and put his hands over his face. 'It's my fault. I should have done more to stop her marrying him.'

'Do you think that he is responsible for your daughter's murder?'

Bowles looked up sharply. He seemed confused and glanced down at the newspaper then back to Jellicoe.

'We will be releasing Chester Johnson while we investigate further. He was never under arrest. This newspaper should not have printed the story,' explained Jellicoe.

The Bus Stop

'Do you think he killed her or not?' snapped Bowles once more.

'We have not discounted him or your son-in-law from the inquiry. Can you tell me more about Derek?'

'What do you want to know?'

What did they want to know? Everything and anything that would help point the finger of blame at Derek Sutton and bring an end to the investigation. Was this too much to ask, thought Jellicoe?

'Perhaps tell us about when they met, why they married and why you were opposed to the match. Tell us about him, what he is like. Is he capable of murder?'

Bowles eyes blazed once more.

'I shall answer the last question first. Yes, I believe he is capable of murder. He is a rogue. He married my daughter because he wanted to be wealthy. When I threatened to cut my daughter off, we saw his true colours. I think he mistreated her. We begged her to return home, but she refused. I think she was in fear of her life.'

'But why stay when he was at sea? She could have left then,' pointed out Jellicoe.

'She could have but she chose not to,' replied Bowles acidly. 'I have never understood women. I never shall. What she saw in this man I will never know. Why she stayed we will never find out. I despise that man. I suppose he would be considered good looking. He had a way of pleasing women. I saw through him almost immediately.'

'Where did she first meet him?'

Silence fell on the table as Bowles fought to control his emotions. He was a man not given to public display. Yet now guilt and despair had laid siege to his self-control though anger, through hatred and through love.

'I introduced them.' It was barely a whisper. 'I introduced them. It was all my fault.' Jellicoe glanced down at the bereaved father's hands. They were gripped together so tightly that they seemed as if they might explode.

'It was a party meeting. Trouble was expected. Sutton was one of the men we brought in to make sure that no one could enter and disturb us. I brought Sarah along because I wanted her to be involved in something worthwhile. I wanted her to be something. I educated her myself. My wife died when she had Sarah. It was just Sarah and me. And then she ends up with that, that…'

He couldn't speak any more. The hatred and the grief were too much. Words were no longer enough to convey the maelstrom of emotion swirling inside him. Emotion that he had spent a lifetime suppressing. There was seemed little else that could be gained from questioning him further.

'I'm sorry for your loss, Mr Bowles,' said Jellicoe.

Bowles looked at him again, but his eyes were lost. Then they focused momentarily, and he frowned. He regarded Jellicoe for a moment as if trying to remember a name or a place.

'Have we met before?' asked Bowles suddenly.

Jellicoe was surprised by the question. He shook his head and replied, 'I don't believe so. Why do you say that?'

Bowles shook his head but ignored the question. His mind had moved on. Then he turned towards the sea and studied it as if answers could be found in the white-foamed waves crashing on the shore.

'I suppose he's escaped.'

The Bus Stop

15

The man stepped off a bus and walked ten minutes to his house. The brown suitcase weighed a ton and felt like it was pulling the arm from its socket. He glanced up at the sun which was threatening to peek out from behind the clouds. It was warmer today, but he still had his coat buttoned up and a scarf. The walk warmed him up so much that he wished he'd taken off his mackintosh and carried it over his arm. By the time he reached his house, sweat was beading his forehead. Eventually he stopped and took off the coat, then continued his way back to the house.

He stopped again just as he rounded the corner at the top of the street. A police car was parked outside; its blue light rotated lazily on top. One policeman stood guard outside *his* door. His eyes widened and he picked up the pace. By the last ten yards he was jogging. He stopped and stared at his house. The policemen stared back at him.

Constable Fisher had been standing outside the house for most of the morning; just as he had done the previous couple of mornings. He was getting tired of the rubber-neckers coming along, the inquiries on what was happening; the cups of tea were welcome. The lady next door was a bit of a laugh. Maybe it wasn't so bad.

He looked at the man and then a thought occurred to the policeman. He'd not paid much attention to the photographs that DI Price had shown them. He wondered for a moment. Could this be? Thoughts invariably sped through the constable's head like bread through treacle.

'Can I help you sir?' asked Constable Fisher in a friendly tone. You could never be sure who you were speaking to. It was an article of faith with the young constable that it was better to be safe than sorry. And there was something about the man.

The man's mouth dropped open. He looked ashen. He stared wildly from his house to the policeman then back again.

'What the hell is going on?' whispered the man. He looked as if he would cry.

Two thoughts raced through Fisher's mind at this point. Either this man was from Mars or…

'Mr Sutton? Mr Sutton is that you?' called DS Fogg from the house.

'What are you doing in my house?' yelled Derek Sutton wildly in response.

*

Jellicoe and Yates arrived back at the station. It was quiet and the desk sergeant was on the phone when they arrived. He barely acknowledged them. The two men climbed the stairs and made straight for their office. It was deserted. Yates wondered out loud what was wrong, but Jellicoe knew something had happened. He turned immediately and went to the interview room. There he saw Burnett and Price sitting in front of a stricken Derek Sutton. So, this explained why the room was empty, thought Jellicoe.

But he was wrong.

Burnett caught sight of Jellicoe. His face was grave. Not angry, noted Jellicoe. Grave. Something was wrong. Burnett rose immediately from the seat and strode to the door. Derek Sutton's head was now buried in his hands, and he was weeping uncontrollably.

The door opened and Burnett appeared. Jellicoe didn't ask the question so much as frown it to the chief.

'Sutton appeared at the house this morning. He had no idea what had happened. Claimed he was in London with some of his former ship mates from the war. You'll need to check this. But first get over to Chester Johnson's house the two of you. We need all the men we can use.'

'What's happened?' asked Yates.

'It's only a bloody riot,' snarled Burnett angrily.

*

Riot was, perhaps, an exaggeration. This was Jellicoe's first thought as he arrived at the block of flats where Johnson lived. There were three police cars parked like a barricade and several uniformed men standing at the entrance of the steps that led up to

100

The Bus Stop

Johnson's apartment. Outside the door was another policeman. In front of the flats was a group of around twenty men and a few women. They were shouting insults, but these were as likely to be directed at the policemen as the bus driver who was, presumably, in his flat.

Yates followed Jellicoe up the stairs, but Jellicoe stopped him. He nodded towards the crowd of men.

'Stay here and keep an eye on them. See if you know any of them. Also, can you radio for a photographer to come here. That'll clear them.'

Just at that moment, Jellicoe realised that the photographer may well be Winnie Leighton. For a moment he wondered if he should rescind the order. It might be putting her in the line of fire if her presence ramped up the temperature. By the time he had decided to change his mind, Yates had returned to the car. Jellicoe shrugged and skipped up the steps. He nodded to the policeman standing guard outside the house and soon found himself back inside Johnson's flat.

Chester Johnson was sitting on the sofa with DS Fogg. Neither looked to be enjoying the other's company. Fogg looked up hopefully.

'Do you want to go back?' asked Jellicoe.

That was a question hardly needed repeating. Fogg was up and out of the seat in the beat of drum. He nodded a thanks to Jellicoe and left the stage. It was a very different Chester Johnson that greeted Jellicoe to the one he'd met at the Tulip Club. Gone was the energy and charisma. It had been replaced by a listless, mute despair. What made it all the more difficult for Jellicoe was the resigned acceptance. It felt as if Chester Johnson had been living in a dream for many years and that he'd just woken up to the bitter, acrid reality that he was black in a white man's country. He thought he'd escaped this reality. But you could never do so. Never.

Johnson did not look up at Jellicoe, so the detective sat down. They two men sat in silence for a minute, maybe two, listening to the sound of the crowd chanting outside. They were not giving Chester Johnson a name. Nor were they chanting anything about the case. No, they were demanding that he and people like him

101

should leave. Finally, Johnson looked up at the detective. He tried to smile.

'Friends of yours?' asked Jellicoe.

A smile did form on Johnson's lips, but the eyes told another story: confusion, fear, and deep sadness.

'Yeah, right. Drinking buddies. Always grab a beer when they're in town.'

They were silent for a while listening to the sound of the clock ticking and the crowd chanting. Johnson grinned once more as he listened.

'It has a kind of rhythm, don't you think?' The voice was sad but did not appear to condemn. Jellicoe didn't know how to reply. After a few minutes the chanting appeared to cease. Neither man moved to see if the crowd was dispersing. Rather than chant, a few shouts could be heard. It didn't sound as if many had left.

'I'd offer you a coffee but there's no milk.'

'I'll organise for some supplies to come in. Maybe you can give me a list of things you need.'

'Sure,' said Johnson, almost glad of something to do. He picked up a pen from the sideboard but had no paper. Jellicoe tore a sheet from his notebook and handed it to the bus driver. While he was writing, Jellicoe asked him about the bus company. This brought a derisive laugh from the American.

'Suspended without pay pending the investigation by the police,' replied Johnson. He looked at Jellicoe in the eye and said in a dry English accent, 'I don't suppose you chaps could get a weave on.'

'Derek Sutton, the husband of the murdered woman has appeared.'

Johnson looked at him warily.

'Appeared. You found him?'

'No. He turned up at the house. Claims he knew nothing of what had happened.'

Johnson sat back in the sofa to consider the implications of this statement. To Jellicoe it looked as if Johnson realised that the voluntary arrival of the only other plausible suspect did not auger well for him. The bitter smile was now fixed on his face, papering over the cracks in his belief.

The Bus Stop

'Well, I'll be,' said Johnson after a minute. There was a musicality to the way he said it. 'That sure don't help me.' His voice had a sense of wonder in it. The nightmare was unending. Once more, Jellicoe could think of nothing to say. In fact, worse, he could see no reason for his being there. He was hardly a comfort to this man. Much better that he did something to prove one way or another who had killed Sarah Sutton. He looked at Johnson and indicated with his eyes, the list.

'Oh, yeah,' said Johnson and wrote a few items down before handing the list over. Jellicoe stood up and said he'd arrange for someone to go to the shop. He was desperate to leave now. He stood up and turned to the door. He could hear some booing outside. This made him smile. Then a quiet voice behind made him stop.

'Excuse me, sir,' said Johnson.

Jellicoe turned around to face the American.

'Better make that one pint of milk rather than two. Looks like I won't be here very long.'

*

The crowd outside had dispersed by the time Jellicoe saw the five-foot four reason why. He stepped down quickly and handed one of the policemen the list.

'Can you get some groceries for Johnson?'

The policeman looked at the note, then back to Jellicoe. For a moment they stood looking at one another then a thought occurred to Jellicoe. He took a wallet out of his breast pocket and handed the policeman a pound note. The policeman looked at the pound note then back to Jellicoe. He sighed and handed him a second note thereby emptying his wallet.

'I want the receipt and change,' warned Jellicoe and then he strode off towards Winnie Leighton.

The young woman in question was arguing with a couple of men who were demanding that she hand over her camera roll. She seemed unmoved by the exhortations if her derisive laughter was anything to go by. As Jellicoe drew closer, she turned to him. He could detect the hint of a smile on her face. The two men glanced at Jellicoe and then back to Miss Leighton. They decided to end their suit. A few words of farewell followed on both sides that suggested a shopping trip to choose curtains was unlikely.

'Hello,' said Winnie, the smile leaving her face. 'Do I have you to thank for this assignment?'

'Do you have me to thank for chasing away those hooligans?'

Winnie Leighton's eyes flamed for a moment before she stopped herself.

'Has anyone ever told you how funny you are?' Before Jellicoe could respond, she added, 'I thought not.'

Jellicoe made a show of looking around the, now, deserted parking area in front of the flats.

'You certainly have a way of winning friends,' said Jellicoe, drily. 'I'm impressed.'

'Was that the point of the exercise?' asked Winnie, clearly irritated at having been used in this manner.

Jellicoe was as happy as any man is to lie to a young woman when the situation merits it. This was not one such moment. There was too much enjoyment to be derived from this minor triumph in what had been an, otherwise, ghastly day.

'You did well. I hope you managed to capture some of their faces though. It might be useful. You never know.'

'I thought the criminal coming to the scene of the crime or visiting the man he's framed was a trope of mystery novels.'

'I prefer reading philosophy myself, so you'll know more about that than me.'

Winnie Leighton surprised Jellicoe at this point. She burst out laughing. It was a delightful sound. He hoped he'd hear more of it. When she'd finished, she said, 'A bad day?'

'Awful and I think it's going to,' Jellicoe stopped himself from saying what he really thought. Then he finished his thought, 'it's going to cause a lot of problems for us. For the town.'

This seemed to concern Winnie and she frowned. Then she asked, 'Why do you say that?'

Jellicoe shook his head and held his hands up in a submissive gesture.

'All of it. The narrative is too simple. We're missing something. I can feel it. And meanwhile, all of this,' said Jellicoe, with a finger pointing in the direction of the departing protesters, 'is just going to get worse.'

Winnie Leighton turned to look at the two men who had been arguing with her. A policeman had been standing nearby so she

The Bus Stop

had felt profoundly untroubled by their aggressiveness towards her. Had there not been someone there it would have been a different feeling entirely. She felt just the hint of a chill. Then she realised there was a light breeze blowing now.

'I'll have these for you tomorrow morning,' said Winnie, turning away from Jellicoe and walking towards a green, two-door Ford Anglia and climbed in. She drove off without once looking at Jellicoe or, indeed, indicating, which amused the detective greatly.

16

Jellicoe and Yates arrived back at the police station. Just ahead of them, the squire-like Cecil Lords and Superintendent Frankie were walking into the building. It didn't look like either would be exchanging Christmas cards in the foreseeable future. At least this was one thing in Frankie's favour. Like Burnett he had little time for the newspaper owner especially as he was the one who had broken the story about Chester Johnson. The press had just started arriving at the American's flat when Jellicoe and Yates were leaving. Doubtless they were disappointed to have missed the almost-riot. Jellicoe left instructions that they were not allowed anywhere near the flat.

Jellicoe and Yates headed upstairs to the detectives' office which was being manned by DS Fogg. After a brief update on what had happened at the flat, Fogg laughed uproariously when Jellicoe told him about the arrival of Winnie Leighton.

'I must remember that one,' said Fogg nodding in approval. He lit up a cigarette and returned to typing his report, one finger at a time. When the mood struck him, which was often, he could spend a morning typing half a page.

Jellicoe felt a momentary stab of guilt at the thought that Winnie would become a *de facto* crowd disperser. It was only momentary though. Life goes on and there was much to do. And anyway, Miss Leighton could take care of herself.

'Is the chief still with Sutton?' asked Jellicoe, sitting down at his desk.

'Aye. Ivor is with him. I think they're going to join the press conference soon. He wants you in that one by the way.' Jellicoe's heart fell and the detective sergeant grinned mirthlessly back. 'Thought you'd like that,' cackled Fogg with that smoker's laugh of his.

'Wallace?' asked Jellicoe, looking around the empty office.

The Bus Stop

'He left ages ago with Clarkey.'

Jellicoe was sure he'd given him some order or another but couldn't recall what.

'Where the hell is he anyway?' mused Jellicoe. He looked out the window but as usual, no answers were forthcoming from the sky. There was a hint of sunshine though.

It wouldn't last.

*

Wallace stepped through the woods treading lightly. In his mind he was like Randolph Scott in *Last of the Mohicans*. His dad had taken him to see it at the pictures when he was a kid. His efforts not to make a noise were somewhat undermined by his un-Chingachgook-like partner, Constable Leonard Clarke. The former and, on occasion, still, prop forward for the local rugby club had all the stealth of a stampeding bull elephant. Twigs did not so much snap under his feet as explode. After one particularly loud crack which may well have been audible in Glasgow, Wallace turned to the big constable with a grin.

'I think we've lost the element of surprise, Clarkey.'

Aside from Chief Inspector Burnett, Dr Hilary Taylor, Chief Constable Leighton, Sergeant Crombie and, bizarrely, local gangland leader, Ronnie Musgrave, few people outside the rugby club were permitted to call Constable Clarke. 'Clarkey'. Even DI Jellicoe did not use the nickname although Clarke wouldn't have objected in his case; Wallace despite or probably because of his youth, was a notable exception.

Wallace was something of a star player at Clarke's rugby club. Clarke took full credit for this. After all, he boasted, if it wasn't for the threat of being flattened by the likes of him, how else would Wallace have developed such a turn of speed and deft feinting technique. Nobody, not even Wallace, was prepared to disagree with this conclusion.

Clarke stopped and looked down at the branch which had succumbed to the sixteen and a half stone packed into a frame that was just shy of six foot if you believed him. Nobody did. At a stretch he was five nine. A big five nine.

Clarke shrugged at this and held up his fist. He made a point of looking at the fist and said, 'So what?'

'What if they have a gun?'

107

'You go first, sir,' said Clarke, with a grin that broke like sunshine from a cloud.

Wallace glared at him before breaking out smiling ruefully himself. He strode forward through the thicket out to the clearing on other side. Just in front of him was the canal. On the canal was the oldest looking barge he'd ever seen. Even the rope attaching the barge to the bank of the canal seemed to be rusting. The canal marked the end of the woodland. On the other side were fields and hedgerows.

'Bloody hell,' said Clarke, appearing, as promised, behind Wallace. 'How does that stay afloat?'

'Do you think anyone actually lives on that thing?' said Wallace aloud, thereby eliminating any last prospect of surprising the inhabitants.

'You'd be surprised, young Wallace,' said Clarke approaching the rusting barge slowly.

The barge was one of the three moored along the stretch of water that Wallace could see. The other two were half a mile back or more in the direction of Frimhampton. A red telephone box stood on the bank, fifty yards away on the other side, near a lock.

The barge was at least sixty feet long and was typical in size and shape to most of the other barges that pootled along the canal. The main difference was the utter lack of care that had been taken with its upkeep. On top of the barge was assorted bric-a-brac: a rusting bicycle, bottles with what looked like small boats inside, dead plants, a dead rat if Clarke wasn't mistaken and a plastic hose which certainly had not been used to clean the vessel. Wallace felt a chill as he stared at the boat. It was as if all humanity had been excised from the vessel and replaced with misery.

The two men looked at one another. Clarke put his hand out in an 'after-you' gesture. Wallace thanked him and they both walked toward the barge. There was no sign of life on the vessel, but a table was on the bank and a half-drunk mug of tea. The two men separated and walked to either end of the barge, checking inside the windows. Neither set foot on the boat less for fear of what they would meet than literally putting their foot in it.

'Hello,' shouted Wallace, feeling something of a fool. He knocked on the wall of the barge and asked if anyone was there.

The Bus Stop

A voice from inside shouted, 'Who is it?' It was a man's voice. There was something odd about the tone. It was like a five-year-old complaining to its parent about having to go to bed. Wallace raised his eyebrows at Clarke. The big policeman responded in a similar manner.

'Can you come out, please,' said Wallace. 'This is the police.'

Silence followed. It persisted longer than either Wallace or Clarke could believe.

'Did you hear what I said?' Wallace could not hide the irritation in his voice. 'Please come out and identify yourself. This is the police.'

'Go away. Leave me alone.'

The same pleading child-like tone. Wallace looked at Clarke. Both were confused.

'I won't ask again, sir. Constable Clarke and I will board your vessel and make you come out.' Even to Wallace's ears he sounded like a parent scolding a naughty child.

'Mummy says I can't talk to strangers.'

'Mummy?' expostulated Wallace. But some understanding was beginning to dawn on him.

'Is your mummy there?' asked Wallace. His voice was less demanding as he reverted to a gentler tone. Clarke looked on in approval. He'd just been on the point of suggesting this. The lad was learning.

'No.'

Wallace could almost imagine the man inside folding his arms as he said this.

'Can you come out? Please. We don't mean any harm. Really.'

'No.'

'Why not?' asked Wallace. The irritation had returned to this voice. Clarke, the father of two boys and a girl grinned at this. Kids. He'd learn.

'Mummy locked me in.'

*

'Then what happened? asked Yates, dipping his hand into the packet of potato crisps like he was watching a film at the cinema. Wallace glanced towards Clarke as if in need of moral support. The big constable merely grinned and shrugged his shoulders.

'You didn't just leave him, did you?'

Wallace was affronted by this and sat up more in his seat, 'What did you suggest we do? Break the door down or wait for his mummy?' He said the last word in a cruel mimic of the man in the barge. Yates was not too sure how this would go down with the chief and said so. The three men were sitting in a café near the police station. Outside the sky was darkening. It felt like an omen. The police station was besieged with reporters now as another press conference was in progress. Leighton had wisely left this to be handled by Superintendent Frankie.

'What do you think they're saying?' asked Wallace to Yates.

'I don't think "His Highness" was happy to be called in, but Burnett insisted.'

Yates had taken to calling Jellicoe "His Highness" for reasons that were understandable but still needled Wallace somewhat. He could detect the underlying jealousy. It was unedifying because Yates was his own worst enemy. Wallace rated him highly as a policeman, yet he was fundamentally too willing to take the easy route. The detective sergeant made no secret of his ambition, yet Wallace suspected he would never achieve anything close to what his ability merited until he was prepared to put in the hard work.

They paid for their tea and walked slowly across the street to the police station. The place was eerily quiet. They arrived back at the deserted office and sat down. And waited. Wallace used the time to type up a brief report of the visit to the houseboat.

A noise in the corridor suggested that the press conference was over, and the principals were on their way back, no doubt with a spring in their step and hope in their hearts. The door flew open, and Burnett stalked in like an angry man who couldn't give full vent to the deep well of coruscating rage that was building up within him. Neither Jellicoe nor Price looked much happier. Wallace watched the two inspectors' troop into Burnett's office like men approaching the firing squad. The door slammed shut.

Yates raised his eyebrows and smiled. Silence fell on the group of two men as they tried to catch what was being said in the office. They didn't have to strain their ears too much. Burnett's vocal cords were in excellent nick and being exercised at full volume.

Burnett glared at the two detective inspectors. An independent observer might have concluded that both men were moments

The Bus Stop

away from a carpeting. In fact, Burnett's ire was directed elsewhere.

'Find me the beggar who squealed to Cecil bloody Lords. I will hang him, testicles-first from a flagpole.'

Jellicoe, in fact, had some ideas on that subject and suspected this was not what would happen. For the moment he decided to remain silent. But Burnett hadn't finished.

'I had three phone calls from Fleet Street today. They're coming. I can feel it...'

He didn't have to add 'in his water' but both Jellicoe and Price filled in the gap. A case by the coast involving murder with potential racial over tones was not one that Fleet Street would ignore for long. Part of Jellicoe dreaded their coming and hoped that he might be given less responsibility in this case. The press would see his involvement and rake up the death of his own wife all over again. Another part of him was compelled to continue. He could no more stop himself being involved than he could stop breathing voluntarily. Already he could feel the tentacles of the investigation curling around his senses, his heart, and his mind. They would not let go until the case had been brought to a satisfactory conclusion.

'Johnson?' snapped Burnett at Jellicoe.

'Shaken and afraid,' replied Jellicoe. 'The crowd has dispersed for now, but they'll be back.'

'They'll have Fleet Street following them. That'll make them worse,' observed Burnett, grimly. He reached inside his pocket for his pipe.

'Any chance I can have a chat with Sutton?' asked Jellicoe.

'Be my guest,' came the reply which was, to all intents and purposes, a dismissal.

They left the office and joined Wallace and Yates.

'Sounds in a good mood,' said Wallace.

'As ever,' replied Jellicoe. 'All right, Yates and I are going to have a word with Sutton. In the meantime, can you ask the chief for details of who Sutton was with and then confirm if he is telling the truth.'

'Go in there when he's in that mood?' asked Wallace sulkily. But then the grin returned, 'You're so kind.'

'Don't mention it,' said Jellicoe. He motioned to Yates to follow him to the interview room. When he reached the door, he turned around and said to Wallace, 'Tomorrow morning, first thing, take me to this houseboat. I want to see it for myself.'

Jellicoe paused outside the interview room and looked in. Sutton was still there, drinking some tea. Beside the cup was a plate of untouched digestive biscuits. Sutton was staring stonily at the wall. A policeman sat in the corner of the room. Neither was saying anything.

'I have a feeling about Mr Sutton,' said Jellicoe to Yates. 'I'm going to go rough on him, I think. You let him feel he has a friend.'

'Yes, sir,' replied Yates with a smile.

The Bus Stop

17

Derek Sutton stared sightlessly at the wall. He did not move his head when Jellicoe entered the room with Yates. Instead, he remained perfectly still. Red-rimmed eyes lay deep within his sockets. If this was a performance, then Jellicoe had to tip his hat. It was a good one. The two detectives sat down allowing the uniformed officer a break.

'Afternoon, Mr Sutton,' said Jellicoe.

'Is it?' replied Sutton tonelessly.

'I'm Detective Inspector Jellicoe. This is Detective Sergeant Yates. If you don't mind, I have a few questions that I would like to ask you. Then perhaps you can leave.'

'Where will I go?' asked Sutton. He was probably asking about his accommodation that evening but Jellicoe interpreted a wider meaning within the question. Sutton was not an educated man, guessed Jellicoe, but in times of stress, particularly grief, anyone, no matter what their background, acquires an insight into oneself, into our humanity that would not otherwise be available through reflection alone. His question hinted at the deeper fear that lies within whenever something previously taken for granted vanishes, ceases to exist, or is denied to you. The edifice of belief, of routine, of purpose crumbles. What's left is very often the thing we fear most: an overwhelming awareness of our vulnerability.

'Who did this?' asked Sutton. His voice was a whisper.

Did you? Jellicoe wanted to ask this as he had once been asked.

'We will find this person,' replied Jellicoe without any great conviction. 'I'm very sorry for your loss. I know this is the last place you would like to be right now, but we need your help. The hours and days after a murder such as this are tremendously important. You do understand?'

Sutton nodded but made no reply. Jellicoe studied the man who was despised by the murdered woman's father. At this moment he was clearly not at his best, but Jellicoe could see why he would be considered attractive. Even seated it was clear to see that he would be as tall, if not taller, than Jellicoe. His brown hair was thick and wavy with just a hint of grey at the sides. His eyes were dark as was his skin, the result of countless trips at sea in warm weather climates. His shoulders were wide and hinted at a strength that was not dependent on weight.

'Can you think of anyone that might have wanted to kill Mrs Sutton?'

Sutton shook his head. There was a trace of irritation in the movement.

'I told the other policemen. Everyone loved Sarah. She is, she was wonderful: caring, always smiling. She was wonderful,' Sutton's voice trailed off.

A hard glint came into Jellicoe's eye, but the voice was almost casual.

'When did you last see her, Mr Sutton?'

'Three days ago.'

'How did she seem to you?' This was Yates. His voice was sympathetic. Reassuring.

'Normal.'

'There was a bruise on arm and on her head,' said Jellicoe. The voice was quiet but there was a hint of an edge to it now. If Sutton was aware of this, he didn't show it. His head hung down limply.

'I don't know, I wasn't aware she'd hurt herself.'

'You were on leave, Mr Sutton,' said Yates. 'I gather you went to see your sister in London and some friends.'

'Yes,' said Sutton looking up. 'I told the other cop…other policemen this.'

'So, there was no other reason for leaving,' commented Yates, pretending to make a note.

'No.'

'You and Mrs Sutton never had any children,' commented Jellicoe.

'Sarah never wanted to. Her mother died having her. Put her off,' answered Sutton.

The Bus Stop

'Would you not have liked to have children?' asked Yates. Once more, his tone was concerned and gentle.

Sutton shrugged and his face scrunched up a little, 'You do it if they want to, don't you? I never really thought about it.'

'Why did the office of Neptune Shipping tell us you were on compassionate leave?' asked Jellicoe.

Sutton looked up sharply and eyed Jellicoe closely.

'My sister was ill,' replied Sutton. There was nothing in his tone or manner that suggested this even resembled the truth.

'What was wrong with her?'

Sutton stared wildly at Jellicoe. 'What is this?' he demanded angrily.

'I'm sure she'll confirm that, Mr Sutton. I'll just go and check,' said Yates helpfully. On Sutton's side. Just wanting to get the bearish Jellicoe off the poor man's back. Jellicoe almost grinned. Yates rose from his seat.

'Stop,' said Sutton. His face coloured. A red patch formed on his cheek like a wound.

'It's no problem. We can clear this up in a jiffy,' smiled Yates. He looked hard at Jellicoe as if admonishing the inspector. It was brilliantly done. Jellicoe would have applauded him at any other time. The subtle shift in sergeant's features. An unspoken suggestion that the two men disagreed about Sutton.

'Stop,' repeated Sutton. 'She's not ill. I made that up.'

Yates's face shifted again to anger. But the anger was not at Sutton, it was towards Jellicoe who, in the narrative the two policemen were spinning, had been proven right. Sutton turned from Yates to Jellicoe who was now displaying an undisguised look of triumph on his face. Sutton looked away. The twin shame of what he was about to admit and the fact that this pig was lording it over him was almost too much.

Suddenly Jellicoe stood up. He glanced at Yates and then announced that he needed to pay a visit. Yates sat down as Jellicoe left the room. Jellicoe walked out of sight of Sutton but stopped close enough to the room to hear what was going on inside. He would make a point of commending Yates afterwards for playing his role to perfection. Sutton began to speak.

'Sarah and I have been having problems. I'm away too much. We had an argument a few days ago. A big argument.

'They drive you crazy, don't they?' said Yates lighting a cigarette. He showed the pack to Sutton. He nodded and Yates lit him a cigarette. Just two blokes sharing war stories about being married. Of course, Yates wasn't married but he knew how this line played out.

'Yeah,' said Sutton shaking his head and taking a long, grateful drag on the cigarette. 'No sense. Always demanding things. When I come off from two weeks away, I want to relax. I'm tired. Does she let me?'

'Same here,' lied Yates. 'Can you do this? Can you do that? Oh, I arranged to see the Cravens. Lord, give me a break. I've just had to go and tell a mother her kid's been stealing old ladies' purses.'

'Never ends,' laughed Sutton. Tears appeared in his eyes, though.

'Did you hurt her, Derek?' Yates's voice was soft, regretful. All a mistake. An accident.

Sutton nodded and wiped his nose. The tears were streaming down his face now. Tears of guilt.

'I may have grabbed her a little too hard. The bruise. It might have been me. She bumped her head. It was an accident.'

'These things happen,' said Yates, hoping the hint of anger in his voice was not too plain. 'Nothing else, though?'

'No, nothing else. Ask Deano or Fisher. I was with them.'

'We will, Derek. We will.'

*

Jellicoe nodded to Yates as he entered the detectives' office a few minutes later. The interview was finished. Jellicoe had not returned. It was night outside and they were the only men left in the office.

'Good work,' said Jellicoe.

'Is he guilty?' asked Yates, unsure about how to react to what he'd heard.

Jellicoe shrugged. It seemed the most appropriate response. Yates smiled. He understood all too well that the case currently resembled a jigsaw puzzle with pieces scattered everywhere. Why had Sarah Sutton been killed? Was it a racially motivated attack? A form of revenge for a comment made. Was it a 'domestic' as Superintendent Frankie had indicated? Or was there something else at play here? As ever, the truth was lying just out of reach. An added frustration was the truism that those involved were not telling the police everything even though they may be innocent. How many cases, wondered Jellicoe, had he been involved with where a simple admission might have saved days of work for a large number of men?

'What now?' asked Yates.

'Home,' replied Jellicoe. He'd had enough for the day. Yates slumped onto his chair. For a slight man he made quite a dent. He rubbed his eyes then turned to Jellicoe as he sensed the inspector wanted to say something.

'I want to know tomorrow if Sarah Sutton had life insurance. It might be a motive,' said Jellicoe tonelessly.

'You don't sound convinced. You think it's Johnson?'

Jellicoe half-smiled at this and shrugged once more. His mind was moving slowly. He needed beans on toast and a mug of tea. The thought of this made his heart sink. Was he becoming a beans addict?

'And Sutton? What shall we do with him?'

Jellicoe looked down at the note on his desk. It was a handwritten scrawl by Burnett. He held it up for Yates. It read:

"*If you can find something to hold Sutton on, hold him. Otherwise release him.*"

He showed the note to Yates.

'That answers that, then.'

*

Jellicoe trudged up the steps like he was ascending the final few feet of Everest without the help of oxygen tanks. Something about this case was draining him or perhaps it was his singular diet. He needed to learn how to cook. He needed to learn how to take care of himself. Over his years at university, he had read papers on the impact that poor diet could have psychologically as well as physiologically. It was time he turned this knowledge into something that could inform how he shopped, what he cooked and what he ate. Outside the flat was a familiar figure: Monk was waiting by his empty bowl.

'Give me a minute,' said Jellicoe lifting the dish.

He unlocked the door and stared open-mouthed as Monk flitted in through the opening.

Jack Murray

'Who invited you?' he asked with a grin. Monk looked up at him expectantly.

'All right.' He was too tired to have an argument with a cat. Monk followed him into the kitchen and hopped up onto the table. 'Make yourself at home.'

Monk did so. He flopped down on the table and stretched then yawned. The saucer of milk appeared by his head. He rolled over and rose into lapping position. Jellicoe looked at him lap up the milk with machine-like efficiency.

The cupboard full of tinned beans wasn't going to open itself so Jellicoe finally, with a mammoth effort of will, hooked his finger around the handle, pulled and gazed at the green and black tins.

'Whoopee.'

The hunger he had felt driving home seemed to dissipate. He shut the cupboard door and walked into the living room. For a moment he thought about putting the Thelonious Monk long player on to welcome his guest but that would have required a degree of energy. Instead, he flopped down on the sofa and switched on the radio. The news was on. He listened to a report about Prime Minister Harold MacMillan's upcoming visit to the USSR but soon his mind wandered.

On the coffee table was the half-read book '*Strangers on a Train*'. He hadn't looked at it in the last couple of days. He picked it up again and began to read. Outside it began to rain. Monk popped up on the sofa and curled up. Jellicoe eyed him warily.

'Just shelter. Understand?'

*

Chester Johnson listened to the rain beating against his window. At first it was gentle and then it became harder. Then it smashed his window. He opened his eyes and sat up with a start. Rain drops flew into his living room, but Johnson could not move. He stared down at the brick that had nearly hit his head. There were three words painted onto the brick:

GO AWAY N____.

The message was clear. He couldn't stay.

He stood up and went to the window. Two men were below; they saw him and then turned their backs. The one consolation

The Bus Stop

was they would get wet. Where were the police? Johnson cleared the remaining shards from the window and put his head through the shattered glass to look around. There was no sign of anyone.

Fifteen minutes later he'd put a piece of board across the window and nailed it down. Then he pulled the curtains. They blew a little inward, but the board was doing its job. He thought about going to bed but decided against it. Bed meant sleep. Sleep meant dreams. The dream was back now. Every night. He didn't have to be asleep to see the terrified woman's face or hear her screams.

Johnson collapsed on the sofa and poured some whisky into a tumbler. He downed it. The liquid burned his throat and brought tears to his eyes. He'd never liked whisky. God only knows why he was bothering to drink it now. It's what they did in the movies. Alan Ladd or Fred MacMurray wouldn't feel their stomach on fire. Always white men on the screen. It was difficult to imagine Sidney Poitier slugging down firewater then wiping his mouth with his hand. Harry Belafonte? Johnson laughed at this.

He laughed but it sounded bitter even to his ears. Then he poured himself another whisky. He'd go a bit slower this time seeing as he couldn't drink like those tough white boys. Yes, he'd go slow. What else was there to do?

Sleep?

Jack Murray

18 Thursday

Jellicoe nodded to 'Crumbs' Crombie at the front desk of the police station. It was eight o'clock in the morning and he was entertaining his first visitor. It was old Mrs Bickerstaff reporting yet another crime. Jellicoe smiled his usual sympathetic greeting to the ever-patient sergeant when he was dealing with one of the more eccentric visitors to the station. He overheard her saying that the noise was unbearable first thing in the morning but was through the double doors before the explanation of the noise was made apparent.

Unusually, Jellicoe was the last in that morning. A sea of faces gazed up at him as he entered then resumed their work.

'Heard anything from the Post Office on the telephone numbers?' asked Jellicoe of Wallace.

'No, I'll follow up at nine.'

Jellicoe rolled his eyes. It wasn't Wallace's fault. Dealing with the Post Office was usually a fraught process. Getting anything from them always took a long time. He nodded to Wallace.

'After you speak to them, we'll go to that barge you mentioned.'

An hour later Wallace was driving out of town towards the wood. They drove past the bus stop near where Sarah Sutton had been killed and continued for half a mile to a turning. The sky was overcast and heavy with rain.

'There's a bridge here that can take us along the towpath near the canal. It'll save us a trip through the wood.'

'Lead on Macduff.'

It was another five minutes as the road seemed about as direct as a politician answering a question. Once or twice Jellicoe was on the point of asking if Wallace was sure this was the way. The young man seemed certain, but then again aren't all young men. Age changes things. Uncertainty invades the mind like winter's

The Bus Stop

chill; it pours through the spot where our defences are weakest. Judgement may improve with time because mistakes teach but only if we are prepared to learn. The biggest lesson we learn from failure is to doubt ourselves. Wallace's time would come, reflected Jellicoe.

The young constable took one corner at a speed that Jellicoe deemed on the adverse side of insane. He glared at Wallace. The message was received and soon they were driving at a more sedate speed. Finally, the canal came into view and then the extraordinary barge that the young sergeant had described. For once he hadn't been exaggerating.

'Good lord. Why doesn't it sink?' exclaimed Jellicoe, echoing Clarke a day earlier.

'We were wondering that too, sir,' laughed Wallace.

Wallace pulled up alongside the red telephone box. They stepped out of the car and Jellicoe went straight to the telephone. He opened the door and noted the number. Then joined Wallace as they walked just ahead to the lock which would allow them to cross over to the side where the barge was moored. Jellicoe glanced up at the grey clouds overhead.

'Let's make this quick. I don't like the look of that up there.'

Wallace was all for making this a quick visit. The cold air stung his face or perhaps he only noticed this when standing near the barge. He felt once more the unease he'd first experienced when seeing the vessel. It seemed to suck the very life out of its surroundings. One look at Jellicoe's face confirmed that the inspector was feeling no more chipper about desolate sight in front of him.

Jellicoe stepped forward to the hatch, knocked politely on the door then stood back. There was noise inside. They could both hear talking. Then barking. Jellicoe raised his eyebrows at this. The hatch door opened, and a long-haired Alsatian dog appeared that could well have been the evillest looking creature Jellicoe had ever beheld. Cold eyes surveyed the two visitors. The dog made its mind up quickly. Teeth bared; it began to bark in a frenzied manner.

'He likes you,' said Wallace nervously.

'So I see.'

Thankfully the guardian of Hades was restrained by a chain that might once have been Jacob Marley's. The metal was over an inch thick but to give the hound from hell its due, there was little confidence in either of the detectives' hearts that it could actually restrain the beast.

'Enough Woodcock.'

Woodcock? The two detectives looked at one another. Wallace frowned and mouthed, 'the boxer?' Jellicoe shrugged in agreement. Of more interest now was the voice that had suddenly silenced the dog.

It was a woman's voice.

Moments later a small woman appeared, ducking under the hatch to come out onto the small deck at the end of the houseboat. She was probably no more than five feet tall, slightly built with long grey hair. Jellicoe would have placed her at around sixty years of age. She wore a grey wrap dress that was discoloured by age. There was little welcome in her eyes. She wore her suspicion like a Chelsea Pensioner wears medals: openly and with no little pride.

'Yes?'

Her voice was as sharp with the detectives as it had been with the family pet. Jellicoe was feeling a lot more relaxed now about Woodcock who was clearly a little cowed by the diminutively domineering woman.

'We're from the police.'

'So, you said. What do you want?'

Jellicoe risked a glance at Wallace who was obviously trying to smother a grin. It would have been remiss, reflected Jellicoe ruefully, for the young man not to extract some enjoyment from seeing his boss on the wrong end of the type of righteous indignation that only a mother can bring.

'Are you alone?' asked Jellicoe.

Impatience, then anger, flared in the eyes of the woman. Whether this was because Jellicoe had deliberately not obeyed her or because she was afraid to mention the presence of her son was the question. Jellicoe surmised that she was someone who did not like seeing control taken away from her.

'What's that got to do with you?'

The Bus Stop

'May we come on board?' asked Jellicoe in as polite a voice as he could manage. He moved forward. The growl from Woodcock was only slightly louder than that coming from the woman.

'Don't you dare,' snarled the woman.

'Madam,' said Jellicoe with exaggerated patience, 'a murder was committed less than three hundred yards away from this spot. Now either you let me come on board or I will organise for half a dozen policemen to come here, and we will take you and whoever else is on this vessel into the police station to answer questions related to this crime. Am I clear?' Jellicoe, when the need arose, could inject a great deal of sharpness into his tone too. It had an effect.

'You can't just come on board,' growled the old woman but there was doubt now. Even Wallace could hear this.

'Yes, I can,' snapped Jellicoe climbing onto the barge. This set Woodcock off again. He was positively straining at the leash and the only thing stopping him was the grip on the rusted chain. Was it Jellicoe's imagination or were those the longest and sharpest fangs he'd ever seen on a dog? Beads of sweat broke out on Jellicoe's forehead but the old woman's grip and the chain held firm. Perhaps Woodcock's bark was worse than his bite. Just then his barking seemed to go up a decibel.

Perhaps not.

'Restrain that animal,' ordered Jellicoe, his voice a decibel higher through the genuine fear he felt. This seemed an unnecessary order as the woman's grip was the only thing preventing Jellicoe's certain demise if not from the teeth of the animal, then the coronary that would have ensued by its attack. He stepped forward.

'Gerard,' said the woman, half turning to the hatch.

'Yes mother,' said a man's voice. It was as Wallace had described it to him the previous day. Like a child given a man's voice to play with but unsure about how it worked. The tone was higher than a man's but was not quite that of a youngster either.

Behind the woman, Jellicoe saw the owner of the voice appear. He ducked under the hatch then climbed up onto the deck. He was quite a sight.

It was difficult to relate the small woman in front of him to her son. He was taller than Jellicoe, gangly in the manner of a teenager but he was in his thirties, perhaps older. His hair was short and could only have been cut by the woman before Jellicoe. The fringe was high and cut straight across giving him the appearance of a Friar. He wore a blue shirt, tieless but buttoned up to the top. The shirt sleeves were short revealing thin, hairless arms.

Jellicoe had a rule of thumb, which was unusually prescriptive for a man with a background in psychology. It posited the notion that a man wearing trousers that were obviously too short for him probably had a screw loose. The taxonomy lacked a certain academic rigour, but the hypothesis had merit. He hadn't shared the theory widely at university but his anecdotal observations both at Oxford and since joining the police had yet to encounter an exception to the rule. The man before him had trousers that he had probably outgrown twenty-five years earlier.

'What do you want?' The voice of the woman was a little more fragile now.

Jellicoe tried to sound less business-like and more sympathetic.

'May we come on board and speak to you about what happened. Someone was murdered quite brutally nearby. We are still trying to find the person who did this. I can see that you have a guard dog…'

Woodcock growled as if to say, 'Damn right they do.'

'…and your son, too. But the person we are seeking is dangerous.'

The woman nodded to Gerard to go back inside. She motioned for Jellicoe and Wallace to board. Much to both detectives' relief, she led Woodcock away from the hatch and down inside. Wallace allowed Jellicoe to go first which amused the inspector. The inside of the barge was as much a surprise as the outside had been.

It was spotless.

The contrast with the exterior could not have been greater. This was a well-maintained space, and, for the first time, Jellicoe could see why it might be feasible to live on a such a houseboat. It was cramped certainly but there was also a minimalism that appealed to him. An absence of needless possessions, of unnecessary detail. It was elemental, yet what remained was

The Bus Stop

fundamental. Except the odd-looking bottles with the three masters inside. Am I envious, he wondered?

'Would you like a cup of tea?'

Wallace declined but Jellicoe accepted. Once more the older detective smiled inwardly at the obvious suspicion and fear in the detective constable. This was probably sensible. It might save his life one day.

'Gerard, please make us some tea.'

The tone was business-like, and Gerard obeyed immediately. He trekked through to the other end where there was a small galley. Jellicoe nodded to Wallace to follow Gerard. This brought a frown from the lady.

'You haven't shown me any identification and what is your young man doing?'

Jellicoe smiled ruefully and took out his warrant card to show the lady.

'Forgive me, I think Woodcock threw me a bit.' At this point Woodcock started to bark at Wallace. Jellicoe smiled and said, 'Good guard dog.'

This was met with a stone face. The woman was in no mood for light-hearted banter.

'May I have your name?' asked Jellicoe.

'Mrs Regis. Victoria Regis.'

'This is your barge?'

'Yes.'

'How long have you lived here?'

'Since Gerard was born. Forty-two years now.'

This made Jellicoe look up sharply. He looked into the eyes of Mrs Regis. They were clear blue and troubled. This was an invasion of their home. Jellicoe doubted they'd had many visitors in all that time. 'Why here?' he asked.

Tears formed in the eyes of the woman, but she refused to cry.

'I lost my husband in nineteen eighteen. He never saw Gerard. I was pregnant without any money. I used what the army gave me to buy this. It was cheap. It was all I could afford.'

'You had no family?'

She shook her head. The fire had returned to her eyes. Anger even. It was if she were re-living a memory. Jellicoe suspected there was a family somewhere. He stopped for a moment and listened to the strange sing-song voice of Gerard Regis speaking to Wallace. Then his eyes shifted to Mrs Regis. There was a question in his eyes that he hoped would not be necessary to ask. It wasn't.

'Gerard is my life. He's a lovely boy and will always be just that. Do you understand?'

Jellicoe did. He'd met dozens of youngsters like Gerard while studying at university. There were various ways of describing them because there were various conditions it could apply to. Mentally disabled. Handicapped. Soft in the head.

'My boy wouldn't hurt a fly.'

Jellicoe nodded at this. There seemed no other response.

'You lock him in?'

'Yes. When I walk the dog or go to the town to shop then I keep him inside. He's perfectly happy. He has everything he needs here, and he likes to tidy.'

'It's very clean,' confirmed Jellicoe. The tea arrived at this point brought by Wallace. Two china cups and saucers. One of the cups had a slight chip. Mrs Regis took this one.

'How long will you stay here?'

'Another week. We move up and down the canal. We stop here often.'

This presented a dilemma for Jellicoe. On the one hand, he did not want the Regis pair to move but equally, there was the possibility that a murderer was stalking the forest. Woodcock started growling again which decided Jellicoe that they were probably safe. He drained the rest of his tea and declined the refill offered by Mrs Regis. In truth he was desperate to leave.

The desolate air emanating from the exterior of the barge was as nothing to the void inside. Despite its cleanliness and order, this was a heartrending place. A widow who had devoted her life to bring up a son from a world that would not understand him and certainly wouldn't care. On the walls were some photographs of a young man that resembled Gerard. He was dressed in a soldier's uniform. He was standing beside an officer on horseback. Both were smiling. In the background men were digging trenches.

Mrs Regis saw where Jellicoe's eyes were directed and, once more, she fought to control the tears forming in her eyes.

'My Alec. He joined in nineteen seventeen. Barely lasted six months. Gerard arrived a month after he died.'

126

The Bus Stop

'I'm sorry,' said Jellicoe and meant it. He drank some more tea then added, 'We won't keep you any longer. He rose from his seat but not too much as his head brushed the ceiling of the barge. He nodded to Wallace to come. Wallace fairly flew out of his seat as Woodcock decided to send them on their way with a few well-chosen barks of farewell.

They stepped onto the towpath. Neither Regis came to see them off. The two men passed a tree stump with splinters surrounding it. They looked at it then one another. Jellicoe forced himself to look back towards the barge again. One object caught his eye amongst the junk lying sprawled around the top.

It was an axe.

19

The rain began to beat down onto the helmet of a thoroughly disgruntled Lee 'Ginger' Rogers. The source of his resentment was not just the weather. He could feel cramp coming on, as he usually did, when cooped up in Eddie's sidecar. The occasional and terrifying bang from the exhausted exhaust of the Norton Denominator was doing nothing to lessen this dark mood. While the Creator had bestowed upon Ginger muscles that would have received an approving nod from Charles Atlas, the story from the neck up was a little less praiseworthy. Ginger was not a thinker. He felt things like anger, joy and, at this particular moment, resentment for always being the one stuffed into the sidecar. The fact that he had never learned how to ride a motorcycle was irrelevant.

'Let's go home,' said Ginger. They had been riding around for half an hour and he was sick-sore, freezing to the point of cramp and bored to the point of despair.

'One more street,' suggested his friend Eddie. 'Don't forget. We're being paid by the dog.'

Ginger needed no reminding of this and decided forbearance was better than grousing. The dognapping was turning out to be more lucrative than he could ever have hoped.

The intrepid canine snatchers edged round the corner, and they found themselves in a cul-de-sac. Normally Eddie avoided these as they blocked at least one escape route then something caught his eye as he began to brake.

'Well, I'll be.'

'I'll be what?' asked his moody companion.

'Look,' said Eddie, pointing to a garden with a white picket fence.

Ginger looked and his eyes caught what Eddie was alluding to. There in the front garden was a cocker spaniel sleeping under a tree. No one was around. It was too good an opportunity to pass up. Wisely, given the motorbike's rather annoying predisposition to coughing and random explosions, Eddie shut off the engine. He climbed off the bike and then watched in mild disgust as his friend tried to extricate himself from the narrow confines of the sidecar.

'You should do Yoga, mate,' suggested Eddie.

In response, Ginger suggested that Eddie should do something that would challenge even the most expert yoga practitioner.

'Someone's grumpy, I see,' replied Eddie marching forward towards their prey.

Bessie the cocker spaniel was blissfully unaware that destiny was sneaking up on her with a bag. She was well past the first flush of youth. Her hearing was not what it once was, and she certainly no longer possessed the fleetness of foot that had once terrorised pigeons in the nearby park. Too late she heard branches cracking. At nine years of age, her reactions were but a shadow of past glories. Within seconds, she was inside the bag and barking angrily at such mistreatment. Ginger hurdled the picket fence like his American namesake Lee Calhoun, and he was at the bike in a matter of seconds.

The Norton spluttered to life, coughed once and then the two boys were away following another successful mission. Ginger laughed joyously; all memories of his earlier misery were banished as he considered the reward that was coming his way.

The boss would be very pleased.

*

Jellicoe and Wallace arrived back to find the front of the police station blanketed by press including some TV cameras. This suggested that London's Fleet Street had entered the fray and, most likely, Southern Television which was part of the Independent Television Network. This was unlikely to be bring glad tidings. Rather than run the gauntlet by entering via the front of the police station, the two detectives elected to drive around to the back and use the fire escape to reach their office, both wondering what had happened.

They passed along the corridor and found out the reason almost immediately. Inside one of the interview rooms was Chester Johnson. Standing over him, his face inches away from the American's face, was Detective Sergeant Fogg. He was shouting at the American. Sitting by Fogg was the Welshman, Ivor Price. Outside the interview looking in were Frankie and Burnett.

'Where have you been?' asked Burnett without taking his eyes away from the spectacle inside the room.

Jellicoe told him then asked, 'Has something new turned up?'

'Another anonymous tip off. A man phoned us an hour ago and claimed to have seen Johnson, here, kneeling at the place where the murder took place. It was too dark to see what he was kneeling over, but I think we can guess.'

'Anonymous,' said Jellicoe wearily.

'Anonymous.'

'What does it matter?' snapped Frankie. 'We have something now we can hold him on.'

Neither Burnett nor Jellicoe had the heart to point out that it was not much good without a witness. Frankie had thought of this and sent in Fogg whose style of interviewing was on the aggressive end of the threat spectrum. The aim was clearly to browbeat the American into a confession or, at the very least, an admission that he had seen the dead body of Sarah Sutton. To admit this would put him in the dock and give the prosecution just about enough to go on. Then it would be up to a jury to decide. Jellicoe had little doubt what verdict they would come up with.

Fogg strode forward and grabbed Johnson by the collar of his shirt before releasing him when Price put a restraining hand on his arm. Jellicoe had suspected he was as appalled by this as he was. Johnson said nothing. Jellicoe could not see his face, but he could imagine what the American was feeling. It rendered the approach by Fogg futile.

Fogg sat down, perspiration dripping freely from his face. He was breathing heavily as much from the effort of shouting himself hoarse as from anger. Johnson turned briefly to the window. Jellicoe could see resignation etched into his features. Resignation and fear.

'Let me speak to him,' urged Jellicoe.

'Nonsense,' barked Frankie, 'Fogg has him on the run. He'll crack.'

Burnett and Jellicoe exchanged looks then the chief spoke.

The Bus Stop

'Let me and college boy have a try. Fogg looks like he needs a fag anyway.'

Frankie did not look pleased at being second-guessed but decided not to make an issue of it in front of the inspector. Rather than admit defeat he turned and walked down the corridor back towards the stairs that would take him up to his office.

'I suppose that's a yes then,' said Burnett. He rapped the window and motioned for the two detectives to leave. There was no disguising the relief on both their faces, albeit for entirely different reasons.

Burnett and Jellicoe entered. They sat down in front of the bus driver. He had both his elbows on the table and head in his hands. Neither detective said anything for a minute. They waited for Johnson to collect himself. Finally, the American looked up. At this proximity, Jellicoe could see his features were greyer and his eyes were bloodshot. He wasn't sleeping. Why, wondered Jellicoe?

'Trouble sleeping?' asked Jellicoe.

Johnson nodded but remained mute. Jellicoe said nothing hoping that Johnson would say more. Finally, the silence became oppressive.

'Is there a reason you're not sleeping, Chester?'

'I didn't kill her.'

'You were seen by her body, Chester. You knew she was dead.'

Johnson looked away. Veins throbbed on his temple. He squeezed his two hands together. Jellicoe glanced at Burnett. There was the hint of a nod from the chief inspector.

'You went back, Chester, didn't you? You were worried. The bus was late anyway and there was no one on it.'

Johnson's head shot up. He fixed his eyes on Jellicoe. Then he nodded.

'Yes,' he whispered. 'I asked her if she was all right. If she was sure she wanted to get off.'

'She ignored you. Completely ignored you,' added Jellicoe.

'That's right. Why'd she do something like that? I was only trying to help.'

'I know, but some people are like that, Chester. So, you drove off. But something stopped you. You were worried.'

131

'Damn right. No one should be alone there at that time of night 'specially not a woman.'

'That's when you went decided. You went back.'

'It was five minutes. No more. I saw her there. Near the phone box. Just lying there like she's sleeping. I crossed the road and went to her, but I know a dead body when I see one. I could see the blood. There was no pulse.'

'Was there anyone else around? Other cars?'

The American shook his head. Then he covered his face once more with his large hands.

'I stayed for a minute. Shook her. But she was dead all right. I didn't know what to do so I went back to the bus.'

'Then what did you do?'

'I finished my round. It was the last journey of the day. I went home.'

'You were the one that called us?'

Johnson nodded. He looked at Jellicoe again, tears in his eyes.

'She was dead. Was nothing that could have been done. She was gone. I didn't kill her'

Jellicoe nodded to him and sat back in his chair. Johnson needed a lawyer now. This was a long way from a confession, but it was certainly enough to hold him and, potentially, charge him. Jellicoe had seen men hanged for less evidence than this.

The two detectives left Johnson and returned to the office. Price and Fogg were waiting there with Yates and Wallace. They all looked up expectantly. Burnett gave them the good news.

'He's admitted that he knew she was dead.'

Fogg clapped his hands while Price clenched his fists. Both Yates and Wallace remained neutral. In the background a phone was ringing.

'Where's bloody uniform?' asked Burnett, going over to the phone. He picked it up and barked, 'Yes?'

For half a minute he was silent then he put the phone down. His face resumed its usual aspect of suppressed irritation.

'Looks like our dognappers have struck again. I want something done about this. You should have heard Cecil Lords today at the press conference banging on about this like it's the crime of the bloody century. Demanding that we turf the gypsies out. He says its them.'

The Bus Stop

'Why, sir?' asked Wallace, mystified.

'Dog fighting, he says,' replied Burnett.

'And what evidence has he shared with us on this?' asked Jellicoe.

'The square root of bugger all, son.'

'I've been to the camp, sir,' said Price. 'I didn't see any sign of dogs for fighting.'

Burnett's look suggested that this was hardly a surprise, but he said nothing. He motioned for Jellicoe to come into his office.

'Close the door,' said Burnett, sitting down. 'What do you think?'

'About Johnson?'

Burnett nodded.

'I believe he's telling the truth. I don't think he killed her. At least I won't believe he killed her until I know why she was on that bus and why she got off when she did.'

'I know,' said Burnett. 'Get uniform to put something out about the white car Johnson talked about, posters and the like. They went door to door, didn't they? Nothing came from that. Maybe this will. If there really was a white car then someone must have seen it. And get Yates and Wallace onto the dog case. The last thing we need is Fogg sticking his big flat feet into that. We'll be at war with the gypsies before you know it. It's not just bloody Lords who's on at us. Erskine Landers is going to bring it up at the next council meeting. He tore a strip of the Chief Constable Leighton earlier. You should have seen him afterwards. Spitting feathers, he was. I know it sounds nothing, but this is the kind of case where heads roll, son. Trust me.'

'I suspect Johnson will be safer in here than at home anyway.'

Burnett looked up sharply at this comment and growled, 'I could never stand glass half full people. Get out of here and catch some criminals.'

*

After speaking to Sergeant Crombie about using some of the uniformed men to follow up on the white car, Jellicoe broke the good news to Yates and Wallace that they were officially taking over the dog case. Wallace was neutral about this. He didn't see every case as an opportunity to move up the promotional ladder. Yates was appalled. It was bad enough to be moved away from a murder case but to be landed with the 'gypsy' case, as he described it, was the limit.

'First of all, it's not the 'gypsy' case,' said Jellicoe in a tight-lipped manner that warned Yates to watch his step. 'Secondly, it has a very high profile with Chief Constable Leighton and the council if that's what you're worried about. And I suspect it is.'

Yates looked suitably subdued in the face of this quiet anger. He knew, once again, that Jellicoe had correctly read his motives. This felt unfair though. No copper would be happy to give up a berth on a big case for one that was bordering on the ridiculous. Still, he reflected, as he left the police station with Wallace, if the Sutton case was finished then it was better than nothing.

'To the gypsy camp,' ordered Yates to Wallace. 'And be slow about it.'

Wallace grinned at the sergeant, saluted, and promptly disobeyed the instruction. After his experience at the Regis barge, he thought visiting the gypsy camp would be a paddle at the seaside.

He was wrong.

This was the first time the young detective had visited such a place. In the few years he'd been a policeman he'd seen many things that had shocked him. At the same time, though, he'd become hardened to the results of crime. A dead body no longer meant a sleepless night. He could be dispassionate at the sight of death, of violence and grief.

The depravation in the camp was unlike anything he'd seen in the worst housing in the town. This was nineteen fifty-nine. Slum dwellings hadn't existed for a decade or more. Even the poorest in society had a dwelling.

Wallace and Yates had pulled up near the camp. The old caravans, the listless ponies and the smoke that seemed to pervade the atmosphere overwhelmed the senses. Children were everywhere. None, as far as Wallace could see, wore shoes. None were washed. There didn't seem to be many men around at least until Yates and Wallace had walked some way into the camp.

There were around a dozen caravans. Some were very old with rotting wood painted to look new. Others were more modern but had undergone many repairs for rust. The more Wallace looked around the more he felt a creeping despair take hold of

The Bus Stop

him. That such misery could exist was beyond his experience of life so far. Yet were they unhappy? Dirty they may have been, but the children were laughing. It wasn't just youthful vanity that made him realise that some young women had appeared and were looking at him in a way that might provoke trouble should any of the young men or fathers appear.

Wallace felt like he was on main street in an old western town. Gary Cooper going out to face destiny. Perhaps not Gary Cooper, thought Wallace. A bit old. Still, he pulled Grace Kelly. Old enough to be his daughter. Katherine Hepburn would have been better. Or Ingrid Bergman. No, too foreign.

Shut up!

Wallace tried to put an end to the wild irrelevancies pinballing around his mind as he fought to stave off the anxiety he was feeling. Some men had appeared. Their faces were hard, cold, and unwelcoming. Fear gripped the young detective constable. These were men used to violence. They had been fighting the world and each other from the moment they were able to walk. Leaning against many of the caravans were pieces of wood that resembled hockey sticks but were, in fact, used to play Hurley. Wallace doubted that any of the sticks had ever touched a ball.

Wallace saw one tall, loose-limbed man jogging over to a large, modern caravan in the middle of the 'street'. He knocked and then entered. Moments later he reappeared. Another man followed him down the shallow steps. The second man looked like an older version of the first one.

The older man walked forward. He wore a plaid shirt and jeans. His hair was grey and thinning on top. He was unshaven but it was not a beard. At least six feet tall, he was lean but there was a quiet power emanating from both his frame and, particularly, his eyes. He was one of the most unkempt men the young detective had ever seen and yet also one of the most impressive. The man's eyes were blazing black, and they were fixed with a ferocious intensity on the two policemen. Oddly this was only the second most unsettling meeting of the day for the young man. The combination of Gerard and Woodcock took some beating.

The thought of Woodcock made Wallace look around the camp site. There were a few dogs. Mostly of the Staffordshire Bull

135

Terrier breed. In all but one case they were off the leash and either playing with children or sitting among them. The parents clearly had a confidence in the dog that Wallace would never have had.

'What do you want?' said the older man by way of greeting. The accent was Irish. There was no question that he knew they were policemen. Gypsies and policemen were natural enemies in Wallace's book. He wondered how Yates would handle this. The answer reflected well on Yates. There wasn't a trace of anxiety in his voice.

'We've come to look around,' said Yates calmly.

'Again. You lot were here two days ago.'

'I know. The dogs are still missing. We'll keep coming here until we find them.'

'Suit yourself,' smiled the man. The smile revealed a set of teeth that resembled rotting tree stumps. He turned his back leaving Yates and Wallace standing in the middle of the camp surrounded by women and children. And the Staffs, much to Wallace's increasing concern. A few men now appeared at the doorways of the caravans. Must have been a late night.

One of the dogs began to growl at the policeman causing some of the people to laugh. This set of a chain reaction and the other dogs began to bark. They may not have known why they were barking but once they started there was no stopping them. Yates looked at Wallace.

He was smiling.

Wallace couldn't believe it. His face must have asked this question.

'Don't worry. They won't do anything. They're on borrowed time anyway.'

Wallace wasn't sure whether he meant the travellers culture or just this particular camp site. Yates wasn't finished though.

'Hey, Jake,' said Yates in a voice just loud enough to be heard by the older man. 'We'll be back.'

The man Yates had called Jake spun around. There was no anger in his eyes. But the glint of hatred was there.

'We'll be waiting.'

The Bus Stop

20

'Where do you think you're going?' asked Burnett, as Jellicoe began putting things away on his desk.

This clearly wasn't a question, a fact which Jellicoe was grateful for because the truthful answer was an empty home, a tin of beans and a book about murder. Whatever image Burnett may have had of the young detective from Scotland Yard, this would have shattered it forever. Burnett, he was no keener on the idea of staying on to work if his face was anything to go by. Then again, his repertoire of facial expressions was limited: angry, angrier and a cruel smile. As appearances went, he was more Edward G Robinson than Cary Grant.

'Where am I going?' asked Jellicoe, a trace of a smile on his lips.

'You're going to the town hall tonight. Erskine Landers is giving a speech.'

Erskine Landers was a senior figure on the town council, but his ambitions lay far beyond dealing with municipal monotony. The palace of Westminster was his goal, and few doubted he would achieve this with General Elections likely to be held later in the year. Jellicoe had not met Landers yet but had seen him once at the police station. He was a regular fixture in the weekly newspaper. He seemed like the young, good-looking, illegitimate, son of the newspaper owner, Cecil Lords, if the attention he was given was an indicator.

Landers had been highly vocal about the spate of dog snatchings principally because his own Yorkshire Terrier, Felicity had been among those taken. Sadly, Jellicoe doubted that this was the likely subject of his speech. There was another topic which inflamed the passions of the prospective candidate for the town.

'I see,' said Jellicoe. 'I can hardly wait.'

Burnett cackled and replied, 'I would have thought a trendy metropolitan type like yourself would love this stuff. I just wanted to make sure you weren't outside protesting with all the other CND types and hand-wringing liberals.'

Jellicoe grinned but decided not to provide oxygen to Burnett's, admittedly light-hearted, banter.

'What time is he on stage?'

This made Burnett smile. Stage was a good description for a consummate actor like Landers.

'Seven,' replied Burnett.

'Just time for a…?'

*

They left the pub at seven on the dot. Burnett's insistence on buying another pint at ten to seven despite Jellicoe's warnings meant they might be late. Burnett disagreed. As they headed out the doors into the cold air he said, 'Trust me it won't start on time. A few of them will be up there wanting to be reflected in his golden halo.'

There were around a dozen people outside the town hall holding placards which had a general theme around 'shame'. They were making quite a din, aided partly by a man playing a trumpet and another with a bass drum which added a percussive intensity to the chant, 'Go home, Landers.'

One or two of the protesters had their own variation on this, of course. Burnett passed by one of them fixed him a glare. The man reverted to the original version. They edged towards the door. On the wall outside the hall were posters featuring the good-looking Landers and, in heavy black lettering underneath, a slogan that he had been using in connection with Windrush and immigration

ENOUGH IS ENOUGH

There were a few people trying to gain access but who were refused by the doorman. Burnett pulled out his warrant card. Jellicoe did likewise. They had no trouble from the man at the door. Burnett turned to Jellicoe and said as they passed him, 'One of Johnny Warwick's boys. I should have guessed Landers would be in cahoots with Johnny-boy.'

The Bus Stop

The interior of the main hall was hot, stuffy with cigarette smoke, and probably full if the presence of people standing at that back was anything to go by. Burnett's acid assessment of the likelihood of a late start was accurate. It was ten past seven and Landers was still being introduced. On the stage, sitting at a table behind him was Cecil Lords and, noted Jellicoe, Mr Bowles, the bereaved father of Sarah Sutton. The long table had a Union Jack draped threateningly over it.

A few people in the crowd were holding up banners. One banner had the same slogan as the poster: ENOUGH IS ENOUGH. Another said: WE WILL NOT BE REPLACED. Underneath was the name of a group – Patriotic Action. Another banner by Patriotic Action read: WHITE BRITISH MINORITY. The white banners threatened to block Jellicoe's view of the stage. And not just his. A few shouts followed by a few whistles saw the banners taken down. This was just in time to see Landers rising from his seat and striding confidently to the dark wooden lectern.

The packed hall broke into loud cheering. Landers stopped and took in the acclamation. For some reason, Jellicoe had expected him to be expensively attired in the manner of a successful car salesman. Instead, he wore a well-cut but unshowy dark suit with grey pin stripes. It was as if he wanted to eschew any hint of vulgar charisma in favour of gravitas. A serious-minded man discussing sorrowfully a sober reality affecting the country. There were many young and mature women in the audience. The appearance of the unmarried would-be politician played no small part in this. He was tall, well-made with black hair greying at the sides. He called to Jellicoe's mind the actor Richard Todd.

He approached the lectern, unsmiling. This was unusual as most of the pictures Jellicoe had seen of him were of a man, enjoying a social whirl in London or on the coast invariably accompanied by a beautiful actress or socialite. His father, Gregory, was the reclusive owner of the plastics factory. The family were multi-millionaires. Landers was a board member and, apparently, a first-class salesman. His success in selling Landers Plastics abroad was ironic given the subject that he was likely to speak about tonight. At least, this was Burnett's view. Burnett made no secret of his Labour leanings. Jellicoe was less sure and was curious to hear what Landers had to say.

'Ladies and gentlemen,' began Landers as the hall stilled. 'Thank you for taking the time on such a cold evening to come and, by your presence, make your feelings known to the people of this town and, dare I say it, this great country of ours also.'

Outside the town hall, the protesters were making their feelings known. It was as if they had sensed the main act was on stage. They were loud and the tone remained distinctly uncomplimentary. Landers paused and listened to the muffled protests. The crowd in the hall chuckled as Landers grinned.

'They want to silence me. They won't. They want to silence everyone here in this hall tonight. They can't. They want to flood our country, *our* country, with people who do not belong here. We won't let them.'

He started quietly but by the end he was shouting above the rising noise within the hall. The noise of acclaim. The last four words were spoken in a staccato manner, and he had jabbed his finger as he'd uttered them. The cheer that greeted them seemed to make the building tremble.

Landers waited a moment to let the crowd settle down. He used the time to scan the crowd while nodding all the time.

'If I am selected,' said Landers. There were boos at this. Landers grinned, held both hands up in a gesture of surrender then continued in a higher pitch, 'When I am selected to represent this constituency at the next election, I will represent your wishes. I hear these wishes expressed every day. Every day more and more of you are telling me enough is enough.'

The crowd roared in approval.

'Here we go,' said Burnett giving Jellicoe a gentle nudge then striking a match for his pipe.

'Enough. Is. Enough,' said Landers. Every word was enunciated like he was performing a Shakespearean soliloquy. 'What do we say to the police who no longer control our streets?'

'Enough is enough,' shouted the crowd.

'What do we say to the influx of travellers who make us feel unsafe in our beds at night?'

The Bus Stop

'Enough is enough,' screamed the crowd in unison. No longer were they a few hundred individuals at a meeting; they were one organism, thinking and speaking as one.

'What do we say to the government who allow foreigners to flood into our great country week after week after week and have the same rights as you and me?'

'Enough is enough.'

Landers, thankfully, moved on from the call and response rhetoric to speak about himself. As the eldest son of the local major business owner, it would be fair to say the crowd knew all too well who he was. His purpose was not to introduce himself so much as make him appear more like one of them. The crowd quietened and settled as his tone became more serious. The aspiring Member of Parliament did a fair job in drawing a veil over his wealth and chose, wisely, to highlight the values he shared with the people of the town. Implied but never explicit was the idea that his family was the backbone of the town's economy.

He was probably right, thought Jellicoe. Tourism might be important but its value to the local economy lasted barely a few months. As sales pitches went, Jellicoe found himself surprised by how effective it was. His own instinct was to distrust politicians, but he had to acknowledge, Landers had more to him than rabble-rousing oratory or fake sincerity.

The showman in him was never going to dwell too long on subjects without applause lines. He was here to entertain his adoring public. And he had a consummate understanding of how to pace the evening. After speaking about himself he returned to the tub-thumping themes that were likely to gin the crowd up.

'Britain loves animals. I am a member of the RSPCA. I donate every year to Battersea Dogs Home. It was there that I met a little lady who became the joy of my life. Her name is Felicity. She's a Yorkshire Terrier. Felicity loves Corn Flakes. She loves watching football with me. She loves chasing birds. She's never caught one, I might add.'

The crowd laughed, enjoying being transported along on a wave that reflected their own values. It was at once soothing and energising. Jellicoe was impressed.

'A few days ago, Felicity was taken from me. Not by some over-enthusiastic dog catcher, not by the good Lord because her time had come. No, she was taken from me by vile criminals who live amongst us. They live amongst us yet contribute nothing except to the workload of the police and the taxes of working men and women. They are parasites, ladies, and gentlemen. Parasites. There is no greater supporter of the police in this town than I. Time and again I have defended them against lies, against unfair criticism, against cuts. But now I ask, why? The police know who has taken Felicity. Oh, yes, they know. And what have they done about it?'

'Nothing,' screamed the crowd.

Landers did not say anything to this. He nodded and smiled grimly. His countenance was one of quiet determination. His posture was the spirit of the Blitz, standing beside the lectern now, feet shoulder-width apart. He'd practiced it in front of mirror that afternoon.

'They are an enemy in our midst. Threatening our homes, our loved ones, the things we value most.'

'Pets,' whispered Burnett with a smirk.

Jellicoe had to shield the smile that appeared as a few men turned around sharply and glared at Burnett.

'We must stand up to this enemy within. If they choose to adopt our culture, our laws, our customs then we will support them. But if they choose to travel from town-to-town inflicting misery on the law-abiding inhabitants then we must stand together and shout in a voice that will be heard the length and breadth of our county.'

'Enough is enough,' screamed the monster that Landers had created. This was followed by a roar of approval as Landers bowed and turned to sit down. Jellicoe exchanged a glance with Burnett who merely rolled his eyes.

'Speak to Bowles,' ordered Burnett. 'I'm going to see if I can have a word with boy wonder over there.'

Jellicoe glanced in the direction of the seated Landers. He was about to be surrounded by a significant proportion of his public. Mostly female; more blue rinse than bobby sox. Jellicoe could not stop from chuckling at this. Burnett saw what he was laughing at and added, 'It's a dirty job sometimes.'

Bowles sat alone, apart from others on the top table. He seemed to be from another generation, another age. Jellicoe approached him at the top table. It took a moment for Bowles to place Jellicoe then he rose to his feet smiled thinly.

'Inspector Jellicoe, this is a surprise. Are you working?'

Jellicoe indicated by a wiggle of his hand that it was not all work. Bowles held out a hand to indicate a free seat that had just been vacated. Jellicoe took him up on the offer.

'I gather you have arrested the American again.'

There was a slight pause before Bowles had said 'American', Jellicoe wondered if he'd thought to say something else, perhaps less innocuous. Bowles half-smiled, as if he read Jellicoe's mind.

'I wasn't going to use a derogatory term if that's what you were thinking.'

It was Jellicoe's turn to smile now. Then he admitted, 'I was. I apologise.'

Bowles waved that away.

'Despite what you may think, Inspector. I don't consider myself a racialist. I doubt Mr Landers would fit that term if you questioned him closely enough. Few people take the time these days to understand better. *Ad hominem* attacks are so much easier and likely to convince those unable to think critically.'

'I wasn't going to accuse of being a racialist, Mr Bowles.'

'Do you understand what we are trying to say though?'

'I understand that for you and Mr Landers the issue is not race so much as immigration. You question why, alone in the world, this country has no definition of its own people. This lack of definition means a native-born Englishman and anyone in the Commonwealth whether it be England or Jamaica is indistinguishable in the eyes of the law of this country. This being the case, we have no ability to control the flow of immigrants from the Commonwealth. You oppose further growth rather than a desire to ship people out.'

Bowles nodded thoughtfully. Then the smile reappeared.

'You have done your homework, Inspector. Or perhaps you are sympathetic to our aims?'

Jellicoe's mind cast back to an evening a couple of years previously when, at Sylvia's insistence, he'd gone to see a Conservative Member of Parliament, Enoch Powell, speak in London. It was not the type of event he would have chosen to attend but, despite himself, he was impressed by Powell's intellect,

143

and he'd learned a lot, particularly around how much television and newspapers could misrepresent the views of individuals they deemed 'the wrong sort'.

'How do you know Mr Landers?' asked Jellicoe.

'He and his family have long provided both moral and financial support to the movement. Sarah even volunteered for him during the council elections. I imagine she would have done so again come the General Election. He's all but been selected by the Conservatives for this seat.'

Jellicoe nodded and filed this piece of information away. He moved on to another topic.

'Have you seen Derek Sutton?'

Bowles nodded in acknowledgement at Jellicoe's deft change of subject.

'Yes, briefly. At the funeral home,' replied Bowles. 'We commiserated with one another. I shan't see him until the funeral two days from now. I daresay I won't see him in my life again after that. Do you believe that the American killed my daughter?'

'I think we have enough now to press charges.'

'That's not what I asked.'

'Did you believe Derek had killed your daughter?'

'Derek? I suppose you know better than I that we are all capable of murder in a given situation.'

'I suppose you're right,' agreed Jellicoe.

*

Burnett met Jellicoe outside the town hall. Jellicoe had seen him have a few words with Landers, but he was one of a dozen. He doubted Burnett would have made whatever point he wanted to make to Landers. The pavement was crowded now. Attendees of the meeting were arguing with some of the protesters. The atmosphere was febrile. Burnett pointed to a group of men from the meeting who were engaged in a vocal and certainly foul-mouthed debate with equally vocal and foul-mouthed opponents. Burnett strode over to the group brandishing his warrant card.

'I suggest you,' said Burnett indicating the pro-Landers supporters before turning to the protesters, 'and you, move on or I'll have you on public order offences. Understand?'

They did. Burnett could be a fearsomely unhinged sight when the mood took him, and he was certainly in that frame of mind just then. A few others heard the commotion with Burnett and decided that it was time to withdraw. Points had been made on both sides. Inevitably, understanding and empathy evaporated in the heat of anger and intolerance.

Jellicoe stood with Burnett and tried to mimic his glare. It was more of an academic challenge for him. It seemed to work but he had to acknowledge that Burnett was a master of this dark art.

'How is Mr Bowles?'

'I found out something interesting which we should follow up.'

Burnett turned to Jellicoe as they walked away from the hall, 'Go on.'

'Sarah Sutton knew Erskine Landers. Not just as a supporter. She may have volunteered for him. Shared interests.'

'I wonder how shared those interests were.'

'Me too,' admitted Jellicoe. 'The pregnancy for a start. I wonder how we can find out.'

Burnett stopped and turned around. This caught Jellicoe by surprise, and he was two steps ahead before he turned around too.

'Where are we going?'

'To see Tristan Harvey.'

The name was familiar to Jellicoe, but he couldn't quite place him. He looked uncomprehendingly at Burnett.

'Tristan Harvey is the social columnist for the weekly newspaper. Well, most of the weekly newspapers along this stretch of the coast. He was at the meeting tonight. He probably doesn't care a fig for the politics but where Landers is concerned there's always interest. He'll have gone to Hector's for a post theatre supper.' Burnett said the word supper in a broad impersonation of BBC English.

'He'll speak to us?'

'He'll speak to me all right. He owes me one.'

The nature of the debt was not elaborated upon, and Jellicoe reluctantly decided to inquire no further. They walked for five minutes through a maze of short cuts until they arrived at a small but obviously popular French restaurant that Jellicoe had heard about but not yet frequented. He was not a fan of French cuisine either in the fussiness of the presentation or the generosity of the portions.

Jellicoe walked ahead and into the restaurant. He was immediately accosted by the head waiter who un-accosted him when Burnett appeared scowling at him.

'Friend of yours?' asked Jellicoe.

'We've had history,' said Burnett, scanning the room. Then he spotted his quarry sitting in a dark corner at the back of the room. Jellicoe followed Burnett to the table. The newspaper diarist looked up as if sensing the elephant-like charge of the chief.

'Chief Inspector Burnett what a pleasant surprise,' said Harvey. He almost sounded sincere. He stood up to reveal that he was quite tall although running to some plumpness around the midriff in a manner that made him look like a Cordon pear. He was at least fifty and, if Jellicoe was not mistaken, wearing just a hint of eyeliner. Harvey cast his eyes over Jellicoe and appeared to like what he saw for his face broke into a very welcoming grin.

'For me, inspector?'

'If you tell me what I want,' laughed Burnett good-naturedly. Jellicoe was less amused by the implication of the exchange. Harvey gestured for the two policemen to sit down.

'Can I offer you something? We don't have to be unsociable, do we?'

'Don't mind if I do,' said Burnet agreeably.

A waiter appeared like genie from a bottle and took down the order of a martini for Jellicoe and a whisky for Burnett. A large one. When the waiter disappeared, Harvey put his two elbows on the table, fixed Burnett with a stare, steepled his fingers and said, 'I saw you there tonight. Worried you might be losing a friend?'

'I suspect we'll only be friends as long as he thinks we're of use to him.'

'A rather neat summary of the man, chief inspector. You should consider sketch writing in newspapers. Perhaps not. You are a little too angry.'

This seemed a good summation of the chief in Jellicoe's view.

'Now, if we may get down to business,' said Harvey after the drinks had arrived. 'How can I help you? Something sordid I hope.'

Burnett took a long sip of the whisky then placed the tumbler down carefully.

'Mr Landers is unmarried I believe,' said Burnett.

The Bus Stop

'Yes,' replied Harvey in a drawn-out fashion A smile creased the corner of his lips. 'What are we possibly suggesting? If it is what I think it is, I can assure you that red blood flows thick and fast through his veins. Sadly.'

Burnett nodded as if approving a neat parry from his fencing opponent. He leaned forward to make himself difficult to hear from any potentially interested ears.

'That being the case, are you aware of any liaison he might have had with the young lady who was murdered earlier in the week, Sarah Sutton?'

Harvey actually clapped in delight at this.

'I say, chief inspector, you are really bringing gifts tonight. How juicy. Of course, I have no idea. What makes you think that they may have made the frightful two-backed monster?' The final part of the sentence was said with a dramatic relish that bordered on lascivious.

'Can you find out?'

'I can if I you say that I can print it if it's true.'

'All yours, Tristan. All yours when the case is over. How soon?'

Harvey ran his finger around the lip of his wine glass and smiled.

'Well, I do have a young friend who is close to dear Mr Landers. I'm sure he will be very open with me.'

Harvey's breathless delivery threw up several possibilities about how open the friend would be and in what circumstance. Jellicoe decided not to think about this but rather on the potential intelligence that might be gleaned.

They parted soon after this promise. The night air was set to chill and, for once, Jellicoe was ravenous enough to look forward to the tin of beans that awaited him back at his flat. He left Burnett and walked ten minutes home. Monk was outside curled up on the welcome mat. He didn't move so Jellicoe had to step over to him to enter his own flat. Just before the door closed, Monk sprang to life and flitted inside.

Normally after giving him some milk, Jellicoe would open the door and allow the cat to go outside. On this occasion, Monk stood at the door and decided against leaving. Jellicoe remained at the door unsure on what to do next. He tried persuasion. Monk ignored him. Then he stooped down and picked him up, repeating the message that it was time to leave. This was undermined somewhat by the fact that he was speaking in the manner of a parent to a recalcitrant child that they are secretly proud of. This was treated with the disdain it merited. Jellicoe set him down outside, but Monk strolled back in without so much as a glance up at the detective. Jellicoe shut the door on the unequal battle of wills.

It was nearing the weekend. He had no money to go out; just a cat, a record collection, and a book to finish.

The Bus Stop

Friday morning. Jellicoe awoke to find Monk curled up sleeping on the bed. Over the weekend, the cat had spent more time inside the flat than outside. In this he had company. Jellicoe's only ventures outside involved a shopping trip and an instantly regretted trip to the bookmaker to back a horse that fell at the fifth fence.

Jellicoe went through his usual morning routine of tea and toast before coming back into the bedroom to insist with all the authority that a policeman could bring to such a situation that it was time for the cat to leave. Monk opened an eye, glanced at Jellicoe then returned to his nap.

'I'll leave the window open, sir,' said Jellicoe in a tone that he hoped the cat would recognise as sarcastic.

It was a dry, crisp morning and the walk into work was made to the sound of seagulls crying overhead. The streets were empty save for a few delivery vans and the occasional bus. The sight of the bus made Jellicoe wonder again about Chester Johnson. He would be charged today and that would bring with it some problems. Attention would shift away from investigating the murder in the whole to a more focused drive to prove that Johnson was the killer. Jellicoe did not believe this, nor, he suspected, did Burnett. An idea was forming on how to deal with this.

When he arrived at the office, he offered a consoling smile to Sergeant Crombie who was dealing with the indefatigable Mrs Bickerstaff. He took the stairs two at a time, impatient to see Burnett. The chief waved him into the office when he arrived.

'I'm going to let Price take over from here,' announced Burnett.

'I was going to suggest this,' said Jellicoe.

'I'm sure you were,' replied Burnett, lighting his pipe.

149

'I was so,' said Jellicoe, drily. This made Burnett glance up, but he manged to suppress the smile that half formed on his lips.

'I'll speak to Harvey,' announced Burnett. 'This can't go further. We don't know if he was the father. For all we know it was Sutton and she didn't tell him. And anyway, if she lost the baby or went to some back street to sort things out, then clearly nothing came of it.'

Jellicoe wasn't so sure. An idea had now occurred to him. At least he had the freedom to pursue the investigation without interference from Frankie. But any satisfaction at this was mitigated by the realisation that if he failed, then Chester Johnson was in serious trouble. How difficult would it be to convict him on such circumstantial evidence? Given his colour, Jellicoe suspected the answer was 'not very'. It could also mean the death penalty. The prosecution would certainly go for it.

The stakes for Chester Johnson were now very high.

*

Duff Ballantyne had spent the last twenty-four years as the bank manager in the town's only bank. The day that a second bank appeared on the horizon would be the day that he handed over the keys to the vault to a younger man, gratefully accepted his gold watch and walked out with head held high to the acclaim of staff and customer alike.

Over Ballantyne's tenure as bank manager, they had faced only two robberies. The first was just before the war when a singularly inept attempt was made with two men wielding toy guns. When the teller had stopped laughing the police arrived to take the men away. They were given suspended sentences claiming, not untruthfully, that an excess of alcohol may have been a contributing factor to the attempted robbery.

The second had happened the previous month. This was a more serious affair and the bank had lost some money as a result. Thankfully the bank's head office in London had taken a mature view that there was nothing Duff Ballantyne could have done to prevent a robbery carried out by explosives-wielding ex-army men, expertly led, well-drilled and benefitting from a town and a police service in chaos dealing with a potential riot.

Ballantyne greeted warmly the arrival of the man widely credited with foiling the attempted robbery. He was accompanied

The Bus Stop

by the new officer from the Met that he'd read about in the 'Sundays'.

Yates shook the hand of Ballantyne warmly and introduced Jellicoe. The bank manager was around Jellicoe's height but thinner and greyer of hair as well as skin. They retired to the Ballantyne's office to allow the reason for the visit to be explained.

'Mr Ballantyne, thank you for seeing us on short notice,' began Jellicoe. 'We have a request which may breach protocol, but I hope you will appreciate it could provide tremendous assistance in an ongoing investigation.'

As he was saying this, Jellicoe wondered how big a crime he was committing against the language of Shakespeare and Austen. The police were as indirect in their requests and explanations as they were direct in their questioning.

'You wish to see the account transactions of one of our customers?'

'Correct. A former customer, sadly,' said Yates, leaning forward with a face full of innocent hope mixed with a certain doe-eyed 'you-owe-me'.

'Ah, would this be the young lady who was murdered?'

'Correct,' replied Yates

Ballantyne sat back in his chair and managed to look uncomfortable while snuggling against the leather upholstery.

'Well, there are a number of protocols that must be followed you understand,' said the bank manager, slowly. He was wrestling with his conscience. But Ballantyne had not spent twenty-four years managing this bank without developing a certain feeling towards where the boundaries between protocol and discretion lay. This was his bank. It was widely respected, highly profitable and a friend to the forces of law and order.

'I can see that this is both important and urgent,' said Ballantyne with a smile. He had read recently about the Eisenhower Matrix, a technique used by the President of the United States and former wartime general to manage his time effectively. 'I shall have someone look at this right away.'

Ballantyne pressed an intercom. Moments later his secretary, Mrs Chesney, appeared. The bank manager requested that the account details of Mrs Sarah Sutton were located. He also requested some tea which was an additional sign to his visitors that Mr Ballantyne was very much the man in charge.

The tea arrived accompanied by some digestive biscuits. A few minutes later an attractive bank teller brought in a thin file with a few sheafs of paper.

'Is there something in particular that is of interest?' asked Ballantyne opening the file.

'Are there any unusual transactions?' asked Jellicoe. He did not elaborate on what unusual meant and Ballantyne did not ask. Instead, the bank manager began to leaf through the pages.'

'She opened the account in October 1955, I see, under her married name. There may be an account under her maiden name shall I ask for it also?'

Jellicoe shook his head saying, 'No, we're interested principally in the last two to three years.'

The banker continued to leaf through the file, extracting a piece of paper every so often. Finally, he came to the end of the file and his eyebrows rose more than a notch or two. This was observed by both detectives, and they exchanged glances on this. A neat row of paper sat in the banker's table. He pushed it forward for them to read. Jellicoe reached for the top piece of paper first. Yates had to content himself with the other pieces of paper.

Jellicoe could see immediately why the transaction had so surprised Ballantyne. The banker regarded Jellicoe carefully as he prepared to field the inevitable question.

'This is quite a large sum of money, Mr Ballantyne. Am I reading this right? It was cash?'

'Yes, three thousand pounds in cash, two months ago.' Ballantyne was smiling and he turned his attention to Yates.

'These are all cash too,' said Yates, putting the sheafs of paper down.

'Three thousand?' exclaimed Jellicoe.

'No five hundred pounds every two months or so. All cash.'

'Was she employed?' asked Ballantyne. There was a hint of regret in his voice at having to ask. When he'd first started out as a teller and then risen to be the manager, he'd known all his customers. Over the last few years, he'd lost that personal connection to them. Many of his older and richer clients were

The Bus Stop

dead. The younger ones no longer sought his guidance in managing their affairs.

'No,' replied Yates.

'Strange she should have such a regular source of income,' commented Ballantyne, in the hope that it might prompt a more forthcoming response. It didn't. But it did give rise to the possibility that they would need access to Derek Sutton's accounts.

They thanked the banker and made the short walk back to the police station across the road.

'What do you think?' asked Yates, as they entered through the double doors at the front.

'It could be blackmail, or it could be a benefit of being a rich man's mistress. Hush money, perhaps. The large sum at the end might have been…'

'A final payoff and goodbye?'

'Yes, but we don't know for certain that she was seeing Landers and it doesn't mean that he murdered her. If anything, it's less likely he would have killed her if he did pay her off.'

They arrived at the office and caught the attention of Burnett. He waved them in and greeted them with the news, 'Just heard from Tristan. Mrs Sutton and Landers were at it all right. Anything from the bank?'

Yates updated the chief inspector on what they had uncovered on the bank. Burnett's eyebrows fairly shot up when he heard about the three thousand pounds. He sat back when Yates had finished and whistled.

'I think that we should pay a visit to Mr Landers, don't you think?' said Burnett. He noticed Yates looking excited and his next comment immediately dampened down any expectation of him joining them. 'Not you, Yatesy my lad. You, son, are going to the dogs.'

22

To add a little bit of heft to the police car going to Lander's Plastics, Burnett persuaded Constable Clarke to drain his second cuppa of the morning and drive them to the factory. It was an excuse, as Jellicoe discovered, to talk about football and another disappointing season for Tottenham Hotspur. Both Burnett and Clarke were long-time fans.

'Nicholson has to go. Should never have brought him in,' said Burnett.

'Rubbish Reg, you don't know what you're talking about,' said Clarke to his superior officer before adding, 'as usual'.

'You see that,' said Burnett to Jellicoe, his finger pointing to Clarke in the front. 'Do you see the respect I get from the ranks?'

'They're in awe of you, sir,' replied Jellicoe in a tone that was desert dry. Clarke burst out laughing.

'Give them a chance, Reg. Young Mackay looks good and Danny…'

'Blanchflower is past it. Mark my words. He'll be dumped soon,' interrupted Burnett.

On such important matters did they pass the ten-minute drive to the edge of town where the plastics factory was located. The factory, like the adjoining head office, competed against one another to see which was an uglier blemish on the landscape. To Jellicoe's eyes the office and factory were like two enormous concrete slabs fly-tipped into the middle of a large carpark. What possible joy could be gained from working in such an environment, wondered Jellicoe as they were waved through the security gates.

They parked in a guest space and stepped out of the car. Burnett noticed a van outside the factory serving tea. He glanced over at Clarke and said, 'Third cuppa of the day methinks, Clarkey. See if you can find out if our friend Landers likes to put it about. Just say we're investigating some of the trouble at the meeting last night if you're asked.'

Burnett led the way to the reception desk. They were told that Landers was in a meeting but that it was scheduled to finish around nine thirty. This would mean a ten-minute wait. The lady behind the desk caught Jellicoe's attention. Unfortunately, his reaction to her good looks was noticed by Burnett.

'Come along, lover boy,' said Burnett turning towards the stairs that led up to Landers' office.

They waited fifteen minutes. Now in the scheme of things this was probably no great inconvenience. The problem was Burnett's mood was calibrated to waiting ten minutes. With each passing minute past the ten he'd mentally allotted to the wait his impatience grew in direct correlation with his irritability. Jellicoe noticed this with people. Anger, anxiety, and everything in between was often a function of the gap between hope and reality. He'd write a general theory on it one day. Maybe win a Nobel Prize in something or other. Maybe not.

Burnett was on his feet now pacing back and forward. He glared at the elderly secretary outside Landers' office. She shrugged and lit a cigarette and proceeded to blow smoke rings. How do people do that? They continued waiting until finally the lady spoke.

'Not my fault, dear,' said the lady whose name plate read Mrs Moring. Goering more like, said Burnett afterwards.

Finally, the door opened, and several well-dressed men of a foreign persuasion exited the office with '*merci*' and '*au revoir*' filling the air. It seemed that alongside his good looks and wealth, Landers had a very good command of French. So much to love in the man, reflected Jellicoe, vaguely amused at his own jealousy.

The door closed and Mrs Moring popped her head in to announce the new arrivals. This initiated another few minutes of waiting. Jellicoe felt genuine concern that he would have to physically restrain his irascible chief from barging into the office. Mrs Moring reappeared and motioned for the two detectives to enter.

'Tea?' she asked in the manner of Lucrezia Borgia speaking to a soon-to-be former lover.

'No thanks, love,' replied Burnett. 'Your smile is refreshing enough.'

They marched into the office and, for the first time since arriving at the concrete violation of the landscape, Jellicoe was genuinely impressed. As ugly as the exterior was, there was no question that young Mr Landers had not stinted in making his working environment as amenable as possible. Jellicoe felt like he was in an apartment in Knightsbridge.

Art deco was the inspiration behind the décor. It was minimal enough to avoid clutter but there were enough objects of art to avoid making the overall impact cold and dull. Behind Landers seat was a large painting by Tamara de Lempicka. It wasn't Jellicoe's taste, yet it matched the office decor seamlessly and suggested restrained taste.

The politician's smile on Landers' face irritated Jellicoe immensely. Or perhaps it was a further sign of envy. He was unquestionably attractive. Tanned skin, flawless teeth and an expensive suit that contrasted markedly from the 'man-of-the people' garment from the night before.

'Chief Inspector, so soon? This is an unexpected pleasure.'

The tone of voice suggested it was unexpected but far from a pleasure. Jellicoe moved the dial on his dislike up a notch to abhorrence. Among Jellicoe's many pet peeves was an aversion to powerful men who spoke as if they had a movie camera on them. This level of egocentricity would have been interesting from a psychological point of view were it not for the observer's own feelings, in this case Jellicoe's, blocking the path to objectivity like a trigger-happy doorman at a posh night club.

'I'm sure it is,' said Burnett drily and Jellicoe could have cheered. A moment later he was not so sure

Burnett briefly introduced Jellicoe which earned the detective a nod and a half smile from Landers but no handshake. Jellicoe decided that he detested the man heartily. He forced himself to smile back at Landers.

'Is this about the matter we spoke of last night?' asked Landers, sitting down. His tone was business-like. A frown creased his forehead. The edge in his voice acted like a red light flashing to Jellicoe's senses.

The Bus Stop

What matter? Jellicoe's face must have betrayed his curiosity, but Burnett quickly shut down further inquiry as he responded angrily to the son of the most powerful man in the town.

'Do you know why my job is so difficult, Erskine?' asked Burnett, anger bursting at the seams of every syllable. He didn't expect and answer so pressed on regardless. 'It's that people who should tell me the truth don't. And everyone else, lies.'

'I'm sorry to hear that, chief inspector. May I ask why you are telling me?'

'Did you know Sarah Sutton?'

This appeared to dent the air of self-possession so much so that it was all Jellicoe could do to stop himself from clapping.

'The young woman that was murdered?'

'Don't give me that, Erskine?' growled Burnett. 'I have Frankie crawling all over my backside and I can tell you I wouldn't wish that on anyone. So don't waste my bloody time. Was she having your baby?'

It was quite an achievement, really. The tanned features of Landers seemed to turn pale in the face of the onslaught from the untranquil chief inspector. But how did Burnett get to call Landers Erskine? Landers looked from Burnett to Jellicoe and then back again. Some colour returned to his skin. In patches. It was a combination of anger and acute embarrassment, like a schoolboy caught leafing through his dad's collection of 'art' magazines.

'What are you suggesting, Burnett?'

The edge had returned to his voice: a man cornered by his own folly. The implication of Burnett's accusation went far beyond the case they were investigating. It was nothing less than the potential ruining of his carefully cultivated image of a man in control of his limitless future. In the face of such an implied threat from Landers, many men would have backed down. Burnett leaned forward, put both hands on the table and yelled at Landers.

'Give me one bloody reason why I shouldn't haul you down to the police station, Erskine. One bloody reason.'

The door opened moments later and in walked a man who was dressed like lawyer, who walked like a lawyer and when he spoke, confirmed that he was a lawyer. He wore a three-piece suit, had dark brylcreemed hair and half-moon spectacles that he gazed over with all the cheerful bonhomie of a headmaster seconds away from dispensing six of the best.

'Hello,' said Burnett turning around to the lawyer. 'Who's this? Perry Mason? No, don't answer. Just kidding.'

'Erskine, you are under no obligation to answer any questions from these men.'

'Policemen,' said Jellicoe, looking not at the lawyer but at Landers. 'Policemen investigating a murder. Mr Landers knows what we want to know. He has a choice now whether he listens to you or he answers the question which we can repeat in front of you now.'

This hit home with the business owner in Landers. A situation was developing that needed to be controlled. Could he trust the police to do this? No was the answer if he was unwilling to help them. Everything he was working towards could be destroyed with one loose word. He put his hand up and it was directed at the lawyer not at Burnett or Jellicoe.

'It's all right, Bernard. I cannot claim to be a supporter of law and order if I am not prepared to answer questions from time to time to clarify misunderstandings.'

The last word was emphasised, and he held Burnett's gaze as he said this. He nodded to the lawyer who turned a colour that Jellicoe assumed to be puce. Bernard was on the point of saying something when Landers shook his head, effectively ending the discussion. The lawyer spun around and strode out of the office, a cloud of anger and humiliation surrounding him.

'Cheerio, Bernard,' said Burnett with a chuckle. Then he turned to Landers. The smile was gone. 'What happened?'

'This doesn't go beyond this office, understand?'

'We'll see about that,' replied Burnett.

'Yes, I knew Sarah Sutton. She volunteered for me at the last council election. She believed in what we were saying. Later she introduced me to her father. This was a pleasant surprise.'

Burnett rolled his eyes and shifted in his seat. His index finger made a circular 'get-on-with-it' motion.

'We saw each other a number of times and yes, things went further than they should have.'

'Did you know she was pregnant?'

'I did.'

The Bus Stop

'Did you ask her to get rid of the baby?'

'No, I wasn't convinced the child was mine.'

'So, you paid her five hundred pounds a month for it not to be yours?'

Landers sat bolt upright and slammed the table, 'That's a lie. I did no such thing.'

'She was blackmailing you,' cut in Jellicoe.

'No, she wasn't. I did give her some money. I suppose you would characterise it as hush money, but she was not blackmailing me. In fact, she nearly refused the money. It was me who insisted. She wasn't the blackmailing type.'

'How much did you give her?' asked Burnett.

'I think you already know, Burnett,' replied Landers through gritted teeth. He sat back in his seat and appeared to calm down. His voice when he spoke again was even and controlled. 'The baby was not mine. Am I clear? It was not mine. Anything said on this topic is vile muck raking. And trust me, if it gets out, it won't be Bernard the police will have to deal with.'

Jellicoe glanced at Burnett. Landers seemed adamant that he had not been blackmailed. If true, this ruled out a motive for Landers to kill Sarah Sutton. Of course, this would have been apparent to Landers, too.

'Why should we believe you weren't paying her blackmail money?' asked Jellicoe.

'There are three thousand reasons why you should believe I was not being blackmailed. She only told me about the pregnancy a month ago. Why would I be paying her before then? I mean, how long were these payments you're referring to going on? I only met Sarah eight months ago.'

Burnett nodded at this which Jellicoe suspected meant an end to the questions on this topic. For all his dislike of Landers, Jellicoe did not believe he was looking at the killer or someone who could have ordered one. Landers, sensing that the interrogation had run out of steam, leaned forward once more.

'I have been honest with you. I hope that you will respect my position. This does not have to be aired in public. I'm sorry about Sarah's death but it was a fling. No more. Sarah was no sorrier it ended than I was. I assumed when she ended things it was because the baby was her husband's.'

'She ended it?' asked Jellicoe.

'Yes. I was relieved mind you. Saved me having to do it.'

Jellicoe understood this all too well. The final months of his marriage before Sylvia's death had been the worst of his life. Back then he'd hoped that she would just put them both out of their misery. He'd not had the courage to. He may no longer have loved Sylvia, but he did love the flat in Kensington and the lifestyle her father helped provide. It hadn't taken him long to tell his son-in-law that he had to give up the flat and make his own arrangements. It was one of the last times he'd spoken with his father-in-law.

A heavy silence fell in the room. Landers stared defiantly at the two detectives. He felt back in control.

'Why are you questioning me about this. You've found the killer, haven't you?'

'Maybe,' replied Burnett standing up.

'And what about my pet? Are you any nearer catching the dog thieves? I doubt it,' said Landers. 'Cecil's right, you know. You're losing control.'

'Yes, going to the dogs,' retorted Burnett.

Jellicoe couldn't bring himself to look at Landers after that comment from Burnett. There was no handshake. Burnett simply turned and walked to the door followed by Jellicoe. The lawyer and Mrs Moring were waiting outside the office. They watched as Jellicoe and Burnett passed them on their way to the stairs.

They met Clarke outside. He was sitting with a few of the factory workers on a wooden bench. If the purpose of his chat was to obtain information on Landers, then it seemed to have gone awry as they found the constable in the middle of a story that had the men slapping their thighs laughing. Clarke saw the two detectives, drained his tea, and finished off by saying, 'Duty calls.'

'Bye, Clarkey,' chorused the men. One of them was black, noted Jellicoe. His accent, distinctly Caribbean.

Clarke joined Jellicoe and Burnett. The chief said wryly, 'Instilling fear and respect as ever.'

'You know me,' replied Clarke. 'Speak softly but carry a large truncheon.'

They returned to the car at a jog as the rain which had been threatening began to fall. Once inside Clarke confirmed that the

160

men liked Landers. They rarely saw the father these days, so Landers was the boss in their eyes. No one mentioned seeing him with women in the office or from the factory. There were no feudal rights imposed on the female employees, which was another reason why he was respected.

All of which was very well, thought Jellicoe, but he was more interested in the relationship between Burnett and Landers rather than the women who worked for him. As if sensing this Burnett turned to Jellicoe with a wry smile.

'You may have been wondering why I know him so well?'

Jellicoe's raised eyebrows answered this question.

'A few years ago, old Mr Landers' daughter was running a little wild. Hanging out with some of Johnny Warwick's thugs. Teenage rebellion they call it. She was implicated in an assault. Now if you've ever seen Beth Landers, there's no way she could've been involved. It was one of her boyfriends. Anyway, I made sure she wasn't put on the charge. And before you say anything, I have no regrets. She's a slip of thing. You'd fancy her, I can tell you. She's off at university somewhere, probably where you went. She'll come out a doctor or something like that rather than have her life ruined because of some bad choices when she was seventeen.

Bad choices, reflected Jellicoe, were not confined to teenagers. Love or, more likely, lust heightened your senses but dulled your thinking. He knew that as well as anyone. There was nothing to say to Burnett. The choice to protect the young woman was a human one. He'd have done the same.

Burnett lit his pipe and sat like an older, angrier version of Maigret staring out of the car window. As they neared the police station he spoke.

'Clarkey, do you remember the Dilys Michaels case a couple of years ago?'

'I do. We never found her, did we?'

'No, we didn't. Do me a favour, Nick lad, while Price and Frankie are tying up the loose ends of the Sutton murder. Have a look at that case file. That bag we found. I wonder if it was hers. Might be worth following up.'

'When was this?'

161

'Two years ago. She disappeared. Was never seen again. We searched high and low. Put out public appeals, posters. You name it, we did it. A few witnesses came forward but nothing that we could use. But one of them I do remember said something of interest.'

'What was that?' asked Jellicoe.

'She'd been on a bus that day from Frimhampton.'

The Bus Stop

23

The file on Dilys Michaels was thick suggesting a significant effort had been made to find her. The story was a familiar one. A young woman had gone out on the morning of the February 24th and not returned. She was seen on a bus in the early afternoon. Later that day, she was sighted in town, but this was by no means confirmed and Burnett had scribbled question marks all over the witness's statement. The bus driver was not Chester Johnson and, anyway, he had no memory of seeing her.

Jellicoe retrieved the handbag from the storeroom and looked around at the empty office. Yates and Wallace were questioning the owners of the missing pets so would be out for the afternoon. Price and Fogg were interrogating Johnson. Jellicoe couldn't bring himself to look in at the interview room. His stomach felt empty from more than just the lack of lunch.

He took a police car and drove slowly to the nearby town of Frimhampton. Meeting the husband of Dilys Michaels would only dredge up unwelcome memories of his own loss and the failed investigation. Perhaps it was hunger but the prospect of meeting a man, like himself, who had lost his wife made a torpor descend over his body.

The file said that Ian Michaels worked at travel agency on the high street of Frimhampton. Jellicoe spotted the travel agency sandwiched between two estate agents. He parked the car and walked in, leaving the handbag in the police car.

A man sitting behind a counter looked up. His face fell when he saw Jellicoe enter. There was no question this was the man he was looking for nor any question that Michaels knew that he was a policeman. Michaels had never been under suspicion due to an alibi and an absence of any motive.

'Mr Michaels?'

'Yes. Are you with the police?'

Jellicoe nodded and said, 'Could I possibly speak to you for a few minutes outside?'

Michaels looked towards a colleague, another man, who nodded. He rose from his seat and accompanied Jellicoe outside.

'I'm here in connection with another crime. We found a handbag near where the victim was murdered. We've established that it did not belong to her.'

Jellicoe went over to the police car and brought out the handbag.

'Do you know if this belonged to your wife?'

Michaels put his hand to his mouth in shock. He nodded and whispered, 'Yes. That's hers. I'd bought it for her for Christmas.' He looked at Jellicoe and then back to the bag.

'What does this mean?' asked Michaels.

Jellicoe wished he knew the answer to that question.

*

Wallace and Yates were back in the office when Jellicoe returned. Wallace was as cheerfully untidy as ever. Even Yates had his top shirt button open, and tie loosened. Jellicoe smiled at his unusually unkempt appearance. Yates rolled his eyes at Jellicoe. It had been one of *those* days.

'Fun?'

'Wonderful,' replied Wallace.

'Wonderful,' confirmed Yates.

'Is that your report?' asked Jellicoe.

Yates sighed and began to relate the highlights of their day. It didn't sound as if there had been many.

'So, we saw half a dozen of the pet owners. Same story. They are angry. They want action. They don't understand why we haven't raided the gypsy camp. We told them that we'd been there, but they'd stopped listening and were showing us pictures of their bloody pooches.'

Not quite a murder investigation, conceded Jellicoe. He slumped down in the seat and updated them on what he'd found out about the handbag. No mention was made of Landers. For the moment, that subject was off limits.

'Two of the owners reported hearing a motorcycle nearby but they didn't see it.'

'Old?'

The Bus Stop

'It backfired.'

'Master criminals obviously,' said Jellicoe. 'Well, tell uniform to be on the lookout for an old motorcycle. This is an odd one. If it is someone from the gypsy camp, why are they running such an obvious risk? What are they doing with the animals? Are they being used for fighting or sold off as pets somewhere else in the country? None of it makes much sense to me.'

Just then the door flew open, and Burnett strode into the room. In the corridor they could hear Superintendent Frankie shouting for him to come back. Burnett ignored him and went into his office and slammed the door shut. The three detectives looked at one another and shrugged. It was not an uncommon sight for Burnett to be angry about something involving the superintendent. Rarely, though, was the man in question near such a public display of displeasure. Frankie was not a man to be outdone in the volatility stakes. He followed Burnett's footsteps and walked into his office. His attempt at slamming the door met with failure as his hand slipped off the handle.

Undaunted by this slip up, he closed the door. The three detectives sat back and made themselves comfortable. The explosions between Frankie and Burnett were surprisingly rare but provided excellent entertainment for those fortunate enough to see them. No amount of soundproofing was ever going to contain the volume of the discussion nor the content. They were charging Johnson and making a statement about it in the next hour. The shouting match raged for less than two minutes without any obvious sign than an accommodation had been reached. Then Frankie ripped open the door and stalked out saying, 'And if you don't like it, do you know what you can do?'

This question offered quite a few possible answers despite which no one was under any illusion that it was meant to be rhetorical. After Frankie had left the office, Burnett waved Jellicoe in.

'That man is a moron.'

'Speaks highly of you, too, sir' responded Jellicoe.

'I'm sure he does. What about the bag?'

'It is Dilys Michaels' bag all right.'

Burnett exhaled and shook his head. A shadow passed over his face. The ghost of regret that haunts every policeman when a killer has gone free.

'I'll bet you a pound to a penny that she was murdered and murdered by the same person at that.'

He rubbed his eyes as much in exasperation as any carryover fatigue from the argument. For once his ruddy complexion had an unusual pallor, his expression worn. Having to deal with stupidity daily inevitably led to strain. Or was it his response, anger? The two men turned and looked at the rain rattling against the window. Jellicoe walked over to the window and stared into the gloom. Mute grey-clad figures swarmed along the street. The only colour Jellicoe could see was a lit Coca-Cola sign.

'Thoughts?' asked Burnett after a while.

Jellicoe's leaned against the window. Thoughts? He had lots of them but there was no coherence to them yet. Too many things unexplained. He turned to the outer office and saw Wallace lighting a cigarette with a lighter. This was a surprise. When had the young sergeant started smoking? Perhaps he always had. He handed Yates a cigarette and lit it for him. Walking over to the door, he opened it and asked Wallace, 'Has anything arrived yet on the phone records?'

'They posted it.'

Jellicoe's response to this was unlike him and brought some life back to Burnett. He chuckled and reached into his pocket for a pipe.

'Johnson could have done it,' said Jellicoe reluctantly. 'He was there roughly when it happened. Motive might have been anger at something she said. He was seen beside the body. And he lied to us. I could make a case from that.'

Burnett nodded. So could the prosecution.

'Derek Sutton has an alibi but that doesn't mean he didn't have someone kill his wife.' Jellicoe paused for a moment and then grinned. He thought of the book sitting on his coffee table.

'What's so funny?'

Jellicoe waved his hand and then continued, 'Then we have the white car. Who owns it? Who was Sarah Sutton meeting when she got off the bus?'

'We only have Johnson's word on that,' pointed out Burnett.

The Bus Stop

'True,' agreed Jellicoe. He went back to the door and called out to Yates and Wallace to come in. The two men stubbed out their cigarettes and trooped in.

'It's the paw-lice,' cackled Burnett who seemed to have recovered some of his old cynicism. 'Had any luck sniffing out the trail of the devious dognappers?' Wallace grinned at this, but Yates was less pleased. This brought another laugh followed by a fit of coughing.

'Not yet, sir. I've asked uniform to keep an eye out for a man or a pair of men using an old motorcycle. A couple of the victims claim to have heard one backfiring nearby,' said Yates.

Burnett's moment of good humour was over, and his face resumed its look of exasperation. The dogs were proving to be every bit as big a headache as the Sutton murder case. If it was the work of the gypsies, then they were making a bloody good fist of covering their tracks.

'Is anyone keeping an eye on the camp?' asked Jellicoe.

'Yes, sir,' said Wallace. 'But they saw no one come or go with any animals and this was after the last theft.'

'It's not them,' said Jellicoe. 'We'd have found something by now. Anyway, we're just discussing the Sutton case. Have we heard anything back about the white car?'

'Nothing, sir,' confirmed Wallace.

Jellicoe shook his head in irritation. Burnett shrugged; his face showed scepticism about its existence.

'What about the mother and son on the barge?' asked Yates. 'Do you think there's any chance that one of them could have killed her? They were near enough.'

'All very Oedipal,' replied Jellicoe. Burnett frowned.

'You what?'

'It's a psychoanalysis concept to explain desire and jealousy in a child. Freud. It's based on the Greek myth of Oedipus accidentally fulfilled a prophesy that he would kill his father and marry his mother,' explained Jellicoe. He could see Burnett's face change from a scowl to a look of horror.

'Was there a happy ending?'

Jellicoe glanced to see if Burnett was joking but the chief had already started laughing and nudging Yates.

'You should be on stage, sir,' commented Jellicoe.

'You started it with your dirty stories,' replied Burnett defensively. If nothing else, Burnett seemed in a better mood now. 'So, if Johnson is the wrong man, how will we prove this?'

Now they were reliant on two things, neither of which offered much in the way of hope that they would shed new light on the case.

'The telephone records from that phone box and the white car,' said Jellicoe. 'Although I would like to investigate Sutton a little more. Was he aware of the money his wife received? It might be a motive for him to have had her killed assuming he really was in London.'

Burnett turned

to Yates and said, 'Go up to London. Confirm Sutton's alibi. Don't just rely on his mates. Can anyone else vouch for where he was on Sunday?'

This brightened Yates up considerably.

'What about me, sir?' asked Wallace brightly.

'Find Fido,' said Burnett before breaking out into a mirthless laugh once more.

The Bus Stop

24

'What are you doing now?' asked Burnett to Jellicoe as Yates and Wallace exited the office.

'I might have another natter with our friend across the road at the bank,' said Jellicoe. Burnett agreed and glanced at his watch. Jellicoe did so too and realised the bank would be shut. He hurried out of the office. Burnett picked up the phone after Jellicoe had left. He dialled a number and waited. Finally, someone answered.

'Put me through to Mr Landers. It's Chief Inspector Burnett. He'll take my call, believe me.'

Jellicoe rushed to join Yates who was heading down the stairs.

'Go to London tomorrow and speak to everyone that Sutton would have seen.'

'That'll take a day, sir.'

'Fine. I just want to be able to discount Sutton. In the meantime, come over to the bank with me. Let's see if we can find out about his finances.'

They stepped out into the drizzle. It was dark now, too. The two men jogged through the traffic towards the bank. It was shut, of course. On the assumption that there was always the chance that someone would be inside, Jellicoe rang the bell and waited. Eventually a woman opened the door and peeked her head though. She informed them that the bank was shut. Jellicoe had his warrant card ready.

'We've come to see Mr Ballantyne. Is he still here?' asked Jellicoe in his politest voice. Like most people he had a range of voices and tones that he could deploy depending on the audience which ranged from small children to difficult subordinates and petty officialdom. In fact, the latter could enjoy the full spectrum depending on gender, age, and attitude.

The lady made little attempt to hide her irritation which confirmed to Jellicoe that they would be able to come in. They were led behind the counter to the office of Mr Ballantyne. The lady spoke briefly with the secretary they'd met earlier. Her reaction was no more welcoming. Jellicoe smiled at her. She disappeared into Ballantyne's office only to reappear a few seconds later.

'Come this way, please.'

'Thank you. Most kind,' said Jellicoe innocently.

Ballantyne rose to meet them. His smile of welcome, at least, had some measure of sincerity.

'Gentlemen, twice in one day. We are honoured.'

Jellicoe doubted that either he or the bank was in the least bit honoured, so he ignored the flattery and came straight to the point.

'I'm sorry to disturb you again, especially outside business hours. We have another small request.'

'Go on.'

'The transactions you mentioned earlier in Mrs Sutton's account are for the most part unexplained. We were wondering if there were similar such cash deposits into Mr Sutton's account. I accept this is highly irregular, but it is a murder investigation.'

There was no hiding the conflict that the bank manager felt at this request. Of course, they could ultimately apply to the court for the right to see the transactions. To force them down this path would seem churlish given the fact that they had saved the bank a great deal of money and him, personally, a not insignificant amount of inconvenience.

'I can look for you,' decided Ballantyne, 'but of course, I will only confirm if similar has occurred. I won't be able to show you. Will this be sufficient?'

'Yes, Mr Ballantyne. We are very grateful,' replied Jellicoe.

Ballantyne asked his secretary to come in and requested that she find Derek Sutton's bank statements. Polite conversation followed on the progress being made rebuilding parts of the entrance damaged by the bomb the previous month. This gave the bank manager the opportunity to bemoan the attitude and capability of the building firm being employed, Osbourne and Son. Interestingly, the firm was one of Johnny Warwick's many

The Bus Stop

business interests. Ballantyne struck Jellicoe as too shrewd an individual not to know that the building firm was part-owned by one of the two main gang leaders in the area. He was also wise enough to accept that this limited his options when it came to complaining about the work.

The file arrived much more quickly this time. Ballantyne thanked his secretary and waited until she had left the office before opening it up to view the contents.

'He opened an account on the same day as his wife. Interestingly they decided to forego a joint account. Perhaps they both had doubts about whether it would be 'til death us do part.'

He began to leaf through the pages scanning each page slowly and deliberately but saying nothing. The file was noticeably thicker than Sarah Sutton's which may have partly been because Sutton was ostensibly the chief wage earner and receiving a salary. When Ballantyne had examined the last page, he looked up at the two policemen. Jellicoe could have smiled at the way he was drawing out the moment. Possibly they deserved this. It was somewhat irregular and, anyway, a small price to pay.

'Aside from what I am guessing is his salary which was paid monthly by cheque from Neptune Shipping there is also a bi-monthly payment of seven hundred pounds. In cash. Just like Mrs Sutton. I can't say more as to its provenance. There are no other one-off deposits or any large withdrawals. Both Mr and Mrs Sutton have accumulated a not inconsiderable amount of money, Inspector. I had no idea. Their mortgage payments are regular and judging by the size of them, I would hazard a guess that they live well within their means.'

Ballantyne looked at the address on the front of the file. His only comment at seeing it was, 'Good Lord.'

Jellicoe raised his eyebrow at this.

'Why do you say that?' asked Jellicoe although he already knew the answer.

'If they live where I think they live, then I must confess to being surprised. They could have afforded something much better, believe me.'

There was nothing else to say so no one said it. The two detectives merely thanked the bank manager and left the bank and returned to the rain and the cold.

'Can you give me a lift back to the flat?' asked Jellicoe. 'You'll be off early tomorrow.'

They returned to the police station. Jellicoe waited in the car park while Yates took the car keys for the Wolsey.

'What do you make of these money deposits?' asked Jellicoe as they drove out of the car park.

'Of course, it could be very innocent. Her father is quite wealthy. Perhaps he is supplementing their income.'

'Or maybe one of them has a rich uncle,' laughed Jellicoe.

'Indeed,' said Yates with a grin. Neither explanation was in the least plausible to them.

'Well, I will speak to Bowles tomorrow,' said Jellicoe, 'but I'm willing to give five to one he hasn't the first idea about this. To be serious for a moment, I doubt he's given them a penny. He doesn't like Sutton and he made that fairly plain. I'll pay a visit to Derek Sutton tomorrow as well and shake the tree a bit.'

They arrived at Jellicoe's flat a few minutes later. Yates whistled when he saw it which made Jellicoe laugh although the satisfaction at living there had worn off in the face of the realisation that he was living beyond his means.

'Come up, I'll show it to you if you like,' offered Jellicoe.

Yates replied, 'Have to admit I am curious. I remember these when they were being built. Always thought they looked very nice. I'll need to be a detective inspector before I can afford something like this.'

Jellicoe felt like saying he couldn't afford it either but decided not to pour oil over the young man's enthusiasm. When they entered the flat, it made Jellicoe realise once more how impressive it was. Yates didn't stint on his praise for what he saw although he did ask how it was possible to live without a television set.

'It's on its way,' explained Jellicoe.

Yates noticed the book sitting on the coffee table. He picked up Jellicoe's '*Strangers on a Train*'.

'Is that from the film?' asked Yates.

'The book came first.'

'Good film,' said Yates absently. He was reading the back cover when he turned to Jellicoe his eyes wide.

'This might sound silly, but you don't think Derek Sutton did something like this?' Jellicoe looked at him, a slight frown appearing on his forehead. Yates grinned and shrugged his shoulders before forging ahead. 'What if Sutton had someone kill his wife while he did something similar in London? You never know.'

It was more speculative than serious by Yates. Jellicoe smiled and agreed that they should not discount anything. A similar thought had occurred to Jellicoe.

'Can I borrow it after you've finished?' asked Yates heading to the door. 'Nice flat, did I say that?'

Jellicoe laughed, 'Once or twice.'

The two men headed out of the flat. As Yates opened the front door, Monk darted in under his legs. Yates looked at Jellicoe for an explanation. The detective inspector shrugged and said, 'I think I've been adopted.'

*

Around five in the evening Burnett left his office to head back to the domestic haven he called home. There, Mrs Burnett would be waiting for him wearing a suggestive smile and not much else.

He could dream.

The reality would be somewhat different. Nearly forty years of connubial bliss meant their relationship was more Abbott and Costello than Anthony and Cleopatra. In truth, Burnett wouldn't have it any other way. He could still dream about Rita Hayworth if he wanted to. Maybe, somewhere in her lonely Hollywood mansion, she dreamed of life with a sour, overweight copper.

He passed Wallace in the corridor. He was carrying two boxes. Behind him was a postman carrying another two boxes.

'What's that?'

'The phone records have finally arrived. The idiots have sent me every phone box in the town. Last three bloomin' years.'

Burnett blew out his cheeks and shook his head.

'I'll leave you to it then, Wallace. Goodnight.'

Burnett went down the stairs. At the bottom of the stairwell there were half a dozen other boxes. Wallace was in for a fun evening and morning by the looks of things. He wondered if there was any point to it. For a second, he thought to head back up the stairs and tell Wallace not to bother, but something stopped him. A whisper from his intuition.

Leave it. You never know.

Jack Murray

The Bus Stop

25 Saturday

The day that both cases were solved started off like any other for Jellicoe. A hurried breakfast of tea and toast. An argument with a cat about leaving the house, which he lost. A walk through the puddles left by the previous evening's rain, arriving at the office to see Sergeant Crombie entertaining Mrs Ada Bickerstaff. He ran past them, keen to avoid being dragged into whatever fantasy the poor lady was relating to the peerlessly patient Sergeant Crombie.

Jellicoe took the stairs two at a time because he knew one day even one at a time would be an effort. He arrived at an office that looked like it had been hit by a cyclone. All the desks were being used as dumping grounds for masses of printouts. In the middle of the maelstrom was Wallace. The last remnants of the puppy dog passion were being worn away by the reality of police work. If he retained even a scintilla of enthusiasm for the job after this, Jellicoe decided he would eat his hat. It would make a pleasant change from beans.

'You look busy,' said Jellicoe, aware that it was a statement of the obvious and perilously close to being patronising.

Wallace glanced up and the expression on his face confirmed that it was both. 'They sent three tons of records for every bloody phone box in the town. Been here since six and that was after leaving near midnight last night.

Jellicoe decided anything approaching sympathy might be treated as another patronising comment. So, he left Wallace to it and popped his head into see the chief. Just for a change, Burnett was in a bad mood.

'Yes?' snarled Burnett.

'What's wrong with you?' asked Jellicoe with a smile he hoped would enrage Burnett further.

It did.

175

'Cheeky sod. Why aren't you out catching murderers or dognappers?' said Burnett. He held up a newspaper. It was a special edition of the weekly newspaper. On the front page was a picture of Erskine Landers and a headline that read:

ENOUGH IS ENOUGH

'Ah,' said Jellicoe, taking the paper and scanning the editorial written by Cecil Lords underneath the headline.

'The police have shown themselves to be inept…gypsies are running rings around them…immigrants are drug dealers, criminals, rapists and murderers. Right now, a black American is being held in custody for the brutal murder of a white woman. We are living in fear…blah, blah and more blah.'

Jellicoe set the paper down and looked at Burnett who was still seething. The chief lit a pipe in the forlorn hope that it would help calm him down.

'If I ever see that toffee-nosed fathead anywhere near this station, I'll pop him one.'

Jellicoe decided to ignore this obvious wish fulfilment make-believe.

'Can't Leighton have a word with him. This is borderline incitement. I thought he and Lords were buddies.'

Burnett looked even more sour at this comment than normal. This put a thought in Jellicoe's head that was confirmed moments later.

'Oh, they're buddies all right. As much as I like Laurence, and I do like him, I think Cecil Lords is only saying what Laurence thinks about the gypsies. He wants to get rid of them and he's using Lords to get public support behind sending in the police, the army, the Americans and whoever.'

'I didn't have the chief constable down as a racialist. His daughter's dating a black man. Or at least they seemed fairly close.'

Burnett snorted at this.

'Good luck to him. Princess Winnie can be a right madam when she wants. I pity the man that ends up with her. And yes, son, take that as a warning. You think dating the daughter of a

The Bus Stop

chief constable is a way to promotion? She'll eat you for breakfast.'

Jellicoe had no intention of dating anyone, any time soon. Eight months had passed. Eight months away from a woman he'd grown to hate. Yet why did he feel so empty? Guilt, probably. Hating someone who is dead is merely a proxy for the true object of your loathing. Jellicoe knew this too well to bother being in denial.

'Do you think the chief constable was the one who fed Lords about Johnson earlier in the week?'

Burnett's expression indicated you should know better than to ask that. This was interesting. If Leighton had been the one who had tipped Lords off, then he was probably aware of his daughter's choice of company. Leighton hadn't been present at the meeting where Landers spoke, but he was clearly sympathetic to the cause espoused by the prospective Member of Parliament. There was nothing in this for him, so he moved on to other matters.

'I'm going to see Bowles now and then Sutton. I asked Yates to go to London and interview the people Sutton claims to have been with.'

Burnett nodded then added, 'We have today and then that's it. Frankie will pull us off this case I guarantee you. You know that he applied yesterday for a court order to remove the gypsy camp. If they push that through, and after this,' said Burnett, indicating the newspaper, 'they will almost certainly find against them, then it'll be all hands, on deck, to have them removed. Frankie and Leighton will want to make them someone else's problem.'

Jellicoe left the room and walked past Wallace who was on his hands and knees at this point. He thought to say something but left it. Anything he said would have seemed like a provocation to the young man at that moment. The phone on Wallace's desk was ringing. Rather than disturb him, it felt only right that he helped by answering it. Jellicoe stopped and reached over to the phone.

'Hello, Jellicoe speaking.'

A voice at the other end of the line said, 'Sir, this PC 167, Bradfield. I met a woman last night who claims that her son saw the white car that you're after. He even has a number plate.'

'A number plate?' expostulated Jellicoe delightedly. It seemed too good to be true.

'Yes. He writes them down for some reason. Don't ask me. Anyway, have you a pen and paper. I'll give it to you now.'

Jellicoe scribbled down the number.

'He didn't really see the man. Said he had a moustache and dark hair. He was more interested in the car. A Jaguar, no less. A few years old if the number plate is any guide. The man had popped the bonnet up and was tinkering with something. Then he put it down again and drove off. He said the car still sounded a bit ropey so he wouldn't have been surprised if it conked out again.'

'Where and when was this?' asked Jellicoe.

'On the Frimhampton Road, sir, after four o'clock. He was heading out of town so it could have passed the murdered woman.'

'Very good, Bradfield. Thanks. What was the name of the boy?'

'Billy Miles.'

'We'll be sure to reward Billy if something comes of this.'

Jellicoe immediately picked up the phone and rang down to the desk. Unusually it was not Sergeant Crombie.

'Hello, can you radio to DI Yates to come back to the station. Tell him he must trace a white Jaguar 863UXU. This is the man that Chester Johnson may have seen on Sunday. Have you got that?'

Jellicoe popped his head into Burnett's office to update him on the news about the white Jaguar. It prompted a hint of a smile, but Burnett was never going to be upbeat for long. A long day lay ahead, the highlight of which would be possible run-ins with the male gypsies at the camp. He'd done it before and had the scars to show for it.

'Come back here when you've spoken with Bowles and Sutton. We're going to need you, trust me.'

This sounded ominous but, for the moment, the most important thing was understanding the source of the cash that the two Suttons were receiving. An idea had already formed in Jellicoe's mind about this. He needed time to think it through. On the way downstairs he saw Constable Wilkins.

'Do you fancy taking me to the Clifftops hotel?'

178

The Bus Stop

'If you insist. How long will we be, sir? I saw the superintendent last night. He thinks…'

Jellicoe put his hands up and rolled his eyes to indicate he knew all about the police action later. They passed through to the front of the station. Behind the desk was Ramsay.

'Where's Crumbs?' asked Wilkins on the way past.

'Didn't you hear? He and Clarkey went with Mrs Bickerstaff.'

Even Jellicoe stopped in his tracks. He turned to the young constable manning the desk.

'Really? Where on earth have they all gone?'

*

Sergeant 'Crumbs' Crombie watched Jellicoe enter the building at his usual early morning time. If you must get up very early in the cause of catching criminals then Detective Inspector Jellicoe would catch many over his long career, thought Crombie. Then he turned to Ada Bickerstaff, to whom he'd only been half listening, She, too, was an early riser. Alas, her record in catching criminals was unlikely to be so impressive. Yet today, for the first time in the recorded history of the town, Ada Bickerstaff was to play a key role in the uncovering of one crime and assisting on another.

Crombie's attention, which should have been on the words of wisdom pouring from the mouth of the elderly crime stopper, was taken by the newspaper in her shopping bag.

'Is that the morning newspaper?' asked Crombie, interrupting the narrative flow from Mrs Bickerstaff.

Temporarily stunned by the interruption, Mrs Bickerstaff replied, 'Yes.' She took the newspaper out to show Crombie. The sergeant wasn't an avid reader of the weekly newspaper. He rarely looked at it, partly because he did not like the owner Cecil Lords who was a bit too high and mighty for his liking. Yet was rare that the paper would go to print twice in a week. Crombie thought it worthwhile seeing why.

He read the headline not once but twice and then the editorial immediately underneath. His hackles began to rise. How dare that man criticise an undermanned police force. Whether or not it was undermanned was a moot point that Crombie was too agitated to consider just then.

Jack Murray

The angry silence from Mrs Bickerstaff allowed a door to open in Crombie's mind and a shaft of light entered the darkness. The editorial was talking about the stolen dogs. Of course, Crombie had heard about this, but he had never imagined that it was quite such a widescale problem nor worthy of such profile. Right at that moment the sheer enormity of what was happening hit home. Because one other thought had now struck him. A thought so powerful and yet frightening in its implications that he could barely breathe as it swirled around inside his head.

Mrs Bickerstaff might know where the dogs were being held.

Constable Ramsay, moving behind Crombie, found a hand on his forearm.

'Hey, lad. Do you mind holding the fort for a while? Do you know where Clarkey is?'

'Having a cup of tea. You know what he's like.'

'I do. Go get him then take over. Me and Mrs Bickerstaff here are going to crack a case together.

Mrs Bickerstaff had now overcome her initial dismay at being interrupted. Her eyes took on the look of the hunter. This was her dream, and she was going to enjoy every last minute of it. Ramsay returned a couple of minutes later with the large figure of Clarke in tow. Ramsay had clearly tipped him off that not only was Crombie venturing out into the field, but it would be in partnership with the legendary Ada Bickerstaff.

'You all right, Crumbs mate?' asked Clarke, nodding in the direction of Mrs Bickerstaff.

'Never better, Clarkey. Fancy taking me and my partner here to where she tells us?'

Clarke helped Crombie off the stool and soon the sergeant, with the help of his crutch, was hobbling with his two partners in law enforcement towards the exit.

'Hope you're right, Crumbs. Frankie wants a few of us to head up to the gypsy camp later. He thinks they're holding the dogs.'

'Let's find out,' said Mrs Bickerstaff, leading the way to the police car. Clarke looked at Crombie again and hoped his old friend hadn't lost his marbles.

After helping his two passengers into the back, Clarke flumped down on the driver's seat and asked the big question at the forefront of both his and Crombie's mind.

The Bus Stop

'I can hear the dogs howling from my back garden on Masefield Close. If my guess is right, Constable Clarke, they must be somewhere in Fenton Woods. They sound a fair few miles away.

The car set off at a stately pace. Clarke was in no rush to get back. The prospect of turning over the gypsy camp was a grim one. Never one to walk away from a fight, neither was he the man to pick one. There was no question in his mind, trouble was coming if Frankie got his court order.

They headed out of town on the Frimhampton Road, passing the bus stop near where the Sutton woman was murdered. As they sped along the road, two young men riding a motorcycle and a side car passed them from the other direction. They saluted the police car in a fashion unlikely to find favour with senior officers, but Clarke grinned all the same. They continued for another five minutes arriving at a small road that led into the wood.

'Shall we try here?' asked Clarke.

'Makes sense,' suggested Crombie, looking hopefully at Mrs Bickerstaff. She nodded back, her features set, and that setting was Kit Carson.

The road was barely the width of one car. It wound deep into the wood. Soon they were enveloped in gloom as light found it difficult to penetrate the heavy canopy of leafless branches. The road came to an end near an abandoned hut.

'What shall we do now?' asked Clarke, turning to his old friend.

'Wind the window down, perhaps we'll hear them,' suggested Chief Inspector Bickerstaff of the Yard. It seemed like a good idea. Three windows were wound down and they sat there, in the dark, deep in the forest listening to the sound of their own breathing.

For a minute the only sound they heard was wind rustling through the trees, perhaps a bird. Then silence. Even Mrs Bickerstaff began to feel the chill of doubt. Not that she for one second did not believe there was a pack of dogs somewhere in the forest. This was now an article of faith. The problem was whether they were in the right place. She was about to say as much when she heard it.

A dog was barking.

Jack Murray

Dogs are chatty animals, given a chance. No dog is happy to hear another hog the limelight. Another bark and then another started a chain reaction. Soon the sound of barking was echoing around the wood. The look of triumph on Ada Bickerstaff's face was complete.

'Let's go,' she ordered. The two World War II veterans obeyed.

Clarke and the lady of the moment helped Crombie out of the car. The three of them began to move in the direction of where the barking was coming from. After a couple of minutes Crombie uttered the immortal line, 'I'm only holding you up. You go on without me.'

Just as Clarke was about to dismiss this idea out of hand, Mrs Bickerstaff said, 'He's right. Let's get weaving before the barking stops. It's getting louder. We're on the right track.'

Clarke shrugged at Crombie who, it must be said, was grinning like a madman. Over a decade on the force and he was about to crack wide open his first case. There was a skip in his step which was no mean achievement given he was missing one leg. But if Crombie was like an excited puppy, then Ada Bickerstaff was a bloodhound. The seventy-two-year-old was virtually racing across the terrain as the sound of the barking grew louder.

The wood was thick with trees, so their journey was rather akin to a skier in a slalom. Visibility was poor given the lack of light and the fact that ten yards ahead was the next tree. But the sound of barking echoing around the forest was all too plain.

Finally, after clearing a particularly dense part of the wood they came into an open space and were met with a sight that had all three of them staring open-mouthed.

The Bus Stop

26

Ginger Rogers was the first to see the police car travelling along the road. He was riding, as ever, in the side car. Cramped, cold and cantankerous barely covered his physical and mental state at that moment. The sight of the police car perked him up. He tapped Eddie on the forearm and pointed to the police coming in the other direction. The two men waved using just two of their fingers. The old cop in the front seat actually laughed at them which somewhat undermined the feeling of elation from their moment of joyous rebellion.

'I hate it when they do that,' said Eddie.

'I know. I think I've seen him around before,' replied Ginger, shouting over the noise of the engine.

'Me too. Big lad.'

'That's the one. Say what's going on with the engine?'

The motorbike's engine was making sounds that neither God nor mechanics ever intended. Both were used to the tubercular rasp of the engine and its smoker's cough. At this moment it was straining like a constipated elephant. Then it gave one loud belch and stopped dead in its tracks. Smoke billowed from the engine accompanied by a strange popping sound. It was the latter that grabbed the attention of both boys.

'I'm no expert in bikes,' said Ginger and never were truer words spoken, 'but that doesn't sound good.'

Eddie was off the bike in a moment kneeling towards where smoke was coming from. A few moments of investigation and then Eddie looked up.

'There's a leak. No water. Engine's overheating.'

Despite Ginger's earlier assessment of his ignorance on the topic of bikes he pointed out in words unlikely to mollify the owner of the machine that even he could see this.

'Worst comes to worst we can leave it here and take a bus back to town to get something to fix it,' said Eddie when he'd finished punching his friend for his comments. Despite giving his friend a few stone and several inches, he was very much the dominant partner in the relationship. 'It's not like anyone will want to steal it.'

'If it's just water, perhaps we can just go to the canal and get some.'

Eddie looked at his friend with something approaching affection. They'd known one another a lifetime and he'd long accepted his friend had not been especially blessed up top. No, even Ginger would have been the first to agree that acumen and intellectual aptitude were not his forte; if he'd known what any of those words meant, that is. He was happy to let Eddie, for the most part, deal with planning. Eddie gave his friend an affectionate slap across the back of the head.

'What was that for?' asked Ginger stung less by the blow and more by the implied criticism that was surely heading his way.

'How do you suggest we carry it?' asked Eddie, not unreasonably.

Ginger looked around him and realised there were no convenient buckets or jerricans either on the bike or on the road. In fact, the only things he could see were the bus stop and a phone box. His mind was spinning through possibilities though. One as bad as the other. They couldn't phone the AA. They couldn't use their helmets to carry water. They couldn't use their hands. It was all a bit useless, and he was increasingly aware that Eddie was grinning triumphantly. Then it hit him.

'There's barges on the canal. We can borrow a bottle or two from them.'

The grin was wiped immediately from Eddie's face. The rug had just been metaphorically pulled from underneath his feet. This was a first for Ginger. Never before had his pal so completely blind-sided him with an idea that he had not thought of first, Yet, his initial feeling of annoyance, was replaced by something else.

Pride.

Genuine pride in his friend. He clapped Ginger on the back.

'Ginger, mate. You're a genius. I'd never have thought of that,' said Eddie and meant it.

184

The Bus Stop

Ginger beamed with pleasure. It was one thing to have a good idea but what was the use of that if no one else knew? Especially a mate. He shrugged modestly, like it was all in a day's work. Nothing to see here, just a brilliant idea. Regular as buses they are.

'What are we waiting for?' said Eddie. 'Let's go and see if someone can lend us a bucket or bottle or something.'

They walked across the road, past the telephone box and the bus stop towards the wood. Eddie drew Ginger's attention to the barriers that had been put up around the area where they'd read about the murder. Out of curiosity they went over to where the woman had been found. Nothing remained to indicate that a murder had taken place beyond what the police had erected. The lack of blood and other gruesome remains reduced their interest in what was there, and they proceeded into the wood.

One look overhead told them that they had to move quickly. Rain was threatening. The last thing they needed was to get caught in a rainstorm. Their feet crunched over the twigs and branches as they moved through the wood. Ahead, peeking out through the trees they could see an old barge. It wasn't until they broke through to the other side that they saw just how old it was.

'How does it stay afloat?' laughed Ginger.

'Bloody hell,' agreed Eddie. 'You're not wrong there, mate.'

They looked along the front of the barge. It seemed as if no one was around. Ginger walked over to a pair of open side doors. He popped his head in and saw that it was a store for chopped wood and coal for the engine while Eddie was surveying the junk on top of the barge. His face erupted into a huge grin.

'Hey, Ginge, I think we've hit the mother lode. Look at this.'

Ginger stepped back from the coal store and walked towards Eddie. He stepped up onto the side to look. There, arrayed in lines of three were around a dozen bottles, each containing masted ships.

'I'm sure they won't miss a bottle or two. A couple of those to fill up the water and a couple in reserve. Stupid bloody hobby anyway.'

'We can always bring them back,' pointed out Ginger before regretting his suggestion when Eddie shot him a look of utter derision. 'Just sayin', like. How would you like it?'

185

'Do I have to point out to you that we've spent a week nicking dogs from their owners?'

'We haven't harmed them though and we'll give 'em back. He said we'd give 'em back.'

Eddie, though, had stopped listening. He lifted a couple of bottles and nodded at Ginger to do the same. Just then they heard a noise behind them. The two boys turned around. Standing there was an old woman and a tall, distinctly strange looking man. Neither of them looked very happy at what they were seeing. More pertinently, she was holding onto a very large and freakishly furry German Shepherd.

Upon accepting the engagement from the old man to begin their crime wave, both Ginger and Eddie had insisted that certain types of dogs were outside the brief. In particular, they identified Rottweilers, Alsatians and, frankly, any large dogs as *canis non grata*. The old man had used these words and laughed at their perspicacity. Neither of the boys understood a word of this but they suspected that he agreed with them on this point. Small dogs were to be the order of the day.

The dog was muzzled which was a relief. Of more immediate concern was that both the woman and the man were holding small axes by their sides. The woman looked in a mood to use it.

'What do you think you're doing?' snarled the old woman.

Eddie's eyes had already widened at what he saw. The woman's evident anger set his heart racing. He tried smiling. If anything, this made matters worse because, if he was not mistaken, the man, who was at least six three and around two hundred pounds and looked more than a little agitated.

'I'm sorry, missus,' said Eddie. 'We was just looking at your collection. I was just sayin' Ginge, how do they do that?'

'You were, Eddie. That's right,' said Ginger who was every bit as rattled as his friend.

'No, you weren't,' shouted the man in a shrill voice that nearly caused Eddie to have an accident. 'You were going to steal them.'

He burst into tears at this point.

This was so unexpected that for a moment, Eddie, Ginger, and the old woman were at a loss as to what to say next. The dog was not so uncertain. It began to strain at its leash. Had it not been for the muzzle it would have been baring its teeth in a

186

The Bus Stop

manner likely to unsettle the bravest of men. Neither Ginger nor Eddie fitted into this category. They were, by now, terrified.

'We're very sorry,' said Ginger, the first to recover his senses after the outburst of emotion.

This was always going to be doomed to failure, but the reaction was still unexpected. The old woman ripped off the muzzle on the dog. Now that it was free, the animal began to snarl and strain at the leash. With only the axe-baring old woman to hold the animal back from tearing them limb from limb, Ginger was the first to move.

His choice of escape route was unfortunate and proved to be the source of much recrimination for the next few hours between the two friends. He immediately jumped into the coal store. Without thinking, rather like Ginger in fact, Eddie followed suit. He jumped into the coal store too, landed painfully on his ankle. This was as nothing in compared to the realisation that they could not have chosen a stupider place to hide.

'What the hell did you come in here for?' asked Eddie between gritted teeth. The pain was blinding.

Ginger closed one of the doors over and was in the process of closing the second when he saw the look on the face of the old woman. It was somewhere between triumph and astonishment. She was managing, just, to keep the killer dog under control. Ginger closed the second door which meant they were now temporarily safe from the beast but trapped. This was something that Eddie lost no time to point out.

'You bloody idiot, Ginge. What do we do now?'

The answer was taken out of their hands when they heard a heavy bolt sliding across the two doors effectively confirming their incarceration. The full horror of his choice was now laid bare to Ginger, although Eddie added a few more Anglo-Saxon words to emphasise the level of stupidity displayed by his friend. Ginger's temperature gauge was rising, and this meant violence was not far away. In the first instance it manifested itself on him banging the door and demanding to be let out.

The dog began to bark again which acted as a salutary reminder of what awaited them if his wish was granted. They were truly stuck between a rock, in this case coal, and a hard place.

'She'll see sense soon and let us out,' said Eddie in a more soothing tone. After all, they had only intended borrowing the bottles to add water to the overheating bike. She'd come over and chat in an adult manner and good sense would carry the day. That was Eddie's view.

And he was wrong.

*

Detective Constable Wallace was neck deep in piles of paper scattered across five desks in the detectives' office when he saw a grim-faced Burnett exit his office. Burnett took one look at Wallace and seemed on the point of saying something when he changed his mind. Instead, he shook his head and continued outside. He was met in the corridor by Superintendent Frankie. There was a look of anger in the superintendent's eyes.

'I've heard word from the judge's office, it looks like they're going to approve us going in and clearing the gypsies out.'

Burnett was surprised by this reaction.

'So, I heard. You don't look too pleased by it.'

Frankie looked appalled. He shook his head angrily and pointed to the interview room. Inside Chester Johnson had shrunken into his seat and DS Fogg was pacing the room like an expectant father.

'Why should I be? Complete waste of time. We're only doing it because of that prat Lords and Erskine bloody Landers. He snaps his fingers and everyone around here jumps to attention.'

There was a certain amount of truth in this. The only surprise was hearing it come from Frankie. Unless Burnett missed his guess, he reckoned a few words had been exchanged between Frankie and the chief constable. While this was hardly a first, it certainly made a pleasant change to see Frankie on the right side of the argument.

'Don't get me wrong, no one would be happier than me to see that lot go. But we have absolutely no proof they're responsible for all these dog thefts.'

'I agree. How's it going with Johnson?'

'No change. He says it wasn't him. He only found her. Fogg's been shouting at him for the last half hour. I've spent the last half hour wanting to shout at Fogg to shut up.'

The Bus Stop

'Where's Price?' asked Burnett. He felt a little awkward asking as, technically, Price was his man.

'I sent him to get the written confirmation from the Judge Patterson. Then he must get a written order from Laurence. I am damned if a single uniformed or non-uniformed man is going in there without explicit and written instructions that they do so. By the way, I popped my head in there a few minutes ago. Why has Wallace turned the office into a dumping ground? In fact, for that matter, where are all the others? They can't all be after the damn dogs.'

Burnett hesitated a moment. To admit that they were still investigating the case would likely cause an explosion from Frankie. Not to do so would probably make things worse.

'We're following up on three leads related to the murder. Sarah Sutton and her husband have been receiving large amounts of money into their bank account over the last two years or so. All cash. Jellicoe's on this. We've had an identification of the white car that Johnson claims to have seen that night. Might be nothing but Yates is on that. Wallace is checking who Sarah Sutton was speaking to at the phone box that night. Those are the phone records for all the phone boxes in the area. They took their sweet time coming, and they sent everything.'

Surprisingly Frankie said nothing. His face was grim but then it usually was. He nodded before replying, 'Very well. Keep me posted on all three. I don't like any of this. Large amounts of money you say?'

The two men looked inside at the American. His head was in his hands, and he was weeping. Burnett felt his chest tighten. It was an instinctive reaction when he knew something was not right.

'Yes, sir. Very large.'

27

'Looks like you've cracked the case, Ada,' said Sergeant Crombie. There was a grin on his genial face that could probably be seen from the moon.

The group was standing in the middle of a slight clearing in the forest. Before them was a semi derelict house with makeshift wooden barriers covering the windows, the door and the side of the cottage which appeared to be missing. Peeking out between the spaces in the barriers were at least a dozen dogs or more. All barking with abandon at having human company.

'We'd have cracked it sooner,' pointed out the pensioner, 'if you'd listened to what I told you instead of ignoring me as usual.'

Crombie raised his eyebrows and glanced at Clarke. The big constable gave him a 'that's-told-you' look by way of support. This was undermined by the fact he was suppressing a grin. 'Crumbs' Crombie knew that this moment would become a favourite story of Clarkey's for years to come. The day Ada Bickerstaff solved the case of the deadly dognappers. Although, by the sound of the barks, the dogs seemed in remarkably good spirits. This was confirmed a few minutes later when they went inside and saw that there was plenty of food and water scattered about in bowls around the cottage interior. Whoever had taken them had certainly not meant to harm them.

The dogs were delighted to have company. The wagging of tails was almost enough to create a gale of goodwill from the captive canines. Their exuberance was becoming overwhelming with a few jumping up on Ada Bickerstaff. Now there was no one in the town who had greater love for her four-legged friends than Ada, but decorum had all but been abandoned. The little woman put her finger up and yelled, 'Sit!'

The Bus Stop

All at once half a dozen dogs went quiet and sat down. A few of the others continued barking and running around. Ada blamed their owners.

'Some people need training more than their pets,' was Ada's only comment.

'They know who is boss when you're around,' said Clarke with a smirk.

Ada Bickerstaff knew she was being lampooned and gave Clarke a sour look. This was enough to make Crombie stifle a chuckle. He got the look from the little woman too. This had the effect of transferring Crombie's smile over to Clarke.

They couldn't stay together. As much as it was a pity to leave them, they had no choice. Clarke looked around the dogs that were there. He counted eleven. This matched the number of dogs reported missing. One of them was a Yorkshire Terrier. He bent down and picked it up. A quick glance at the tag around her neck established this was Felicity.

'We'll bring this one back and radio the station,' said Clarke.

'Is that Landers' dog?' asked Crombie. He received a nod of confirmation from his old friend who was now on the receiving end of grateful licks and stern advice from Ada Bickerstaff that it was not very hygienic. With great care they left the cottage, one by one and replaced the barrier. The parting from the dogs was, of course, a cause of mayhem for the poor animals who sorely missed company. The level of noise went up several notches as the howls of grief grew louder.

The three aging detectives picked their way slowly back to the car. It wasn't easy for Crombie with his leg and the cold was beginning to bite. He was looking forward to being back at the police station. Only one thing left to do, he decided. They reached the car. Crombie used his eyes to indicate to Clarke what should happen next. He gave Ada Bickerstaff her instruction. She sat down beside Clarke at the front.

'Press that button,' said Clarke. Felicity gave a yelp of encouragement in the background.

'Hello, this is Special Constable Ada Bickerstaff calling. Are you receiving?'

There was some static and then a disembodied voice replied, 'Mrs Bickerstaff. Is that you?'

191

'Didn't I just say it was me?' She looked at Clarke to indicate what kind of idiot are they employing in the police. 'I'm with Constable Clarke and Sergeant Crombie right now in Fenton Wood. We've found the kidnapped dogs. Repeat, we've found the kidnapped dogs. Are you receiving?'

Felicity, not wanting to miss out on the announcement began to yelp her heart out. There was silence for a moment and then some static.'

'Receiving Special Constable Bickerstaff. Good work. Over.'

Clarke took the radio from a very proud pensioner and with great gentleness pretended not to notice the tears that were in her eyes.

'Clarke here,' said the big constable. He then proceeded to give instructions as to where they could find the dogs. A few minutes later, Burnett's voice could be heard.

'Chief Inspector Burnett here. May I speak to the special constable?'

Ada Bickerstaff wiped eyes from her eyes and took hold of the microphone. She pressed the button.

'Bickerstaff here, sir.'

She'd heard something similar on Dixon of Dock Green.

'Why don't you come back here for a cup of tea. It sounds like you've earned it,' said Burnett.

'Yes, sir,' said Special Constable Bickerstaff.

*

DS Yates sat in the back of the police car as Constable Patrick Hayward drove. They sped along Frimhampton They passed an abandoned motorcycle and side car parked off road. He thought about stopping but decided that the murder was of more importance than the dog thefts. He made a mental note of the number plate and kept driving.

'Radio in Hayward and tell the station about that motorcycle we passed a moment ago. It resembles the motorcycle used in the reported thefts of the dogs. Let them know where to find it.'

It was as he reached the small town of Frimhampton that he heard the good news that the dog case had been resolved. His job now was to find Matthew Timpson.

Timpson had been identified as the owner of the vehicle with the registration provided by Jellicoe. The address was residential just on the outskirts of the town. Ten minutes later, Yates drew up outside a bungalow in a cul-de-sac. The houses were not especially large, but they were all well maintained except one. Timpson's house was noticeably the only one without a well-tended garden. There was an absence of flowers and shrubbery which was in marked contrast to the care with which the street's other residents tended to their gardens.

Yates stepped out of the car and walked along a gravel path to the door. A swift look through the window and the absence of any car suggested the house was empty. A minute of fruitless knocking confirmed this. There were signs of life in the other houses, so Yates went next door.

He rang the doorbell, and it was opened a few minutes later by a man that had to be ex-army. He stood tall and erect even though he was probably well under six feet. His moustache was as clipped as his speech.

'Yes?' snapped the man giving Yates the once over and apparently not liking what he saw.

'Sorry to disturb you, sir,' said Yates. 'I am Detective Sergeant Yates. I was looking for Mr Timpson, but he appears not to be in. I don't suppose you can tell me where he works.'

'Timpson's Garage,' said the man curtly. 'Take the first left out of here, continue to the crossroads and you will see him on the right. Anything else?'

'Am I right in thinking he drives a white Jaguar.'

'Yes. That's him.'

Yates thanked the neighbour and returned to the car. He gave Hayward the directions and the car set off again. A few minutes later, it pulled up outside the mechanic's workshop. Parked outside was a white Jaguar with the numberplate identified by young Billy Miles.

*

Matthew Timpson was tall with a trim moustache, trim hair, and a trim figure. He was good looking; he knew it, and this gave him an air of confidence that he used to successful effect with the opposite sex. He had never married and saw no reason to, at least for the time being when his occupation brought him into close, often intimate contact, with enough members of the opposite sex to keep a man happy.

He looked at the man in front of him. The man was as wealthy as he was chinless. How else could you explain the new Bentley and the spectacular blonde lady sitting in the passenger seat.

'Brand new,' said the man. 'Just running her in.'

'I'll bet you are,' replied Timpson to the man before winking towards the girl, unseen by her beau. She turned away in disgust. Win some, lose some, thought Timpson. It was a numbers game in the end. You got to be in it to win it.

'I'm not happy about the sound of the engine though. Can I book her in, and you'll take a look?'

'She looks a beauty from here. You've done well for yourself. I'd love to take a look under the bonnet.'

Timpson glanced one more time at the girl in the passenger seat. He'd spoken loud enough once more for her to hear what he said and understand what he meant. Her face was set in stone. No go there, that was for sure. Timpson decided to focus on the customer instead. He went into his workshop and took out a large diary. He was recording the name of the man when he saw Yates step out of the police car and walk towards him. This hastened him towards moving the man back to his car. He walked with him and shook hands.

'I'll see you next Tuesday if that's all right. I'm sure she'll be fine until then.'

'Thanks awfully,' said the man climbing into the car.

Timpson took a deep breath and turned to face Yates who was standing waiting patiently for the customer to leave. The man Timpson saw was sporting a beige raincoat and a trilby. Short of twirling a truncheon he could not have done more to look like a pig, thought Timpson.

'Mr Timpson?' asked Yates.

'Yes, that's me. How can I help?'

'My name is Detective Sergeant Yates,' said the detective showing him a warrant card. 'I'd like to ask a few questions if I may.'

A nod from Timpson confirmed that this was not a problem.

'Can I ask where you were on Sunday between midday and six pm?'

'I went to see a lady friend who lives near the beach, if you must know.'

The Bus Stop

'May I have her name and address?' asked Yates taking out his notebook and pencil.

This seemed to make Timpson agitated. He took a cigarette packet from a nearby stool and fished out a cigarette. He didn't offer one to Yates. He lit the cigarette.

'What is all this? Have I done something wrong?'

Yates fixed his eyes on Timpson for a moment and said nothing. Then he indicated the notebook.

'Look officer. I want to know why you're asking me. The lady is married. I don't want to involve her in a police matter especially as I've done nothing wrong.'

Yates nodded towards the white Jaguar and replied, 'Your car was seen on the Frimhampton Road on Sunday afternoon. Doubtless you'll have read about the murder. We just want to eliminate you from the inquiry.'

Timpson snorted at this.

'What's all that got to me with me? Haven't you some 'spade' locked up anyway? The bus driver or something like that?'

'We have someone in custody but there are some doubts about whether he was responsible or not.'

'He was responsible all right.'

'Why do you say that?' asked Yates, frowning. 'Did you witness something?'

'I wasn't there. No, I mean, look at him. What you can you expect from these people?'

Timpson tried to laugh this off, but Yates's face was immobile.

'So, can you give me the name of the lady then?'

'Look here, I wasn't anywhere near the damn murder, and I didn't see the lady in the end. My car broke down and by the time I'd fixed it I was dirty and not in the mood. I went home.'

'Did you spend any time with anyone between those hours?'

'No,' came the surly reply.

'Do you know Mrs Sarah Sutton?'

'What? Look this is ridiculous. I'm not having someone come in here and accuse me of murder.'

'You are more than welcome to have a lawyer present,' said Yates sharply. He sensed Timpson was hiding something. 'Did you know Mrs Sutton?'

'Why should I know her? That's quite enough. Any more questions will have to be with my lawyer. You can't do this.'

'I can, Mr Timpson. Rest assured I can. If need be, I will be back, and you can contact your lawyer then. Good day.'

With that, Yates put his notebook away and turned away from the fuming mechanic. Timpson watched as Yates returned to the car. The policeman climbed into the back and said a few words to the uniformed driver. The two men glanced back at him. Timpson threw his cigarette down to the ground with great force, spun around and marched back to the workshop. He heard the police car starting.

'Damn and blast,' he shouted. He was breathing heavily now, and his heart was racing. Unsure of what to do, he went over to his phone and dialled a number. He waited for ten seconds and was on the point of hanging up when someone answered finally.

'Hello, Derek. It's Matthew. We have a problem. The police have just been to see me. It's about Sarah. They saw my car on the road that day.' He waited a moment then said, 'Yes, get back to your sister's house for a day or two 'til things calm down. Come back for the funeral.'

Timpson put the phone down, turned around and immediately froze. Standing there looking at him was Yates and the other policeman.

'Mr Timpson,' said Yates. 'We both know you were speaking to Derek Sutton just now. I think you need to accompany us to the police station and explain why.'

The Bus Stop

28

'I can assure you Inspector Jellicoe,' said Bowles, 'I haven't given my daughter a penny since the day she was married, and I certainly would not have given that man anything either.'

Jellicoe was sitting with Mr Bowles in a small library located at the Clifftops Hotel. Both had declined the offer of tea from a waitress. Each sensed the meeting was not destined to be a long one. Bowles looked out the window, visibly angry. Then he turned back to Jellicoe.

'Am I to assume your visit indicates there is a doubt about Chester Johnson's guilt?''

Under normal circumstances, Jellicoe tended to avoid answering questions. It was his job to do that. Yet a part of him accepted that Bowles was owed at least some explanation.

'There remain some things that need to be explained. They do not necessarily point to Johnson being innocent but there is more to your daughter's death. We are just trying to find out the truth.'

'I should hope so,' said Bowles through teeth that were rigid with suppressed anger.

'Have you any idea who or why money was being paid into the accounts of both your daughter and Derek Sutton? Money that was entirely separate from your son-in-law's work.'

'I think you should ask him don't you think?' retorted Bowles. 'I have no idea.'

Jellicoe nodded at this. He believed Bowles did not know. For the first time he sensed something else in the austere man before him. He'd always thought of Bowles as being a relic of Victorian rectitude. He combined primness of manner with no little self-righteous indignation at a world going to hell in a handcart. Derek Sutton was merely the harbinger of the triumph of the irrational. Soon his like would be usurped by the something arguably worse, the ascension of a liberal elite; Brahmins who would lead the country down a path of multiculturalism where permissive values would slowly erode the moral fabric of the country. He realised Bowles was looking at him, a half-smile on his lips. It was as if he was reading his mind. A mind that was not so very far away from the man facing him.

'You are looking at me strangely, Inspector. I wonder what you are thinking. That I seem cold and uncaring about my daughter? Nothing could be further from the truth. I cared. But in this day and age, it seems caring must be public; demonstrative if you will. It can be manifest only on what you give freely: money, love, attention. I come from a world that believes caring for someone can also exist in what you deny them. Does that seem strange to you?'

Jellicoe shook his head. He understood this. His own family upbringing had combined the overwhelming, overpowering love of an Irish mother and a distant, remote father. In the end it was his father he took after because what his father was, and how his father was, and what he stood for became, for Jellicoe, a map of the territory he had to navigate when growing up. He watched Bowles light his third cigarette.

'In some respects, I could almost have admired Sutton,' said Bowles before taking a long, satisfying drag on his cigarette. He blew a large plume of smoke towards the window overlooking the sea.

'Had he not married my daughter, that is. He was born to be led. And his instincts, while base, and untutored, were essentially correct. He fought for his country, too. If he had just stayed away from my daughter, I could have liked him. For a while I tried to reconcile myself with the thought that he, at least, was not a man educated beyond his capacity to think critically. At least he could be a hard worker. By dint of his own enterprise, he could rise above his humble inheritance. I was wrong. Those hopes were quickly shattered. He lacked vigour. Like so many of his ilk, he wanted things handed to him.'

'There was nothing else to him. Just a man with enough native guile to use his good looks to entrap a fairly wealthy and certainly bright young woman at a point in her life when she wanted to break free. Another year and she may have laughed at the idea of the two of them. By then it was too late. I don't know why she

The Bus Stop

stayed with him, Inspector. I don't know if that black man is the one who killed her or not, but it would not have happened had she been with another man.'

Jellicoe wondered if that last comment was meant for Bowles himself. What role had he played in making his daughter turn away from him? There seemed nothing else to gain from staying. He had found out what he needed to, so he left Bowles alone with his cigarettes and his guilt.

Derek Sutton and his wife had been ill matched by dint of class and, if Bowles were to be believed, intellect. Yet she had stayed with Sutton. People did that, though, didn't they? He had stayed with Sylvia not because she was beautiful or clever, she was certainly both, but because life with her promised to be easier. He had no qualms about living off the wealth of Sylvia's family, as Derek Sutton had wanted to live off Bowles. Jellicoe was no unconscious hypocrite in this regard. He'd married if not for love, then for lust. Yet this became a means to an end. It would allow him to focus on what he wanted to achieve without fear of penury. To ask his father for a penny would have been as unthinkable then as it was now. In this he was like Sarah Sutton. This was his act of rebellion, he supposed. Most rebellions fail.

*

'Where to, sir?' asked Wilkins as Jellicoe stepped into the police car.

Jellicoe glanced up at the fuming sky overhead then gave him Derek Sutton's address. He ducked into the car. If Sutton was not receiving money from Bowles, and Jellicoe at no point believed this ever to be the case, then a suspicion was growing in his mind about the source of this wealth. The question was how it could be connected to the brutal murder of Sutton's wife? As they were travelling, Wilkins updated Jellicoe on the latest developments related to the gypsy camp.

'Just been on the radio, sir. It sounds as if they intend pressing ahead, sir, with the ejection of the gypsies.'

'Why?' exclaimed Jellicoe, shaking his head in frustration. 'Haven't they found the dogs? Do they have any proof it was even them that did this?'

If he was feeling this level of exasperation, then what must Burnett have been feeling at that moment? Even Frankie. Surely common sense would prevail, and they would hold off from doing more until they could find the proof required to justify the eviction. As they entered the estate where Sutton lived, the radio crackled to life. It was Yates's car,

'Message for Detective Inspector Jellicoe, are you receiving?'

Wilkins picked up the microphone and spoke.

'This is the inspector's car, receiving.'

The voice of Yates could now be heard on the radio.

'Yates speaking. I am bringing Matthew Timpson in for questioning now. He knows Derek Sutton and Sarah. Over.'

Wilkins handed the microphone over to Jellicoe who leaned forward in his seat.

'Good work, Tony. We're turning into the street where Sutton lives.'

'Hurry, sir. We caught Timpson phoning a warning to Sutton. He might make a break for it.'

'Understood. Over.'

The police car turned onto the long street banked by the relentless beige-ness of the prefab houses either side. At the far end of the street, Jellicoe spotted a figure carrying an overnight bag. It was Sutton. He was wearing a navy pea coat and woollen hat pulled over his head. It's difficult to be anonymous on an empty street.

'Quickly,' ordered Jellicoe, spotting the overnight bag.

Wilkins pressed his foot down on the accelerator and by the time Sutton had registered the car, they were alongside him. He stared at Jellicoe. Then he looked down at the bag. For a moment Jellicoe thought he was going to make a run for it but, instead, he put the bag down and waited for Jellicoe to climb out of the car.

'Going somewhere?' asked Jellicoe.

Sutton stared at Jellicoe and then at the bag. It was pretty obvious that was his intention. The question was where and, more pertinently, why?

'I was going to spend the night in London with my sister and then come back down with her for the funeral.'

'She can verify this?'

'I hadn't arranged anything. I can just turn up when I want.'

The Bus Stop

'Can you come with me, please? We have some more questions we need to ask. I might add we have a friend of yours. Matthew Timpson is joining us.'

Sutton's eyes widened and he seemed on the point of saying something but at the last moment wisely chose to stay silent. Jellicoe indicated the open door. Sutton looked at the police car and then back to Jellicoe.

'Can I leave my bag back in the house?'

Jellicoe smiled and said, 'No. I think you should just come along with us.'

Sutton's face changed colour from a deep red to a pale grey. It was such a dramatic shift that it made Jellicoe wonder what was in the bag. He suspected the answer was all too obvious. They would need permission to search the bag. He doubted it would take long to obtain.

The police car set off and a silence fell between the two men in the back. Sutton set the holdall on his knees and gripped it tightly. He stared out the window; his breathing, laboured. Jellicoe kept his eye on the direction of Sutton's gaze. He was staring at the door as if contemplating the idea of absconding. Good luck with that one, thought Jellicoe. He sat back in the seat and relaxed.

They arrived at the station without any incident. Jellicoe ordered Wilkins to drive around to the back as there were still a few pressmen at the front. By now, Sutton was clinging to the bag like it was loose timber from a shipwreck.

Wilkins held the passenger door open for Sutton and stayed close to him as they entered via the fire exit. Jellicoe walked behind them. They walked up the stairs as if they were taking the final few steps onto the summit of Everest so slow was Sutton's movement.

They arrived on the second floor. The corridor was empty but there was a muffled noise coming from the interview room where Chester Johnson had taken up virtually full-time residence. Wilkins led Sutton into an interview room next door to where Johnson was being questioned. Jellicoe left them and stuck his head through the door of the detectives' office. There was no sign of either Burnett or Wallace, and the room was in a state of disorder the like of which he hadn't seen since his arrival a couple of months previously.

'Where the hell is Wallace?' asked Jellicoe to no one in particular. He shook his head and turned his attention to the interview room where DI Price and DS Fogg were standing over Johnson. Behind them was Superintendent Frankie. The American's head was in his arms, and he was sobbing. Frankie caught sight of Jellicoe and went to the door. He opened it and joined Jellicoe in the corridor.

'Where is everyone, sir?'

'Well, if you can credit it, that mess has taken a turn for the worse. We received word earlier that a gang of men have gone up from the town to remove the gypsies themselves. That bloody newspaper article has them up in arms. Burnett has taken a bunch of the uniforms there to stop a riot.'

'I'm not sure I would have fancied tangling with them. Do we still have to move them?'

'No. Thankfully Laurence saw sense and didn't sign the order. He wasn't happy about it mind. It's a stay of execution rather than cancellation. Of course, once we heard about the vigilantes, that was it. We had to go up there anyway. We've called for help to Frimhampton. Their two men and a dog will no doubt be on their pushbikes now. What an absolute mess.'

Jellicoe couldn't have agreed more. He wasn't sure how his news would be received given Frankie's certainty that Johnson was the murderer of Sarah Sutton.

'We found Sutton trying to abscond to London. He has a bag that I think is stuffed with money. We need a warrant urgently to search it. Yates has connected Sutton to Timpson, the man with the white car that Johnson claims to have seen. It looks like he's telling the truth about that.'

Frankie nodded dully. The morning dealing with the forced expulsion as well as the desolate American appeared to have sapped the life from the superintendent. He glanced back at the men in the interview room before turning to Jellicoe.

'I'll see what I can do about the search warrant. Tell Wilkins to stay with Sutton. He's not to let him out of his sight. Let him stew there for a while; we need you in here,' said Frankie, indicating the interview room holding Johnson.

'Why? What's happened sir?' asked Jellicoe.

'Go in there and see for yourself.'

The Bus Stop

Jellicoe stared at the superintendent for a moment and then went inside the room. He shut the door behind him loudly, but Chester Johnson did not look up. He was too busy sobbing, repeating the same thing repeatedly. Price and Fogg turned to Jellicoe. Price shrugged. Jellicoe leaned in closer to confirm that Johnson was saying what he thought he was saying.

'I killed her. I killed her. Lord help me, I killed her.'

29

'I killed her,' repeated the American. His hands were balled into fists.

Jellicoe sat down on the seat vacated by the two detectives. Price nodded to Jellicoe and motioned to Fogg. They left the interview room. Jellicoe watched them leave and decided for the twentieth time that month that Price was a good man. How it must feel to have a man like Fogg as a colleague, though?

'Chester, it's Nick Jellicoe.'

Johnson said nothing to Jellicoe; his head remained cradled in his arms. His body jerked as each hopeless sob wracked his body.

'Chester, we need to know. Are you saying you killed Sarah Sutton?' Chester, please. Who are you saying you killed?'

Finally, Johnson raised his head. His eyes were red, his nose was leaking like a burst pipe in the ceiling. Jellicoe handed him his handkerchief. The two men studied one another, and silence settled in the room. Johnson was visibly calmer now. After a period of quiet, Jellicoe spoke again. His tone was gentle and non-accusatory.

'Who are you saying you killed Chester? Not Sarah Sutton?'

Normally Jellicoe did not lead questions in this way, but he still did not believe that Johnson was the killer.

The American shook his head. Tears began fall once more but then he shook his head. He said, 'No. I didn't her. I didn't kill Mrs Sutton, sir.'

'Who are you talking about Chester?' asked Jellicoe quietly. 'We need to know.'

Johnson's two large hands covered his face; fingers buried in eyes as if he was trying to shield himself from a memory that refused to die. It took a few moments for Johnson to collect himself. Then he began to speak in a leaden tone of capitulation.

*

The Bus Stop

Her screams grew louder.

She wouldn't stop. His eyes widened. Sweat beaded his forehead. His old foes, heat, and fear. He wasn't sure how he would be able to stand it. He'd survived hell already, or so he thought. In fact, the landings were only the beginning.

The noise outside the house was deafening. It never ended. It never would end. This would be what it was like. If not every day, nevertheless, it would be a constant threat hanging over him and then it would be reality. The gunfire; the explosions; the killing. What would one more death be?

He looked down at the girl, but his eyes were blinded by sweat and tears. He could no longer take the terrified screams, the begging. Everything was drowned out by the sound of his heart beating and his conscience yelling at him. Outside he heard the door banging. They were shouting.

He put the gun to her chest and fired. Her body went still immediately. The banging outside stopped but the explosions were growing louder. He stared down at the dead French woman. Her injuries were horrific. What fear and agony had she experienced in those last moments before she had begged him to kill her? All around the room were the dead bodies of her family. An old woman and an old man. A young man. Her brother? Husband? Lover?

Hatred rose with the bile in his stomach. Hatred for the war. Hatred for the Nazis that had brought him to this hell hole. Hatred for the Allies who had decimated this French town. And most of all, hatred for himself and the woman whose life she had begged him to take; to release her from the fearful pain caused by the bomb. Tears stung his eyes, for himself, for the guilt he would feel because of this single act of mercy. Another explosion rocked the building. The Germans had their range now. He had to leave. He looked at the young soldier staring at him. He, too, was crying.

'It wasn't your fault, Ches,' he said. 'It wasn't your fault.'

Johnson nodded just as another explosion sent clouds of dust falling on them from overhead.

'We have to go, Ches,' said the soldier gently. Johnson looked at him as if seeing him for the first time. He was a boy. Just like him. A white boy caught up in the middle of a nightmare. Johnson nodded. He felt the boy grab his arm and lead him to the door. He couldn't stop himself looking back at her. It would be a sight that he knew would haunt his dreams for the rest of his life.

He owed her that.

*

Jellicoe listened in silence as the story spilled out from between the sobs of the American who had, once more, buried his head in his arms. It was a story that he'd never heard before, a story that was as horrifying as it was all too plausible. He steeled himself to be objective in the face of such misery. The truth of war laid bare and the long-lasting reaction to it from those who had fought. He put his hand on Johnson's arm and glanced back towards the window. Frankie's face was set in stone. It usually was but there was something else there too. Perhaps it was a recognition that this man was not their killer. Or perhaps it was sympathy. Either way, Jellicoe was now more convinced than ever that this was not their man. He rose from his seat and went to the door. There was little to be gained by staying now. Frankie waved him outside.

'What was all that?'

'It sounds like he performed a mercy killing when he was in France. A woman was horrifically injured by one of our shells in a French town. Her family was dead all around her. He's clearly been traumatised by this. I can't say I blame him.'

Frankie exhaled as a picture of what it might have been like passed through his mind.

'Should we believe him?'

Jellicoe looked at Johnson. He was still now; elbow on table and head in hands. There was little point in answering the question. The former soldier was staring blankly at the wall. And then his body convulsed once more. He buried his face in his hands.

Broken.

A fire flashed in Frankie's eyes, 'Then is it Sutton or this other man? We need answers. I wish to hell I'd stayed in bed this morning.'

He wasn't the only one, but Jellicoe felt they were closer now. If Frankie was prepared to accept that Johnson was not their man, then it freed resource and thinking towards catching the real killer. Just then, Jellicoe could not see past the two men being held in the two other interview rooms.

Jellicoe thought about asking Frankie where Wallace was but decided against it. Perhaps he'd gone to the gypsy camp. It seemed as likely an explanation as any. Leaving Frankie, he returned to the detectives' office.

Price and Fogg were there having a cup of tea with a digestive biscuit. It had been that sort of a morning. Jellicoe updated them on Johnson's story. Price looked relieved. He, too, had not believed Johnson guilty of anything other than being in the wrong place at the wrong time with the wrong colour skin. Fogg shrugged. If it wasn't Johnson, it was someone else. He'd be told who to look for next. Fogg treated detective work like a factory production line. The innocent and the guilty looked the same to him. Someone else did the sorting after he had tested both to the very limit of their endurance.

Next Jellicoe explained about the two new suspects. Once more, Fogg said nothing. Price nodded and said, 'Good work.'

'Have you seen Wallace by the way?' asked Jellicoe. 'Has he gone to the camp?'

Neither detective had any idea where Wallace was as they'd been interviewing Johnson. Jellicoe picked up the phone and called the desk sergeant. Ramsay was still manning the front desk.

'Jellicoe here. Where has Wallace gone?'

Ramsay consulted a book before replying.

'He's taken a car, sir. In fact, he radioed an hour ago. he's gone out to see a Mrs Regis. He said you or DS Yates would know where.'

'Did he say why?'

'No, sir.'

'Was there a constable with him?'

'No, sir. They'd all gone up to the camp, sir. There's another riot brewing sir.'

Jellicoe smiled grimly at Ramsay's comment. There'd been a few jokes in the squad room about how his arrival at the station had prompted a riot.

'Wallace said he would radio in again when he arrived, sir.'

'He would've arrived there three quarters of an hour ago. What the hell is he doing?'

Jellicoe was angry now. It was perfectly clear to him what Wallace was doing. He slammed the phone down and swore, causing both Price and Fogg to look up surprised.

Fogg was sitting on one of the tables covered with printouts from the post office. Jellicoe strode over to it and began to look for some clue as to why Wallace had left. And why he'd been allowed to go. What had Burnett been thinking? There was nothing on the table where Fogg sat. He turned just as Price held up a printout with some writing on it.

'Are you looking for this?'

He handed it over. Jellicoe stared at it for a moment and then his eyes widened. He glanced at Price and then at Fogg.

'Ivor, I'm going to need some help. Sutton and Timpson are sitting in the two interview rooms now. Can you take over the questioning of Sutton? Yates can question Timpson. You just need to coordinate how you get them to talk about Sarah Sutton. How do they know one another? Because they do.'

'Is one of them the killer?'

'I don't know yet if they were involved in her death. I'm fairly certain they and Sarah Sutton were running drugs. I think that Derek Sutton smuggles them in every couple of weeks on the Prometheus. I suspect this is bigger than either Sutton or Timpson, too. This needs careful handling. I've asked Frankie for a warrant to search Sutton's bag, too. Pound to a penny he's carrying a lot of cash in it. Look, Ivor, I don't have time now. Can you square this all with Frankie? And I'll need back up.'

'Of course, happy to help,' said the Welshman. 'What do you need?'

'Can I borrow DS Fogg?' asked Jellicoe glancing at the big detective sergeant.

Fogg glanced at Price and received a nod. He stood up to his full six-foot three height and said, 'Where are we going, sir?'

There was a smile on his face that suggested he was looking forward to deploying his unquestioned natural gifts towards actual or implied violence.'

'I'll tell you on the way,' replied Jellicoe, heading towards the office door, clutching the printout that Wallace had left for him.

The Bus Stop

30

Although it was received wisdom that DS Tony Yates was nakedly and unashamedly
ambitious, few would have suspected that in this respect he had very little on DC Wallace. The young constable was more astute at hiding his burning desire. Few would have guessed that he had set himself a goal of being a detective inspector by the age of twenty-eight and a chief inspector by the time he was thirty. Such a lofty ambitions were never going to be achieved acting as a chauffeur for the other detectives. Perhaps a clue to the young man's desire to rise rapidly through the ranks was already manifest in the manner with which he handled a car. It provided a highly visible clue to his desire go places. Quickly.

Caution is the voice of experience acting as a brake on youth's headlong flight towards impetuosity. Its voice is often quiet, but the message should be listened to and acted upon. It is the misfortune of youth that it rarely does so.

When Wallace realised that there was no back up immediately available to him, it mattered not a bit. The solution was simple. He would act alone. But he was not completely immune to the risk he was taking. He would radio in his whereabouts. His intention was to monitor the situation rather than indulge in any acts of daring. Experience would have told him what Von Moltke had once observed: *No plan survives contact with the enemy.*

Nearing the bus stop where Sarah Sutton's murder had occurred, he noticed a motorcycle with sidecar abandoned at the side of the road. He pulled over to take a closer look. Some smoke spiralled lazily upward from the engine. Wallace touched the engine. It was very hot. He guessed the rider had gone to find some water. The canal was nearby. He circled around the bike. Rather like the houseboat, it was astonishing to Wallace that it could still function. Rust was eating away at every part. This had to be the bike mentioned in the alert posted about the dog thefts. The number plate was barely legible, but he was able to make a note of it.

Wallace returned to the car and set off again along the Frimhampton Road towards the turn off he'd taken with Jellicoe. A voice inside his head finally began to make itself heard. As he drew closer to the canal the louder it became.

Don't engage. This is surveillance only. Wait for back up.

He was clear in this. Crystal clear. He was alone and the situation was potentially a dangerous one. He turned into the narrow road through the wood. His heart was beginning to beat faster. The canal was now visible. He parked the car out of sight of the houseboat. His throat was dry. A cold sweat broke out down his spine. He needed to go outside and check if the houseboat was still there. For a second, he thought to radio in. He picked up the microphone but then stopped himself. What would be the point? If the barge had left its mooring, he'd only look a fool. A windy fool. This wasn't part of the plan.

His heart was racing now. He climbed out of the car and shut the door quietly. A quick scan of the surrounding wood told him he was alone. This made him feel calmer. One last check and then he set off towards the houseboat. He moved from tree to tree like he did when he was a kid. The tightness in his breath and the rapid beat of his heart wasn't fear.

It was excitement.

The chase was on, and he was the hunter. He thought once more about what he was up against. An old woman and an odd son. If Woodcock the German Shepherd was around, he'd surely hear him barking. All thought of the muzzle had been forgotten.

Further forward he crept. Like Hawkeye. Like Randolph Scott. The wood was quiet save for the sound of the twigs being crunched under his feet. Something caught his eye. He spun to his left in time to see a grey squirrel scuttling up a tree. He grinned to himself. The smile of a man that had just had the wits scared clean out of him over nothing.

He took a deep breath and pushed forward again. The spring-scented air tasted good. Crunch went the twigs beneath his feet. He cursed inwardly but he was now within sight of the houseboat.

It was still there.

The Bus Stop

And then he heard it.

Screams.

Hysterical shouting was coming from the direction of the boat. All his training at that moment told him to get back to the car and call for back up. Instead, he pitched forward. Running. No longer in cover he ran forward, tripping over a tree trunk veiled by dead leaves. He picked himself up and careered forward towards the houseboat.

The screams and the banging were louder now. But he couldn't make out what they were saying. It didn't matter though. They were in trouble. Something had to be done.

He was aware of it before he saw it. A brown-black blur. Then a growl and within seconds it was on top of him. Biting, raking his hand with its sharp teeth. He rolled over trying to use his weight, but it was too quick and escaped before once more sinking its teeth into his hand.

He screamed in agony. It felt like his fingers were going to be bitten off. It was through to the bone. A voice. It was calling the dog's name.

And then all went black.

*

Ginger Rogers stopped shouting when he felt Eddie touch his arm. They were now taking it in turns to alert the world to their incarceration. As ever, it had been Eddie's idea and Ginger saw the wisdom of it immediately. For a moment, just a moment, mind you, it made him feel better. It felt as if they were regaining some sense of control in their situation. The good thing was Eddie was thinking.

This was his strong point.

Eddie's analysis of the situation was good. He said they were in a stand-off now. The mad woman and man couldn't keep the boys down here forever. They would need to get coal or wood at some point and then they would have them. Eddie said that if the beast attacked them, they would have access to weapons. He wasn't clear if he was referring to the dog or that strange boy-man. Anyway, he could take him. Just a big child. It was the dog they had to worry about.

'Can't see a bloody thing in here,' said Eddie, rooting around the coal and the wood for a weapon he could use in the upcoming battle. He knew a battle lay ahead and they would be ready. And they would win. He had no qualms about crowning the beast with a stick or a lump of coal. The axe-wielding maniacs were the least of their worries.

Outside they heard the beast snarling at something.

'Can you see anything? asked Eddie.

Ginger had his eyes up to the slit.

'Can't see a thing. Something's happening though.'

That much was obvious. Instinct made Eddie reach down and grab a couple of pieces of coal.

'Grab some coal, Ginge, we might need it.'

'No weapons?'

'Nothing in the wood. Just chunks of firewood. I'll root around the coal later but honest to God, without any light, I've no idea what I'm doing.'

'I need the loo,' said Ginger.

Eddie gave Ginger some fairly pithy advice on his desire that he not unburden himself within the confines of the tiny coal store. It was cramped enough as it was, and the air was full of coal particles. The last thing they needed was for Ginger to add to their olfactory misery.

In fact, the passion of Ginger's shouting had been given an extra something by his own private misery. He couldn't hold on much longer. He was, by now, bursting with something more than indignation or anger.

The sound of the barking grew louder. They were approaching the coal store. Ginger stood back and felt two lumps of coal being handed to him by Eddie. Another good idea. Eddie was certainly the man to have with you in a crisis. And make no mistake. This was a crisis.

Moments later the beast was immediately outside the coal store. The bolt was pulled back and immediately light flooded into the store blinding the two boys. Woodcock was barking and snarling with venomous anger at the world. Ginger hurled his two lumps of coal, but he had no idea what he was aiming at. It didn't sound like they'd connected with anything other than mid-air. Eddie held fire because he couldn't see what he was aiming at. His intention was to use the coal for clubbing purposes anyway.

The Bus Stop

Seconds later something heavy landed on top of Ginger sending him sprawling backwards. The doors immediately swung shut again before either boy could take any action on the escape front.

'What the…?' said a bemused Ginger. He'd been bashed in the front and smacked his head off the side of the barge and hurt his back when he landed heavily on the wood blocks.

'What is it?' asked Eddie crawling forward to his friend.

'It's a body. A man,' said Ginger. 'I think he's dead.'

Eddie felt around the man. He was wearing an overcoat. He touched the man's head and began to search for a pulse like he'd seen in the movies. He couldn't feel anything.

'He's dead all right. No pulse,' said Eddie. Immediately he became aware that his hand was wet. 'What the hell is this? Was it raining outside?'

This didn't feel like rainwater though. It was thick and sticky.

'I'll check his pockets. Maybe he has matches,' said Ginger.

Eddie was about to critique the idea of using matches in a coal store when another horrible thought struck him. He withdrew his arms from the man quickly and began to wipe his hand on his clothes.

'Bloody hell that's blood. They've chopped his head.'

'Found something,' announced Ginger a few seconds later.

'A lighter?'

'No, a wallet.'

There was no more talking. The only sounds that could be heard in the storeroom were the sound of frightened breathing and Ginger conducting a search of the unknown man.

'Found something. It's a lighter,' said Ginger.

Much against his better judgement, Eddie said nothing and waited while Ginger tried to light it. Moments later a small flame appeared. Ginger held it down to the man. His head was a mess. Blood matted his hair; his mackintosh and face had been badly mauled or bitten by the beast from hell.

'He's a goner,' noted Eddie calmly but he was far from calm. In fact, he had never been so scared in all his life.

'He's a copper,' said Ginger, looking at the warrant card inside the wallet.

213

Fear gripped the two boys. The US Cavalry had come, and it had been roundly beaten by the two maniacs and their hateful pet. They needed better weapons than a lump of coal, that was for sure.

'Hold the light over in this direction. We need weapons.'

Everything went dark as Eddie crawled over to large pile of coal. A few seconds later, light returned. Eddie began to haul the coal out of the way to see if there was anything that could be used. For a minute he worked his way through the coal. Ginger, wisely, left him to do it in the dark. No point in using up all the lighter fuel. Then he heard Eddie give a cry.

'Have you found something?'

'Yes, it's a hard stick. There's something stuck to it. Like a rag. There's also something we can hit them with. It's got holes. Yuk. Don't know what it's been in. Slimy stuff on it. Get the light, Ginge. Let's see what we've got, mate.'

Ginger was already snapping the lid open and shut. It took a few goes but soon a flame leapt up from the silver lighter. It lasted barely a second or two as Ginger dropped it, screaming like Fay Wray tied to two poles. It wasn't the sight of the black-faced friend that so scared him, though.

Eddie was holding a skull with bits of dark, rotting tissue in one hand and a human bone in the other.

The Bus Stop

31

Clarke, Crombie, and Ada Bickerstaff sat in the police car listening to the crackle and the hiss and the snatches of conversation drifting over the airwaves like smoke at a bonfire. And bonfire it was if the news coming from the camp was anything to go by.

For half an hour they had been waiting for a van to come and start removing the captive canines but the news they were hearing suggested a long wait lay ahead. Another thought crossed the mind of the two policemen simultaneously. Clarke and Crombie looked at one another. A decision would have to be made soon. Do they abandon the dogs, bring Mrs Bickerstaff home, and join their colleagues on the front line?

'What do you think, Clarkey? It sounds like they might need help.'

'We should ask them,' agreed Clarke. The one good piece of news, if there was any to be extracted from the brewing riot, was that the original order to evict the gypsies from their camp, had been rescinded. This, at least, was a blessed relief that even a man as obviously courageous as Constable Leonard Clarke felt keenly.

The men from the Travellers' camps were fighting men. They learned to scrap, it seemed to him, long before they could walk. It was a rite of passage in their culture. A modern-day Sparta. He hadn't fancied tangling with them. In fact, it made the decision of the vigilantes even more baffling in Clarke's eyes. What sort of idiots would willingly, with eyes wide open, go forth and pick a fight with the hardest race in England? The job of the police was more likely to be protecting the torch-carrying, pitchfork bearing far right supporters than the people they were looking to prey upon.

'Go on then, Clarkey, call in,' said Crombie.

Jack Murray

Ada Bickerstaff looked on fascinated. She'd been following the radio traffic avidly.

'Are we going in?' she asked Crombie as Clarke picked up the microphone.

'You'll be going home, young lady,' said Crombie with a stern face that was undermined by a grin moments later.

*

Chief Inspector Burnett was perched on the bonnet of a police car parked in front of a field on the outskirts of town. He gazed at the unfolding scene with a bemusement that his friend Clarkey would have understood all too well. He, too, found it difficult to fathom why anyone would want to pick a fight with the gypsies. It wasn't until that morning, when he'd read the newspaper, and seen for the first-time references to a group called Patriotic Action that he began to understand who might be so ill-advised. Then he remembered the banners at the town hall. They'd meant nothing to him the other night. But now it was becoming clearer. And he didn't like it. Not one bit.

There were photographs in the paper taken in the hills overlooking the town. A dozen men wearing balaclavas brandishing Union Jack flags like they were weapons of hate. They stood behind a long banner that read: NO MORE WHITE GUILT. Behind them another man was holding his own, homemade banner that simply said: BLACK'S GO HOME.

The only aspect of the photograph that appealed to Burnett was the fact that it had clearly been raining when they had assembled on top of the hill. This, at least, made Burnett smile. He imagined them sitting in their cars waiting for the rain to relent, then a mad dash out to the hill. Quick take the bloody photograph. Back to the car. A pint at the Bricklayer's. Yes, he could see it all. And he thought them pathetic. Pathetic but dangerous; if not to the public, then to themselves, if the men streaming from the caravans brandishing Hurley sticks were anything to go by.

Around half a dozen cars belonging to the vigilantes had arrived. They had parked them in a neighbouring field. In all there were no more than fifteen men. Hardly an army. This made Burnett smile a bit more. Maybe he should just leave them to their fate. And that fate would be hospitalisation. Perhaps they could

216

The Bus Stop

take a few of the gypsies with them. Burnett was no more charmed by the men of the gypsy camp than he was by the vigilantes. Sadly, his head would roll if he were to stand by, and watch a riot take place.

There were around a dozen men from the police in attendance. They formed a cordon across the road. The men who had arrived in the cars unfurled a large banner. It read: GYPOS OUT. Underneath it was the name of the group: Patriotic Action.

They began to chant at the men from the camp who were standing shoulder to shoulder in a parallel line to the police. Far from being dangerous, there was a growing absurdity to the situation. Burnett took out his pipe and struck a match of the bonnet of the police car. Then he spotted a tall, older man from the camp approach the younger men who were forming a barrier. This was who Burnett had been waiting for.

Burnett walked towards the line in front of the traveller camp. His eyes never left the older man. It felt like a scene from one of his favourite films, *Vera Cruz*. He would have been the first to admit that he was no Gary Cooper, but the leader of the gypsies was no Burt Lancaster either.

Burnett walked all the way up to the man until he was barely two feet away. The man fixed his eyes on Burnett's. Then he nodded towards the police and the men they were standing in front of. His accent was Irish.

'So, I'm confused. Are you here to throw us out or them?'

Burnett turned in the direction of the other men and puffed on his pipe a bit more.

'Honestly, if it was me, I'd happily let you kick the crap right out of them.'

The older man broke into a grin. The tension between the two men relaxed immediately. Burnett turned again as the soldiers of Patriotic Action demonstrated a penchant for inaction in the face of the dozen, armed men from the Traveller camp.

'I'm not sure they have the stomach for it after all,' said the Irishman.

'No. Perhaps they were hoping for a few more folk to back them up.'

The Irishman glanced up at the sky before replying, 'Not a great day for it. What happens now?'

217

Burnett's pipe had gone out. He looked rooted around his pockets for a match. Moments later the Irishman held a lit match up to him. Burnett nodded and re-lit his pipe.

'Thanks,' said Burnett before continuing, 'I think I'll go over there and try and persuade these gentlemen to leave. To be honest, I wish you lot would bugger off n'all. No offence, like.'

The Irishman's mouth was set but there was humour in his eyes. He held his hands up, replying, 'None taken.' Then he added as an afterthought. 'We didn't take those dogs.'

Burnett studied him closely then said, 'We've found 'em anyway. They're all in the wood.'

The Irishman's face registered nothing at this. He shrugged and nodded towards the Patriotic Action men, 'Get rid of them. But if they step anywhere near the camp, we'll put them in hospital.'

Burnett looked from the gypsy men to the men from Patriotic Action. There were bound to be a few hard cases in that group too. It wouldn't be quite as one-sided as all that, but Burnett thought better of pointing this out. His only desire at that moment was to ensure the safety of his own men. He turned away and started to walk towards the police cordon.

He brushed his way through the line of policemen and surveyed the group of men in front of him. They would give the gypsies a fight all right. Furthermore, he suspected they were carrying more than just banners. They seemed relatively young judging by the lack of lines around the eyes and mouths that he could see behind the assorted masks and balaclavas. In fact, some were probably teenagers who had already spent time in Borstal. There were not enough of them to challenge the camp, but it could inflict damage on the people stuck in the middle.

Burnett picked out a man standing just front of the group. Burnett walked slowly towards him. This time he put the pipe away as he approached the man. He was wearing a black balaclava, like the others. They regarded one another for a few moments then Burnett said, 'We both know you're not going to attack them lot. Time to go.'

There were a few pig noises coming from some of the other young men, but Burnett kept his eyes fixed on the one in front of him. There was a pre-natural calm about the young man that was

The Bus Stop

unsettling. Burnett did not scare easily but something about the person he was facing made him feel uneasy. His eyes did not blink once. They were clear blue and, unless Burnett missed his guess, he seemed to be enjoying the situation. Finally, he responded. He was quietly spoken and clearly educated.

'We are within our rights. No law against us assembling and expressing an opinion.'

'There is a law against you carrying concealed weapons, son. Don't push it. Understand?'

'Are you going to search us?' replied the young man. The tone was mocking. He was amused. But there was also a trace of curiosity in his voice. How would the policeman react? 'Perhaps you could get your friends in the camp to help you.'

Had Burnett not been so alarmed at the sense of danger emanating from the young man, he would probably have laughed. He always had a soft spot for cheek, even from the people he was going to arrest.

'Or I could take my men out of the way and let you all get on with it. I don't like them any more than I like you, son. I don't doubt you'd do some damage but my money's on them.'

The young man wasn't looking quite so amused now.

'You wouldn't dare.'

'Wouldn't I?' said Burnett before laughing mirthlessly. Burnett turned away and walked back towards the thin blue line of policemen. He gestured towards the police cars. 'All right men. Back to the cars. We're finished here.'

As he said this, Burnett spun around and raised his eyebrows in a told-you-so manner. The young man looked on with growing disbelief as the policemen turned and walked towards the police cars. Clearly visible now was the line of men from the camp. Each one was brandishing a Hurley stick. Burnett looked from them to the men from Patriotic Action. It was difficult to say if they were happy or unhappy about the turn of events. There was no sign that they were going to give way either. This was confirmed moments later by the young man.

'Very funny, pig. But we're going nowhere.'

Just for a moment, Burnett was worried he'd miscalculated. But it was just a fleeting thought. He was now standing alone between the two groups of men. It was utterly silent. Each side waiting for the other to make the first move. For the first time he felt a cold breeze lick his face. Or was it the chill of fear. Neither side was moving or likely to move.

So, that honour went to Chief Inspector Reginald Burnett.

With a quick prayer to the Almighty he walked forward again towards the young men of Patriotic Action. He stood roughly ten paces from them. His heart, it must be said, was racing a little. One thought was in his mind. If this didn't work, he would be in the middle of one hellish battle scene and would likely have his arse kicked both here as well as, metaphorically, up and down the corridors of the station. And not just by Leighton or Frankie either. His only consolation would be that he would deliver the same and worse to DI Nick Jellicoe from whom he had stolen the idea.

He smiled at the men of Patriotic Action and then put his arm out wide. Then he began to motion them to stand closer together. His next action became the stuff of legend back at the nick. He took out Winnie Leighton's expensive Leica camera and pointed it at the balaclava-clad men.

'Say cheese.'

Silence.

Then one by one the men from Patriotic Action began to laugh mockingly. The young man shouted over them, 'Not much bloody use that, copper.' He pointed to his balaclava and made a leering grin at Burnett.

Burnett was remarkably unworried by the abuse being hurled his direction and the hand gestures. He merely shuffled a little over to his right. And then a little more.

'Group together, I'm not getting you all in.'

The men from Patriotic Action laughed louder and began to chant, fingers pointing in the air, 'Gypos out. Gypos out.'

Twenty yards in front of them a few of the men from the camp shuffled uneasily. They were itching to send the men facing them on their way. To hospital. The older man held an arm out. Curious to see what Burnett had in mind. And then it struck him what the chief inspector was doing. A grin spread from over his face.

'Well, I'll be.'

The Bus Stop

The police, looking on, were utterly baffled by the actions of the chief. He looked like an absolute fool just then. Sergeant Timmins gripped his truncheon tightly and was on the point of stepping in when he, too, saw what was happening.

Burnett was edging around the side of the Patriot Action men. They stood back to let him pass. A few were making playing to the camera by making obscene gestures and movements. Burnett kept snapping away and then he swung dramatically away from the men and pointed the camera towards their cars.

It took a few seconds for the men to realise what he was doing. By then, Burnett had photographed the number plates of three of their cars and had turned to walk back to his fellow policemen. He waved at the camera as he walked away.

'We'll be seeing you boys soon, trust me.'

Burnett walked towards the men from the camp. He stopped near the older man who was chuckling away at what he'd seen.

'Tell your men to go back to the camp. We'll handle this.'

The older man shrugged and turned to his men. A few of them appeared unhappy at missing out on the ruckus but the older man held say.'

'Come on, boys. There'll be another day.'

Burnett suspected he was right. It just wouldn't be today. He stayed on the spot and watched the men from the camp turn reluctantly away. This was going to be the tricky part. Patriotic Action would view this as a victory of sorts. In fact, a few began to jeer at this point. When Burnett spun around to face them, he could see that their leader was not one of them. He turned away and walked towards the cars parked behind them. A couple of men followed him and then, one by one, the others.

Burnett watched them go and then re-joined the uniformed men by the cars. Sergeant Timmins approached him with a relieved smile on his face.

'Well done, sir. I thought for a minute we might have to knock a few heads together.'

Burnett waved away the compliment and ignored the obvious point that the men in blue might have had a few heads knocked in too.

'Let's get back to the station. I need a cuppa.'

'Sorry sir, we've just had a radio call from DI Jellicoe. He says that DC Wallace has gone to see a suspect for the Sutton murder without backup. Requesting support. Sergeant Crombie and Constable Clarke picked up the message. They're on their way there, sir.'

Burnett looked askance at Timmins.

'Where?'

The Bus Stop

32

The reassuring voice of Sergeant Crombie crackled on the radio in Jellicoe's car. Jellicoe picked up the microphone.

'Don't worry about the camp. How close are you to the point of the canal near the bus stop where the Sutton murder occurred?' asked Jellicoe.

Crombie responded immediately, 'We passed it a minute ago on the way to the camp. Shall we turn back.'

'Yes, Sergeant. Wait for us. We're a couple of minutes away.'

'Yes, sir.'

Jellicoe heard Crombie's voice in the background then that of a woman and a dog yelping. This confused him for a moment and then he remembered something about Ada Bickerstaff. It was far from ideal that she was still with them, but Jellicoe had a feeling that time was against them. Something in the fact that Wallace had not called back in as promised worried him greatly. The young man was impetuous, well, he was young. But he was no fool either. Something had stopped him from calling for back up.

He looked at Fogg. The big sergeant was handling the car well. Bursts of acceleration where it was permissible ensured they would reach their destination soon. The boy racer in Wallace would have been impressed by Fogg's control of the car. As they were nearing the wood, Crombie's voice came over the radio.

'Located Wallace's car. No sign of him. Investigating further.'

A few minutes later, the bus stop and telephone box came into view. They had a choice now: continue or stop and make their way on foot. It was the sight of the rusting motorcycle that swung it for Jellicoe.

'Stop by the bike, sergeant. This is close enough.'

Fogg pulled over by the bike and the two policemen quickly exited the car.

'Where to?' asked Fogg.

Jellicoe pointed past the bus stop and towards the trees.

'On the other side of the trees. The canal. That's where the houseboat is.'

As they left the car neither heard the radio message from Crombie.

'Calling all cars. Request urgent assistance at Fenton Woods on canal opposite murder scene. Officer down. Repeat officer down. Over.'

A car sped past them and then they jogged across the road towards the wood. Up ahead they could hear barking. This had to be Woodcock. Something appeared to have upset him. This was not an unusual occurrence; the dog had a hair trigger temper even when it was in a rare, good mood.

They reached the wood in time to hear shouting now. The two policemen glanced at one another briefly then increased their pace. There was little point in waiting for the backup. Something was happening by the houseboat.

Jellicoe was breathing harder now. His heart was pumping rapidly, a combination of sprinting and dodging trees while wearing a mackintosh and a suit. His hat had fallen off somewhere near the bus stop. Fogg had fallen behind Jellicoe. His height made him less nimble at swerving and he had one hand on his head to hold onto his hat for reasons that surpassed Jellicoe's understanding.

As they neared the other side of the wood the barking became more frenzied and then, suddenly, it stopped. The reason for this was possibly the most amazing thing Jellicoe had seen in his relatively short career as a detective.

*

'You heard the man, Clarkey,' said Ada Bickerstaff. This caused both Clarke and Crombie to turn around to the old woman in the back of the car. She sat looking at both as if this was the most natural thing in the world.

Clarke was already executing a three-point turn. He thought about putting the siren on then thought better of it. The approach required was stealth rather than the 7th Cavalry. Not that it had done *them* much good. Felicity the Yorkshire Terrier yelped encouragement at Clarke to get a move on.

The Bus Stop

For what seemed like the tenth time that day they passed the motorcycle and then the bus stop murder scene. Clarke shot Crombie a quick look. He received a shake of the head. They would drive around and try reach it from the other side. Crombie would stay in the car and keep the reinforcements, should they be needed, informed via the car radio.

A few minutes later they passed Wallace's car, parked in the deepest part of the wood. Clarke pulled over and stepped out of the car. Mrs Bickerstaff was on the point of joining him when Crombie held a hand up. For once discretion won over the impetuosity of old age. Ada stayed put and waited with eyes fixed on the big constable who was walking around the car. Then Clarke made a quick patrol of the immediate area. There was no sign of Wallace. He returned to the car.

He opened the door just as Crombie was telling Jellicoe and whoever else was listening that there was no sign of Wallace at the car.

'Let's go forward. Slowly. We don't want to scare the horses,' warned Crombie. Felicity began to bark again but quietened when Ada lifted her finger and looked sternly at the little dog.

The car moved forward slowly. Clarke kept his foot off the accelerator and allowed the slight hill to provide momentum to the car. Soon they reached the bridge and crossed over to the other side. They were still out of sight of the houseboat as it was around the next bend in the canal. They drove forward another fifty yards before pulling in.

'You stay here with Sergeant Crombie,' said Clarke, turning around to Ada Bickerstaff.

'That doesn't make much sense, does it, Clarkey?' replied the geriatric gumshoe. Clarke was undecided which to be more amazed about: her desire to join him in the surveillance or being referred to by his nickname.

'Mrs Bickerstaff...' started Crombie.

She held her finger up which silenced the sergeant in much the same manner it did the dogs.

'Sergeant, wouldn't it make sense that I go with Constable Clarke some of the way. If something happens, I can return across the lock and tell you. Then you can let the others know on the radio.'

This did indeed make sense which made the situation all the more surreal from the perspective of the two uniformed men. The point was unarguable as far as Ada was concerned. Crombie's slow exhaling of breath told her that female logic had carried the day as it so often does.

Clarke and his elderly partner climbed out of the car and headed towards the lock. Crombie, meanwhile, levered himself into the driver's seat and wound the window down to get a better view of the stretch of canal ahead. Behind him, Clarke and Ada were negotiating the narrow lock across the canal, the latter refusing assistance from the former. Both made it across without falling ten feet into the water. They moved into the trees for cover and began to pick their way forward.

'Ada, I'm warning you. This could get a bit dangerous. When I tell you to stop, I mean it, all right, love?'

Ada made a harumphing noise that meant "if you say so" in any language. Clarke stared at her momentarily to seal the agreement through eye contact. Ada glared her submission on this point. They reached a point which allowed Ada a clear, unobstructed view of the houseboat, about eighty yards further up. Clarke pointed to a spot behind a large tree.

'I'll keep moving forward. You stay here. First sign of trouble, get back to Crumbs and tell him what's happening.'

Ada saluted Clarke who frowned, unable to decide if she was mocking him or just acting in the spirit of the occasion. Shaking his head, he began to creep forward moving slowly from tree to tree. Ahead he could see no sign of life on the houseboat. There was no sign of Wallace either. He stopped behind one tree and scanned around the forest.

Trees. Just trees.

A blue kingfisher fluttered down near the canal in front of Clarke. For a few moments the two of them looked at one another then Clarke shooed the bird away, fearful it would inadvertently reveal his presence. Then he turned around to check Ada was still there. He saw her peek out from behind a tree. She made the 'ok' sign. Clarke pushed forward.

Thirty yards from the houseboat he heard a dog begin to bark. It was coming from inside the barge. A woman told him to be quiet. But the dog kept barking.

The Bus Stop

It sounded like a big dog to Clarke. He looked around him and saw a large branch that had fallen from one of the trees. Picking it up, he snapped some of the smaller branches from it. It had sufficient heft to act as a club if he needed to defend himself.

The dog was going crazy by now. It knew someone was approaching the houseboat, guessed Clarke. Moments later a woman's head appeared. She wasn't quite the Wicked Witch of the West he'd been led to believe but she certainly looked one ha'penny shy of a shilling. She looked around her but could evidently see nothing.

The dog wasn't so blind though. Nor was it particularly friendly looking. Its eyes were fixed directly on the spot where Clarke was standing. It began to growl again and then the growls became a snarl and then it began barking frenziedly again. The Alsatian was now straining at the leash. Behind the old woman, a man appeared. He ducked under the hatch and joined the woman up top. The man was as tall as the woman was short. Clarke saw what DI Jellicoe had meant about him. If there had been any doubt about the woman, then there was none about the man. Everything from his strange hair to his awkward gangly frame, uncoordinated posture, and strange dress sense acted as a warning to Clarke.

If the sight of the strange inhabitants of the barge had not been enough, another sound distracted Clarke as he hid behind the tree. He could hear banging. It was coming from the direction of the boat. Then he heard yelling.

'What's wrong with Woodcock, mummy?' asked the man in a that curious whiney voice Clarke had heard a few days previously.

'I don't know. But I'm going to find out,' said the woman in a determined voice. The yelling grew in volume leaving Clarke utterly perplexed as to what was going on. He could hear a couple of voices. Was one of them Wallace?

He risked a look towards the barge. His greatest fear was confirmed. The woman was bending down. She unclipped the lead from Woodcock's collar. At this point Clarke heard the words he'd dreaded hearing the most.

'Go boy.'

Woodcock did not need to be asked twice. Freed from the lead he bared his teeth and began to bark again. Then he was off and running in the direction of the trees.

*

Further up the canal, Crombie could hear the wild barking but had no idea what was happening. Ada Bickerstaff was still behind the tree monitoring the scene. And then she wasn't.

To Crombie's utter horror, instead of coming back to tell him what was happening she started to move forward in the other direction. Towards Clarke. This was not part of the plan. A wave of anger rose in the mild-mannered Crombie. Thirty years of marriage had trained him well in the vicissitudes of the opposite sex but even he found their inability to follow basic instructions heartily frustrating sometimes. In fact, Ada Bickerstaff was no longer creeping forward. She was jogging and in the open too.

Crombie grabbed the radio.

'Calling all cars. Request urgent assistance at Fenton Woods on canal opposite murder scene. Officer down. Repeat officer down. Over.'

Replacing the radio, he reached into the back and grabbed his crutch. Pulling it over to the front seat he opened the door. He climbed out of the car with great care. He was used to doing it now after nearly fifteen years minus a limb, but it never got easier.

The noise of the barking further up the canal had piqued the interest of Felicity the Yorkshire Terrier in the back. One moment she had been on the point of dozing off in the back seat, the next she was awake and ready for games. The sight of the open door was all she needed. Before Crombie had his one and only leg outside, she bolted over the front car seat and out the front.

'Felicity,' yelled Crombie angrily. Another woman who wouldn't do as she was told…

*

Clarke heard the snarls and barking from the hairy beast grow louder. His heart was beating wildly now. Gripping the tree stump more tightly he set himself up to do his best to fend off the dog. He'd probably faced much worse in France in forty-four yet right then he could not remember being gripped by such cold fear.

Just as the animal was upon him it seemed to stop. Clarke was too surprised to feel relief. Before he had time to consider what

The Bus Stop

had stopped the animal, he heard another sound that sounded like yapping. It grew louder. It was yapping. He turned to his right and saw Felicity scampering along the other side of the canal. He peaked round the tree. Woodcock had seen the small dog also.

Clarke's eyes widened. Woodcock and the two people on the barge were transfixed by the little dog. It ran parallel to the barge and then stopped and looked across at everyone. Everyone looked back at Felicity. Then Felicity looked around for a way of getting to the other side. This prompted Clarke to raise his hand up in a 'stay' gesture.

The movement of the policeman was enough to remind Woodcock of what his original commission had been. His head snapped round. Clarke saw the teeth of the animal bared and felt his head spinning. It began to bark inching forward slowly, ready to pounce. Clarke drew back the thick branch baseball-style.

The dog snarled and crouched down. Clarke knew the attack was imminent. Across the canal, Felicity was yapping. Out of the corner of his eye Clarke saw the two inhabitants of the barge approach where he was standing.

They were holding axes.

*

The sight of Woodcock being unleashed was enough for Ada Bickerstaff to understand where her duty lay. Constable Clarke was in danger with an animal like this. And only she could help. For Ada Bickerstaff had spent a lifetime surrounded by dogs and was a leading member of the local Royal Society for the Protection of Animals. On this occasion the animal in need of protection was of the human variety but it mattered not to Ada.

She strode forward towards the charging German Shepherd, held one finger in the air and yelled, 'Sit.'

Woodcock slid to a halt and sat down a couple of yards away from Clarke.

Ada walked past Clarke and from the side of her mouth said, 'Put that club down.' Then she turned her attention to Woodcock and knelt by him saying, 'Who's a good boy?'

This was perhaps something of an exaggeration in the eyes of a very relieved Leonard Clarke but there was no doubting that the German Shepherd was a different animal in the presence of Ada Bickerstaff.

229

The banging on the doors of the barge continued. This was a reminder that there were captives nearby. Just at that moment Clarke saw DI Jellicoe and DI Fogg appear from the clearing. They were behind the two inhabitants of the boat. Fogg made his way immediately to the side of the barge to release the prisoners.

On the other side of the canal, Sergeant Crombie approached the Yorkshire Terrier. Alas, 'Here girl,' was never going to cut it with this pampered pooch. Felicity began to yap again causing Woodcock to prick up his ears. He growled but this stopped immediately when Ada raised her finger once more.

'Leave my dog alone,' screamed Mrs Regis, who had regained her voice after the shock of the last few moments. She ran forward towards Ada Bickerstaff clutching the small axe. Her son was rooted to the spot. His eyes were wide. There were too many people around him. He felt dizzy with fear and anger.

Clarke stared at the approaching woman. Ada Bickerstaff was oblivious to what was happening. Her attention was focused solely on the dog. Clarke looked from the woman to the wooden club he had dropped at Ada's insistence.

Jellicoe was moving before he had time to think. Mrs Regis was a few feet away from Ada Bickerstaff when she felt the axe ripped from her hand. Jellicoe lobbed the axe into the wood. There was a wild look in her eyes, anger mixed with hatred and then her face crumpled with desolation. She collapsed to the ground sobbing uncontrollably.

Jellicoe's attention was diverted from the woman to shouting from behind. Two young men with blackened faces appeared. Neither was Wallace. They were shouting angrily at Gerard. They silenced immediately when he turned around to them and they realised he was still holding an axe.

Eddie's eyes met those of DI Fogg. There was recognition from both men then Eddie pointed to the coal store.

'Your man is in there. I think he's a goner.'

A frown appeared in Fogg's face. He jumped down to the prone figure in the shadows. He put his hand on his Wallace's scalp and then lifted it to reveal a palm covered in blood. In a moment he'd pulled himself back up onto the side of the canal. He shouted to Crombie.

'Get an ambulance, Crumbs. Quickly.'

The Bus Stop

There was desperation in his voice. Jellicoe looked at Fogg. There were tears in his eyes. He shook his head. Jellicoe grabbed Mrs Regis roughly and yelled at her, 'What have you done? What have you done?'

But she couldn't speak. It was over. Over for her and for her boy. What would become of him? A life in an institution with people who didn't understand him. Or care. The tears flowed freely as she gave herself up fully to anguish. The wood echoed to her agonised wailing. The sight of such torment momentarily shocked everyone. Gerard was the first to react.

'Mummy,' he wailed. The man in front of him had caused pain to the person he loved more than life itself. His fear turned to wide-eyed fury. He stumbled forward, gripping the axe tightly. His mouth twisted into a snarl.

'Gerard,' said Jellicoe calmly. 'Put the axe down. It's over.'

'No!' screamed Gerard. Flecks of spittle flew from his mouth. The desire for blood was too great now. His mother's desolation drew him forward, axe raised. Clarke was on the move but with a crushing despair that he would be too late to save the inspector. Gerard was too close to him now. Jellicoe had not moved from the side of the mother. He held his hand out.

He could barely breathe with fear but somehow found his voice.

'Drop the weapon, Gerard. It's over.'

He hoped he sounded calm. Jellicoe had made the same calculation as Clarke. He couldn't avoid the first swing. It would kill him. That much was certain. But something else had caught his eye.

'Don't Gerard,' said Jellicoe, softy. Then in a harder, more aggressive tone he shouted, 'Stop!'

Gerard stopped. Jellicoe had gambled on this habitual response, and it worked. Just for a moment. But that was all Jellicoe had needed: just one split second. Gerard didn't hear the rushing footsteps behind him. A moment later, as he raised his axe, he was tackled by Ginger Rogers, full in the back. He hit the ground with a grunt, the axe spilled from his hand. Gerard was unnaturally strong but Ginger Rogers was an experienced street fighter. It was an uneven match. Within seconds Ginger Rogers was sitting on Gerard's back with the man-boy pinned to the ground.

'Thanks,' said Jellicoe. 'And by the way…'

'Yes?' asked Ginger, looking up at Jellicoe from his position on top of Gerard.

'You're under arrest.'

In the distance sirens wailed louder and louder.

The Bus Stop

33

DS Yates saw Frankie arrive at the window of the interview. He motioned with his fingers to come out. Yates had spent a frustrating half hour with Matthew Timpson who simply denied every accusation thrown his way. Even when it was pointed out that telephone records would show that he had spoken with Derek Sutton, he shrugged and claimed it was a wrong number. This deftly avoided outright denial that he knew Sutton. Confidence was returning to Timpson. Yates could see it in his face, his posture; he could hear it in the tone of his voice. It suggested he had more cards to play than Yates was aware of. One would, no doubt, be a good lawyer. He was already demanding to see his.

Yates opened the door and joined Superintendent Frankie and DI Price in the corridor. The look on Price's face suggested he was having no more joy with Sutton that Yates was with Timpson; Frankie just seemed particularly downcast.

'Just heard from Crombie. Jellicoe and Fogg have found the killers. It was the old woman and the man from the barge. They also think they killed Dilys Michaels. That was a case from a few years ago.'

'That's great news,' exclaimed Yates.

Frankie shook his head. His face was grim.

'No, sadly it's not. Wallace has been taken to hospital. The young fool went there on his own. He suffered a bad head injury. It doesn't look hopeful. They think he might not make it.'

Yates immediately felt his stomach empty of air. He liked the young man. Everyone liked him. the look on Price's face suggested he, too, was shocked by the news. A heavy despondency fell upon the three men. Frankie was the first to snap out of the spiral of dejection assailing them.

'We need to get something from these two. They are bang to rights. We'll see how smart Sutton is when we have permission to search that bag. Go in hard on them about the drugs. When Burnett and Jellicoe arrive, they can suggest ways out of the hole they're in.'

Price nodded at this, 'You mean turning nark on the operation?'

'Exactly.'

'No, sir,' said Yates.

Frankie turned sharply towards Yates. Even Price was surprised by Yates' comment.

'What do you mean no?' snapped Frankie.

'What I mean is, sir, wouldn't it be better to hang the murder on them? We have enough evidence that it could have been them. Timpson was there or thereabouts when it happened. We can put Sutton down as an accessory. Like that film, *Strangers on a Train*. The thing is, neither of them know that we have the real killer.'

Frankie stared in disbelief at the suggestion. It was the final point that was the clincher.

'You're right,' said Frankie. 'They know they can avoid being charged for trafficking drugs because we don't have any evidence. I'm sure Sutton can already explain any money he has in the bag. But we do have strong circumstantial evidence against Timpson on the Sutton murder. You're right, Yates. We should push that and see where it leads. If he's facing a murder charge and the death penalty, the thought of a few years doing time for drug trafficking will seem like a walk in the park. Get to work. Price, you tell Sutton that Timpson is being charged for the Sutton murder. Tell him he's an accessory.'

The two detectives re-entered the interview rooms. Frankie stood near the window of the room housing Timpson. Two crimes had been solved in one morning. Ordinarily he would have been jubilant. Instead, he felt empty and angry. Wallace's injuries were a distressing reminder that their work was not without risk. Crombie had been in tears on the radio. He'd not seen the injury, but Clarke had.

There seemed little hope.

Timpson looked up at Yates as he came back in the room. He pointed to the cigarettes on the table, smiled at the detective and said, 'May I?'

The Bus Stop

Yates took the cigarettes off the table, pulled one out and put the packet in his coat pocket.

'I don't know what you're looking so pleased for. If I were in your shoes, I'd be a bit worried,' said Yates while lighting the cigarette.

'Worried about what? You have nothing and you know it. I've never been near drugs in my life.'

Yates sat down and spent a minute smoking, lost in his own thoughts. Then he fixed his eyes on Timpson. He stared at him unblinkingly. The silence that had descended on the room felt like the final curtain at the theatre, the one that signals to everyone that the show is well and truly over. Finally, Yates looked away and shook his head.

'What's so funny?' asked an unamused Timpson.

Yates smiled at Timpson. The mechanic was looking less assured now. This was not the reaction he was expecting from the detective.

'Look, Timpson, why do you think you're here? We know you are running drugs. It's not going to take much effort to connect you and Sutton. Maybe you haven't called him much from your phone at the garage. Fair enough, you might get away with the wrong number line. But you do know Sutton. We both know this. How long do you think it will take us to establish this connection? And if you know Derek Sutton then I daresay you will have known his wife. His dead wife. The one you killed.'

Frankie looking on from the window had to stop himself from applauding. There was no question Yates had ability. There was potential there. Timpson laughed mirthlessly and shook his head.

'You have nothing. You can't pin that one on me.'

'Oh, but yes I can, Timpson,' snapped Yates immediately. He rose to his feet and walked to the back wall, leaning against it.

'You killed her all right. We know you were there. We have two witnesses to this.'

'Rubbish.'

'You were there all right. You know what I think? I think you and Sutton cooked this up between you. You wanted to cut Sarah Sutton out of the number you were running. Derek goes up to London to establish his alibi. Meanwhile you meet Sarah Sutton at your usual drop off and you kill her. We never found her bag.

235

The one that was carrying the drugs. Do you think if we searched your house or garage that it might show up, Matthew?'

Timpson was transforming before Yates' eyes. He was pale now and beads of sweat had formed on his forehead.

'You're fishing.'

'Am I? We're in the process of organising a search warrant now. I can tell you that we'll have it by lunch. You can have your lawyer by the way. He'll be defending you on a charge of murder. And you know what that means, don't you? The death penalty. We'll go for that, and we'll get it. Cold-blooded murder. It'll take the judge no time to decide that.'

'That's a lie,' shouted Timpson. He was angry. More importantly, he was scared.

'You know what's funny, Matthew, though?'

Timpson shook his head.

'While you're dangling on the gallows, Sutton over in the other room will just get a few years. And then he'll walk. You did his dirty and he goes free.'

'Lies,' screamed Timpson hysterically. 'Lies.'

*

Jellicoe had always hated the smell of hospitals. The smell of disinfectant made him want to escape into the fresh air away from it and the unearthly echoing quiet of the corridors. Yet he knew he could not leave. Not while David Wallace was fighting for his life on an operating table. Beside him sat Burnett. Neither spoke. Silence was its own tribute to how they felt towards the young detective. It was also a condemnation. Neither could say it yet but they would later.

Each felt an enormous weight. The knowledge that Wallace's injuries were certainly life threatening and, if he survived, life changing. The realisation of this lay heavy on their minds. Along with the guilt. Not survivor's guilt. Nothing so simple. The guilt of having somehow failed the young man. Failed in their duty to train, to guide, to rein in the impetuosity that made him venture into danger alone.

The clocked ticked loudly, slowly counting the seconds until the news came from the doctor. For an hour they waited silently blaming themselves. The arrival of Chief Constable Leighton and

The Bus Stop

Superintendent Frankie only intensified the sense of failure following the successful conclusion to the two cases.

'Any news?' asked Leighton.

The two detectives shook their heads. Neither could speak. The two senior officers sat down opposite Jellicoe and Burnett. In a low voice devoid of energy or triumph, Frankie updated the two men on what had transpired back at the police station.

'Yates got a confession from Timpson. He's admitted that he and the two Suttons were couriers for drugs, mostly heroin. Sutton would pick it up in Gibraltar and bring it over every month on the Prometheus. Timpson would meet Sarah Sutton at the bus stop, collect a bag and travel to London to drop it off at pre-arranged spot at Elephant and Castle. This drop-off changes every month. He doesn't know who collects it. He doesn't hang around to find out. He collects the cash and off he goes. Sutton is talking also. You were right, Jellicoe. There was money in the bag. Five hundred pounds give or take.'

No one spoke about what had happened at the barge. Jellicoe could not find the words to describe the agonised wailing of the man-boy, the hysterical shrieks of his mother which became like a rabid animal as they took her son away. What had really happened to Dilys Michaels or Sarah Sutton or even David Wallace? Jellicoe doubted they would ever know the truth. Had Dilys Michaels and Sarah Sutton spoken to him on the phone while they waited for a bus? Jellicoe would have wagered his salary on this.

His suspicion was that Gerard Regis used the phone box near the canal to call the only number he knew, the other phone box. This was a desire for human contact denied him by a mother too fearful to allow him into public. Perhaps she sensed there was violence in him. Or a desire to possess and own whatever he found. Including people.

A search of the top of the barge was revealing to Jellicoe. All manner of assorted junk collected over many years rather in the manner a child might collect toys and horde them jealously.

Or were the murders the reaction of a jealous mother trying to protect her son from the insidious influence of the opposite sex? Jellicoe felt certain she would say this to protect her son from the verdict that would almost certainly be reached and the penalty that would follow.

Yet a part of her would be in despair as she thought of her son's future. He would be locked away in an institution. He would never be released into society again. How could he? The torture of knowing that the rest of his life would be spent caged like an animal with people who did not love him. Worse, with people who misunderstood him and would probably mistreat him. The clock ticked; each passing second a contemptuous reminder to the four men of their impotence.

The Bus Stop

Monday morning, Jellicoe took a detour from his usual route to the police station. He headed down to the sea front, past the harbour and towards the pier. He walked along the pier to the end and stared out onto the sea. The wind stung his face. He cast his eyes heavenward, his gaze fixed on a seagull fluttering overhead, impervious to the wind or, for that matter, any obvious sense that it was knew where it was going.

It was one of those mornings that the clouds forgot to appear. The sky was blue, the sun was shining, and the salt scented air gave a veneer of clarity. Jellicoe drank in the air hoping it would somehow cleanse him of guilt, eradicate the self-reproach and return him to his favoured state of penance for the sins he knew rather than thought were his. Sylvia's death he could deal with. For some reason, the idea of David Wallace dying released a sense of weakness in him that he could scarcely believe had he not also seen the same reaction in Burnett.

Thought of the chief acted as a reminder that he needed to go into the station. It was almost nine in the morning. He was already late. He didn't care. Slowly, he ambled back down the pier, past the fishermen, past the mothers with their prams, past the toddlers running ahead happily ignoring the desperate cries of 'stop'.

He arrived at the station ten minutes later and saw Frankie sitting with Burnett. Price and Fogg were in the outer office. Yates had been given an assignment to see Dilys Michaels' husband and give him the news that they had found the body of his wife.

A night's sleep had done little to improve the mood of the office. Burnett waved for Jellicoe to enter. Jellicoe hung his coat up on the rack and joined the two senior men. For once there was no joking about Jellicoe's tardiness. The atmosphere in the room was thick with unspoken remorse. Jellicoe stood by the window rather than sit down. He waited to hear the latest.

'He's alive,' said Frankie. 'If the face on the doctor was anything to go by, this may not be a good thing. We'll know more when, if, he comes out of the coma.' There was nothing one could say to this so neither Burnett nor Jellicoe replied. Frankie continued, 'Thanks to Yates we have Timpson and Sutton, but I don't think there's much prospect that we can cast the net wider. We'll keep an eye on the harbourmaster, though. He's either in on it or lax. Neither Sutton nor Timpson are prepared to bargain with us. We'll try but I think they'd rather take their medicine and come out in a few years relatively rich and, more importantly, alive. Rather that than risk grassing on anyone in this operation. We'll try, of course, but I'm not getting my hopes up.'

They were silent for a moment. Then Burnett spoke. His voice was dripping with contempt.

'Have you seen the statement from Erskine Landers?'

'No,' replied the other two men in unison.

Burnett took a sheet of paper and held it in front of him.

'I won't read all of it. He says, "I am delighted to have my dearest friend Felicity back with me. My thanks to the police force for bringing an end to the misery that has been inflicted on our town by these dreadful thefts." Kind of him, to say so.'

'What does he say about the riot his speech bloody nearly incited?' asked Jellicoe.

'I was coming to that,' replied Burnett. 'He says, "We have to have peace. We have to have law and order. Although I share the beliefs of many among those that call themselves members of the group known as Patriotic Action, I cannot support vigilantism.'

'He can't condemn it either, it seems,' said Frankie. This made Jellicoe and Burnett both smile. *Mine enemy's enemy is my friend*, thought Jellicoe. Burnett set the paper down and shook his head in the manner of a man who had just about reached the limit of his ability to tolerate barefaced impenitence.

The phone rang on Burnett's desk. Burnett picked it up and listened for a second. Apparently that limit was about to be exceeded. His face became a mask of outright contempt.

'Send him up to my office,' snarled Burnett. He slammed the phone down and glanced at Frankie. 'Your guest is here.'

The Bus Stop

Frankie's eyes narrowed, 'Are you sure about this, Reg?'

Reg? When had Frankie ever called Burnett Reg, wondered Jellicoe. He was not alone in this. Burnett's face slowly transformed into a malicious grin.

'Oh aye. I'm sure.'

Jellicoe decided not to ask. Instead, he waited to be asked to leave. This did not happen. A minute or two later, Constable Clarke appeared in the outer office, accompanied by Sergeant Crombie and Cecil Lords, newspaper magnate. Or so he would like to have believed.

The three men entered Burnett's office. Neither Burnett nor Frankie rose to greet the new arrival. Burnett pointed to the empty seat. Lords glanced from the uniformed men to Frankie and then to Burnett who was looking like a man about to enjoy a game of Russian Roulette from the trigger end of the gun.

'Hello, Cecil,' purred Frankie. 'So good to have you join us in celebrating a successful end to the two major cases you've been writing about.'

If Cecil Lords was in a celebratory mood, then he hid it well. Something about the atmosphere in the room and the look of diabolic intent on Burnett's face told him that the champagne was probably on ice somewhere and likely to remain so until after he'd left.

'Well, I'm sure congratulations are in order.'

'I think they are, Cecil,' replied Burnett, slowly. 'I look forward to reading a glowing account of how our little police force uncovered not one but two murders, tore the limb of a drug smuggling ring and cracked the case of the purloined pooches.'

Jellicoe, despite the feeling of dejection had to choke back his laughter at this outburst. There was nothing self-congratulatory in Burnett's tone. Rather, it was snarled in the manner of a man who was at the utmost limit of his ability to restrain himself from violent action. Lords turned red. He was either about to explode with anger or expire with fear. Jellicoe was fifty, fifty on either one. Frankie, like a jealous suitor, cut in on the dance.

'I think Chief Inspector Burnett is being too modest, Cecil, don't you? Your humility does you credit Chief Inspector Burnett. I mean, Cecil, he has neglected to mention his own critical role in halting a near riot out at the Traveller's Camp. You know the one I'm talking about, don't you, Cecil?'

To give Lords his due, you do not become a rich man, a newspaper owner, and a leading political player in the region without having some backbone.

'I do, Frankie. I also know an ambush when I see one. I shall speak to Laurence about this. You can be bloody sure of that.'

'You do that, Cecil, you do that,' purred Frankie. 'And while you're speaking to him, be sure to mention your own role in all of this. You know, sending those two boys to steal the dogs, for one. Paying your bully boys to go up to that camp and start trouble. Yes, Cecil. You go and tell Laurence all about how you've wasted police time, broken who knows how many laws and basically turned this town into a hotbed of racialism and prejudice.'

Lords was on his feet at this: face red with anger, eyes popping out of their sockets like a Looney Tunes cartoon. He pointed his finger at Frankie and was about to threaten all manner of hell to rain down on him when he heard a noise outside. It acted to silence everyone in the room. It was almost as if Burnett had planned it this way, at least that was Jellicoe's conclusion when he saw the suppressed grin of triumph on the faces of both the chief inspector and the superintendent. From outside the front of the police station came the distinct sound of a motorcycle backfiring.

Jellicoe glanced out of the window. Down below he could see Eddie Tilly sitting astride his bike along with Ginger Rogers. Both boys were looking up at the window. Jellicoe heard Burnett rising from his seat and go over to stand beside him. Burnett saluted the two boys. They returned the salute. Then with a cough from the motorbike and a cackle from the chief inspector, off they went.

Lords was staring at Burnett with a level of hatred that Jellicoe had rarely seen outside of a psychiatric hospital. The newspaperman slumped down on the seat.

'Sorry, Cecil, my old mucker,' said Burnett in a jocular tone. 'You were about to say something?'

Lords glared at Burnett sullenly but said nothing.

'C'mon, Cecil, don't be shy.'

The silence from Lords filled the room. Frankie rose to his feet and perched himself on the table opposite Lords. Burnett did

The Bus Stop

likewise. Then Frankie leaned down and snarled in a malevolent whisper.

'We know what you did, Cecil. We know that you put those boys up to nicking the dogs so that you could create a story for your front page and raise this town up against the gypsies.'

Frankie's face was now inches away from Lords. His finger jabbed Lords with each word.

'You are without doubt the biggest ballsack I ever met, Lords. And I could lock you up make no mistake about that. We have more than enough to do this. But you know what? I'm going to leave the case open. We can close it at any time we want. Do you know what that means, Cecil?'

A hateful silence greeted this question.

'Cat got your tongue?' asked Frankie with malicious glee. The superintendent held out his hand with the palm cupped upwards. 'It means, you detestable arserag, that I have both of yours in the palm of my hand. If you step out of line again, the case of the captive canines will be miraculously solved. Do you understand?'

Lords paused a moment, face flushed with anger but then he nodded reluctantly, hate pouring from his eyes like molten lava. He started to rise from his seat, but Burnett's firm hand stopped him immediately. He fell back onto the seat. This time it was Burnett who leaned in closely to the newspaper owner. He said, 'There are two things you are going to do now. The first is you will write a frontpage article praising the bravery of a young policeman who is now in hospital. Of course, you will make a substantial contribution to the fund that we will create should he require care in the future. Then I want names. I want to know everyone in Patriotic Action, Cecil. Names. Addresses. Girlfriends. Boyfriends. The lot.' Burnett grabbed a notebook from his table and a pen. He put them on Lords' lap.

'Start writing.'

*

Chester Johnson put on his jacket. In a few minutes he would be a free man. He laughed at this. A free man? Wherever someone like him went, this was an idea rather that a reality. The police would make all the right noises. The superintendent had already come in to wish him well, but what did any of that mean? The bus company would fire him. They'd find a way. How can you have a man driving your bus who has been accused of murder? People would avoid getting on a bus with him. A man who drives empty buses is like a one-legged tightrope walker. He's heading for a fall.

Then what? The bus company had been his life for nearly ten years. What would he do now? How would he be able to afford to live. He had savings. Not much. A month or two would empty his account. He sat down on his bed and put his head in his hands.

Jellicoe found him like this. Throughout the case, Jellicoe had sensed rather than known that the American was innocent. There was no triumph in having proved it. The life of one man lay hanging in the balance. The life of the man before him had been ruined. This case had probably changed two lives forever.

Jellicoe stood at the door, unsure of what to say. He hoped Johnson would look up and understand that it was time to leave the cell. He suspected trite observations around his innocence would only anger rather than console. He said nothing. For a minute the two men were alone in the room until Johnson finally looked up.

'Time to go?'

Jellicoe nodded. He stood back and opened the door. Johnson rose slowly to his feet and trudged past Jellicoe into the corridor. They walked alongside one another in silence then Jellicoe stopped before they came to the door that led to the front desk of the police station, the exit and freedom. He asked, 'What will you do now? The chief constable has spoken with the bus company and told them what happened. They have to take you back.'

Johnson didn't have the energy to smile cynically.

'Would you let your child on a bus with me?'

There were two answers to this question, but Jellicoe's would probably not have been the majority view.

'The newspaper that broke the story about you has promised to devote a front page to your innocence. They've also agreed to condemn the racialism of groups like Patriotic Action.'

Johnson was surprised at this.

'How the hell?'

Jellicoe smiled and replied, 'Some pressure was put on the owner about this. We owed you that, Chester.'

'How's that boy that got hurt?'

The Bus Stop

Jellicoe felt the emptiness once more. It would stay with him, with all of them until they knew David was safe.

'They don't know if he'll make it or if he does, how he'll be.'

Johnson nodded at this, sympathy in his eyes. Jellicoe opened the door that led to the entrance. The two men went out, past Crombie on the desk. Standing there too was Chief Constable Leighton and Robert Bowles. Leighton's face fell when he saw Johnson. The embarrassment was acute. They he looked at Jellicoe with undisguised fury. Bowles, his back to Johnson, was initially unaware of what had happened. He saw the flash of anger on the features of the chief constable and turned around.

Silence fell on the entrance area like the aftermath of a bomb. Johnson and Bowles looked at one another for just long enough to realise who the other was. Jellicoe held his breath. This could not have been foreseen. Yet somehow Leighton would blame him. He didn't care at that moment. It was the reaction of Bowles that concerned him.

Johnson was clear on what he had to do. He stepped forward with his hand outstretched. There were tears in his eyes now.

'Mr Bowles, I just want to tell you how sorry I am. I tried to stop her; I didn't try hard enough. It was my fault.'

Bowles looked from Johnson and then down to the outstretched hand. And then he could barely see anything except a young girl crying 'Daddy'. This and a hundred other thoughts raced through his mind before he returned to the present day and the reality of the life that lay ahead without Sarah. He stared at Johnson's hand. It took a moment and then he grasped it. His voice was barely a whisper.

'It wasn't your fault.'

The End

245

Jack Murray

About the Author

Jack Murray lives just outside London with his family. Born in Ireland he has spent most of his adult life in England. His first novel, 'The Affair of the Christmas Card Killer' has been a global success. Four further Kit Aston novels have followed: 'The Chess Board Murders', and 'The Phantom', 'The Frisco Falcon' and 'The Medium Murders'. 'The Bluebeard Club', the sixth in the Kit Aston series, launched late 2021. There are two Kit Aston novellas: 'The French Diplomat Affair' and 'Haymaker's Last Fight'.

Jack has also published a spin-off series from the Kit Aston mysteries featuring a popular character from the series, Aunt Agatha. These mysteries are set in the late Victorian era when Agatha was a young woman.

In 2022, a new series will be published by Lume Books set in the period leading up to and during World War II. The series will include some of the minor characters from the Kit Aston series.

Printed in Great Britain
by Amazon

13714037R00150